SITTING ON A FORTUNE

The Sisters, Texas Mystery Series

Book 9

BECKI WILLIS

Clear Creek Publishers

Editing by SJS Editorial Services
Cover by Diana Buidoso dienel96

ISBN-10: 1947686186
ISBN-13: 978-1947686182

CONTENTS

1

The night was black, offering no glimmer of light into the darkened house. The only illumination came from the dim glow of a digital clock.

Earlier reconnaissance revealed the location of objects worth taking. With the house now quiet, save for the occasional groan of settling timbers and protesting pipes, silent feet moved through the space, procuring the items of value.

A slight miscalculation on the width of a cabinet door, and the stockpot clattered to the floor.

"Shh!" The warning hissed from behind clenched teeth. "You'll wake the old man!"

"He could sleep through a tornado."

"With all this banging and clanging, it sounds like one now." The grumbling thief scooped up the copper-bottomed pot, tucking it best he could beneath one arm and cradling it to him. "Better not press our luck," he reasoned. "This will do for tonight."

He stopped to listen, making certain there was no movement from the bedroom. Satisfied, he tiptoed toward the back door and eased it open. Unable to see past his own nose, he nonetheless made a show of peering from left to right.

With an air of authority, he motioned his troops forward and melted into the night.

2

"I'm telling you, that man is crazier than a bedbug!"

"Granny Bert, that's not a nice thing to say." Madison deCordova frowned at her grandmother's blunt outburst.

"What's the truth have to do with being nice?" her grandmother demanded. Bertha Cessna rapped her knuckles on the tabletop with a smart nod. "You mark my words, that man's remote control is missing a few buttons. You could whisper in his ear and hear an echo, there's so much empty space rattling around up there. Forget renting out space. With a draft like that, not even a candle would survive."

"Shh! He might hear you!" Madison cautioned, stealing a covert glance at the man in question.

Tom Pruett sat at a nearby table, spinning yet another tale to anyone who would listen. His current audience was Genny Montgomery, owner of *New Beginnings Café* and Madison's best friend since junior high. A polite smile graced Genny's lips, but her eyes had a glazed-over look of disconnect.

Tom Pruett had that effect on people.

Not for the first time, Madison wondered about the man's age. She guessed him three or four years either side of eighty, but it was difficult to tell, considering everything about the man was monochrome. Thinning gray hair and a wilting mustache did little to complement the ashen pallor of his skin. Beneath shaggy gray brows, his eyes had perhaps once been blue, but were now a faded, watery gray. Even his wardrobe was as bland as his features; he faithfully dressed in khaki work pants and matching shirt. He carried a gray cane to assist with his shuffled gait, but he was still agile enough to come and go as he pleased, darting about town in a light gray Prius.

If not for his vivid imagination and outrageous tales, there would be nothing of interest to set Tom Pruett apart.

Nonplussed by her granddaughter's warnings, Granny Bert insisted, "He's too busy yammering to hear anything but the voices in his head. Listen to him, telling Genny some nonsense about people coming into his house at night when he's sleeping! Like anyone in their right mind would want to watch him snore." A cynical snort summed up the elderly woman's feelings on the subject.

Amusement hovered at the edges of Madison's mouth, spilling into her voice. "To hear him tell it, these people are robbing him blind in the middle of the night. I don't know why anyone would want to take his pots and pans, but that's what he's claiming happened last night."

"Last week, he told Sybil there were Nazi war planes flying over his house. The week before that, he claimed some Hollywood producer was filming a documentary about his life."

Madison nodded. "We've heard that one before. Depending on what version he tells, it's either his daughter, his niece, or some famous yet unspecified producer who's doing the filming."

"Like I say," Granny insisted, "the man is loonier

than a 'toon."

"He's not originally from here, is he?" Madison murmured. "I don't think I remember him from before."

Before referred to her teenage years. While her parents chased after yet another of her father's dreams, Madison moved in with her grandparents. Growing up in the small community was a far cry from the exciting world of racecar circuits (her father's life ambition at the time), but Madison credited it as being the best decision her parents ever made. Life with Joe and Bertha Cessna gave her the stability and support she needed and helped mold her into the self-reliant, responsible adult she was today.

College drew her away, but after twenty years, two children, and the unexpected status of widowhood, she returned and was once more living in The Sisters. The sparkling diamond rings on her finger were proof she had new reason to stay this time.

"He's a transplant," her grandmother confirmed. "He and his wife moved here about the time your twins were born. She took over as school counselor when Glynda Purdue ran off with the band teacher."

"Really? I don't remember hearing about that scandal." Madison twisted her mouth in a rueful expression and confessed, "Of course, I spent the first three months of the twins' life sleep-deprived and completely overwhelmed with my two little bundles of joy. The only clear thing I remember about that time was their uncanny ability to sleep at exact opposite times."

"You had more important things to worry about than small-town scandals, but I must say, that one did create quite a stir."

In truth, it didn't take much to stir the gossip mill in the small community. Even with the two towns combined, the population barely topped two thousand. Despite live streaming and online shopping to fill the gaps, there wasn't much to do in the way of entertainment in Juliet and Naomi, commonly referred to as The Sisters. Madison liked to believe that the locals weren't so much nosy as they were bored. Even when their own lives lacked excitement, they could live vicariously through their friends and neighbors.

And when their friends' and neighbors' lives were just as boring... well, they could always embellish.

Thinking Mr. Pruett's tired wardrobe could use some embellishing, Madison darted a guilty glance at her own attire. Who was she to criticize tired, monotonous wardrobes? Her clothes racks were full of outfits that could just as easily be found in her grandmother's closet. Even with the new, trendy additions from her trousseau, she had dressed this morning in one of her favorite go-to outfits: a blue oxford button-down shirt and black slacks. Not even a stylish pair of sandals adorned her feet.

Have I learned nothing from my stylish assistant? She chided herself silently. Derron would be appalled by her lack of embellishment.

Redirecting her attention away from her boring wardrobe, Madison commented, "I don't think I've ever heard anyone mention a Mrs. Pruett."

"You wouldn't. She passed about five years ago. He's gone steadily downhill ever since."

"Maybe he's just lonely and makes up these fantastical stories to keep himself entertained."

"That's all fine and dandy," Granny Bert huffed, "but he should keep his fantastical fantasies to himself!"

"Children?"

"Just the phantom daughter he mentions now and then."

Madison shook her dark head in empathy. "That's sad. I can't imagine how empty my life would be without the twins—and now Megan—to liven things up." With the addition of Brash's daughter, there were now three sixteen-year-olds keeping her days tapped out at full steam.

"Imagine the joys of having four sons," her grandmother said, her voice colored with shades of sarcasm. "What one didn't think of, the others did. More often than not, your father was the ringleader."

"Yet to hear him tell it," Madison quipped, "he was always the one left holding the bag. He blames it on being the youngest."

Granny Bert pointed a crooked finger her way. "I'm here to tell you. As the baby of the brood, your father got just about anything he wanted. He'd dream up schemes and get his older brothers to do his bidding. Just ask him about the sawed-off leg of his father's favorite easy chair. Fifty years later, and it's still a mystery."

Madison laughed over the rim of her tea glass. She could only imagine the mischief Charlie Cessna stirred up, aided and abetted by three doting older brothers. He did a fine enough job, all on his own.

"Speaking of chairs..." She set the tea down as she changed the subject. "I found one I'd like to buy for Brash. His birthday is coming up next month, and I officially have no ideas on what to get him. I thought having his own chair for the bedroom might be nice."

"Every man needs his own recliner," Granny Bert agreed.

"This one isn't a recliner, but it is over-sized and quite comfy. I found it at *New Again Upholstery*."

"That job you're doing over in Navasota?"

Madison nodded. The restoration and resale shop had hired *In a Pinch Professional Services* to fill in while their key employee, the proud father of a new bundle of joy, took paternity leave. Even though Madison knew nothing about upholstering furniture when she started, she considered her two-week stint there a crash course in all things upholstery. With what she'd learned under the owner's tutelage, she hoped to tackle this project on her own.

"Best of all, they said I could use the employee discount. Which comes in handy, because in just a few more days, I'll be out of a job."

"Not—Not if I hire you."

The words didn't come from her grandmother.

Madison jerked her head up to see a bright-eyed boy standing beside their table, his chin wavering ever so slightly. He could be no more than ten or eleven, even though he was taller than most kids that age. His ruddy, chubby cheeks, rounded belly, and high-pitched voice suggested he hadn't seen puberty yet. When the boy shifted on his feet uncertainly, Madison realized the brightness in his eyes could be attributed to nerves, unshed tears, or both.

She put extra warmth into her smile. "Hello. Who have we here?"

"My name's Monte Applegate. And you're the police chief's new wife, right? The one who solves clues and things. The one who helps people."

"I'm Madison deCordova. And, yes, I'd like to think I help people whenever I can."

"Good. I want to hire you." Monte dipped a beefy hand into his front pocket. After considerable rummaging, he pulled out his fist and opened it over the table. Down rained several crumpled bills, two rocks, a half stick of gum, and several loose coins. He fished out the rocks and gum, pushing the money her way. "There's twenty-two dollars. I'll have another three by the end of the week. Is that enough?"

The boy's expression was so eager and sincere, she dared not smile. Instead, Madison counted aloud as she straightened crumpled bills and sorted change. "Twenty-five dollars is a lot of money," she acknowledged. "What kind of job did you have in mind?"

"I need to find out who killed my dog."

Hazel eyes flew to his. "Someone killed your dog? Deliberately?" she squeaked.

His legs shifted again. "He may not be exactly *dead*," he conceded. Lifting his chin with confidence, he went on quickly, "Yet! But he will be soon, if I don't find him. He won't eat from no one but me."

Madison scooted over, making room for the boy in the booth beside her. "Have a seat," she said, patting the spot encouragingly. "This is my grandmother, by the way. Bertha Cessna."

"I know who Miss Bert is," the youth acknowledged. Like a gentleman, he extended his hand for a proper greeting. "My grandmother is Jean Applegate."

"The artist? Why, yes, I do believe I see the resemblance!" The older woman pumped his hand enthusiastically. "How is that talented grandmother of yours? Still painting, I hope?"

"Yes, ma'am. Every chance she gets."

"I have one of her paintings over my sofa. It's the focal point of the room."

The boy offered a weak smile, uncertain of what a focal point was.

Madison filled the silence with a gentle prod. "Tell me about your dog, Monte."

This, he could do. "His name is Pup. I've had him about three years now. I found him in a cardboard box down at the dump. On Saturday mornings, I like to go down there and search for treasure. That day, I hit the jackpot! Can you believe it? Somebody had thrown that little puppy away! He was all scared and skittish-like, but I finally coaxed him out and gave him the sandwich in my back pocket. I took him home with me, bandaged up his cut leg, and he's been fine ever since. But he won't let no one but me feed him. Now that someone's stole him, I don't know what he'll do."

Despite the boy's glum expression, Madison had the urge to smile. She could picture the boy shifting and sorting through the smelly rubbish of other people's castoffs, hoping to find something of value amid the leftovers. Would a sandwich from his hip pocket even be fit for consumption? She mentally shrugged away the image, trying to keep a straight face. *One man's trash is another boy's treasure*, she reasoned.

Forcing her mind back on track, Madison asked, "Why do you think someone stole your dog?"

"He's a good dog," the boy was quick to point out. "But, sometimes..." he admitted, "he does like to wander about. He especially likes to go over to our neighbor's and nose around. Last time, he was pretty mad about it, so my dad said I needed to keep him tied for a while. Ol' Man Andrews has a temper and threatened to shoot him the next time Pup came roamin', so I took extra care to make sure he didn't get loose. I had him on a rope behind a latched gate. But when I came home from school two days ago, he was gone."

"The gate was open?"

His nod was vigorous. "I made sure I closed it good. I even used a rope to wrap around the latch. I found it untied and on the ground. The gate was open, and Pup... Pup was gone." Monte's chin quivered again, same as his voice.

Madison laid her hand atop the boy's arm. "Have you talked to the neighbor?" she asked gently.

"Me and my dad went over there, but he wasn't

home. We went back the next day, and he said he hadn't seen him. Said he's been out of town for a couple of days. I think he sometimes travels for his job. I put up posters around town and reported Pup missing to the police, but they said there wasn't much they could do about a lost dog. A stolen dog would be different, they said, if I had proof someone took him. But how can I prove someone took him, when I don't know where he is!"

The boy looked so forlorn, Madison's heart prickled in her chest. In her mind's eye, she ran through her schedule for the next few days. Her stint in Navasota would be up on Friday. She was taking the girls shopping in Bryan-College Station on Saturday and promised Blake they would have a fish fry on Sunday, provided he and Brash caught enough fish. But that still left the evenings, now that the April sunshine lingered in the afternoon sky.

She turned to the boy with a suggestion. "Let's do this. If you'll give me a good description of your dog, I'll see what I can do. Do you happen to have a picture of him?"

Monte nodded. "I put it on the poster." He pulled a folded sheet of paper from his back pocket and handed it to her.

"Perfect. I'll share it on social media. Between my three kids and myself, we have hundreds of followers, so that should get us some good exposure. I'll also drive around each evening and see if I can find him. Where do you live?"

"A few miles out of Naomi, out on Sawyer Road."

"And who is your neighbor, the one Pup likes to visit?"

"The old guy who owns *Gold and Silver Exchange*."

"Gerald Adams?" Madison asked in confusion. That man was in prison.

"No, the new owner. Lamont Andrews."

"I don't have a contract with me, but I think we can use this napkin." She pulled a pen from her purse and scribbled out a quick receipt. She wrote a brief description of the job, added both their names and her telephone number, and scrawled 'Paid in Full' across the bottom.

The boy studied it for a moment before looking up with a frown. "Don't we need to sign it, or something? And don't you need a copy?"

"Right. Here, you sign it and add your phone number. After I sign, I'll take a picture, so I'll have it on digital file."

Satisfied with her suggestion, Monte took the pen into his chubby fingers and carefully wrote his name.

"Don't forget to add a number so I can call you when I have news," Madison reminded him.

After doing so, Monte pushed to his feet. "I hope you find him soon."

"Me, too."

Looking more hopeful than when he first came in, Monte shook both their hands and promised, "I'll leave the last three dollars here with Miss Genny, if that's okay with you."

"Didn't I mention the cash discount? Your bill is completely covered, just as I wrote on that receipt. There's also a money-back guarantee. If you find the dog before I do, I'll refund your money. Fair enough?"

A hint of a smile touched his lips, the first she had seen since his solemn arrival. "Fair enough."

Once the boy was gone, Granny Bert proudly beamed across the table at her granddaughter. "Well done. You treated him with dignity and respect, acting as if his money was as important as anyone else's."

"I remember receiving similar treatment about a year ago. Someone offered to sell me a house that was ridiculously out of my price range but made it sound perfectly legit, right down to the one-hundred-dollar monthly installments."

"That sale *was* legit! I sold you the Big House fair and square."

"There was nothing fair about selling me a historical mansion for the paltry sum of five thousand dollars, and you know it. But you made me feel like I was pulling my own weight and actually providing for my family, and for that, I will be eternally grateful."

"You did provide for your family. You own a gorgeous home you can all be proud of."

"You provided the house, and we all know it. But it was a good lesson, and one I try to emulate. Never treat other people as *being* lesser, just because they have less money than someone else."

"That's the kind of lesson that is invaluable," Granny Bert reminded her. She wasn't prone to flowery speeches of endearment, but she made an exception as she lifted her tea glass in salute. "And one you learned well. You do me proud, girl."

Though few and far between, praise like that from her grandmother always made her eyes leak.

3

After leaving the café, Madison took the long route home. Normally, it was a three-minute drive. All she had to do was cross the railroad track that separated the towns of Naomi and Juliet, go two blocks, and pull into her driveway on the prominent corner lot of Second and Main.

Instead, she turned right out of the parking lot and drove a handful of blocks through Naomi to get to the town's outskirts. Taking Sawyer Road out of town, she was surprised to see a new house going up. Last year, the same plot of land was home to a watermelon patch. Since she seldom walked Glitter Thompson's dogs these days, she had no reason to come out this way.

Thinking of the former Vegas showgirl and her beloved poodles, Madison wondered why she never called anymore. Was she no longer traveling, or did she think Madison would turn down such a meager job, now that *In a Pinch* was more established? Madison made a mental note to drop a few lines to the other woman, perhaps with a coupon. Though the job never paid more than a few dollars, those were dollars she had depended on when first coming back to The Sisters. Despite her new title as Mrs. Brash deCordova, Madison wasn't too good now to remember the people who had helped her when she was down.

None of her first jobs had been glamorous, but they had been important. Driving Leroy Huddleston back and forth to the doctor, walking dogs, running errands for Miss Sybil, and a handful of other small jobs had kept gas in the car and service for the cell phones. She slowly worked her way up to bigger and better-paying jobs, most at locally owned businesses. On the police chief's recommendation, she had landed a recurring gig with a Houston-based private investigator who now kept her on a small retainer.

In a Pinch Professional Services would never show up in *Forbes Magazine,* but it was finally solvent, thanks in large part to the people who hired her for the more 'interesting' jobs. Jobs like proving a man innocent of murder, proving the fidelity of a spouse, locating a stolen item, and similar cases best suited for a private detective. Those bigger jobs had helped her get back on her feet, but it didn't mean she couldn't squeeze in a few entry-level jobs now and then.

That was exactly why she was out here now, searching for a boy's lost dog, down a road that brought back unpleasant memories of illegal cockfights and a race for her life through a darkened pasture. Not all jobs were about money.

After a quick search on the internet, Madison easily located Monte Applegate's house. The search had taken just seconds, a scary reminder of how much information was out there for public consumption, often pinpointed on a map.

She noted the chain-link fence with the standard drop-latch closing. She couldn't see the entire backyard, but what she could see was in good repair. No gaping holes to facilitate a curious dog's escape.

Lamont Andrew's humble abode was little over a mile down the road, an easy jaunt for a pup with an adventurous spirit. With no other cars on the road, Madison rolled to a stop for visual perusal. The older frame home had seen better years, but the pier and beam foundation looked solid, and the roof appeared in good condition. Fifties-era pink paint was chipped and fading, a perfect match for once-black doors and shutters in similar condition. A newly constructed deck extended from the back of the house, where Madison caught a glimpse of a huge stainless-steel grill and a colorful umbrella-topped picnic table. An abundance of glass and chrome winked in the bright Texas sun. The deck and its accessories were easily worth more than the large old shed at the back of the property, but she couldn't help but notice the thick chain and padlock wrapped around its doors.

Odd, that a two-thousand-dollar grill sat in plain sight, but an old shed was locked up tight.

"Maybe that's where he keeps his extra stock," Madison mused aloud. "Not sure I would trust that shed in a strong wind, but it looks safe from trespassers. The question is, what would a dog find so intriguing about this place?"

She saw no obvious signs of the owner having a pet, but a girlfriend for Pup was always a possibility. Madison scribbled herself a note.

"If I were a puppy," she continued to think aloud, "I might want to explore the crawl space under the house. Or maybe the shed. As a person—and a rather squeamish one at that—the thought of spiders and snakes and a random skunk or two doesn't appeal to me in the least, but maybe it's just the human coming out in me. Pup, no doubt, finds all of that fascinating."

She peered around for a few more moments, noting the remote location of the house. She saw no other houses in sight, and two sides of the property backed up to a high-game fence. Spotting a herd of white-tail deer on the other side of the fence, including two bucks with impressive racks of horns, she knew the owner of the game ranch wouldn't allow his fence to fall in disrepair, not with the high price of genetic breeding and commercial hunts.

No, Pup wasn't slipping under the fence to run with the deer, and he wasn't cutting through the Andrews property on his way to the neighbors'. Something here held his interest.

"Could be a rabbit," she reasoned.

She lingered for another moment before deciding to turn around and head back to town. A quick glance at her watch told her that if she hurried, she could still make *The Gold and Silver Exchange* before closing.

Madison was ashamed to admit it, but this was the first time she had been inside the establishment. Particularly after last year's fiasco with the Community Angel Tree, when many of the presents were stolen under her watch, she knew the importance of shopping local. The generous merchants of both towns had rallied to replace the gifts, often with bigger and better offerings. Eager to repay their gesture, Madison now made a point to shop local whenever she could.

True, she planned to go to Bryan-College Station this weekend, but the girls needed craft paints and those little pom-pom doodads for one of their cheerleading projects. Her Uncle Jubal's *Five and Dime* did a fair job of keeping up with the times, but they wanted a certain paint they could only find at *Hobby Lobby.* The sly duo had also wrangled the promise of a new shirt out of her, and the selections here in The Sisters were limited. The *Vintage Closet* in Naomi and *Good as New* in Juliet offered clothing in a variety of styles and sizes, but it was anyone's guess what the current selection might be, as all were secondhand. The florist and the local gift shop both carried a few cute t-shirts, and *Hadley's Feed Store* carried a decent selection of western wear, including some from the Sticker Pierce line. But to find the best selection and the best price, the girls insisted they needed to go to the larger city.

Since none of the local stores carried printer ink or her favorite scent of air freshener, Madison needed to run by one of the chain discount stores. While she was there, she knew she would stock up on household staples. Even though The Sisters had a small grocery store on either side of the tracks, when feeding a walking and talking stomach like sixteen-year-old Blake, she needed to buy in quantity. The larger supermarkets were always her best option for feeding her son.

Even to her ears, they sounded like excuses. The idea of shopping local was noble, even when it didn't always make sense. Yet whenever possible, she did stop in at a different store in the community, if for no other reason than to show her support.

This, however, was one business she had missed.

In truth, it wasn't what she had expected. It looked more like a pawnshop. Rows of glass cases lined the walls, filled with jewelry, coins, and shiny baubles displayed beneath brilliant lighting. A few random items were on display in the middle of the room, everything from musical instruments and small electronics to a motorized scooter and an iron bistro set. A slight haze hung in the air, emitted from a large incense burner featuring an intricate golden design and displayed in a prominent location.

Not a fan of patchouli, Madison immediately sneezed.

"Oh, hello. I didn't hear the bell when you came in," the man behind the counter apologized. "May I help you with something?"

"Just browsing. You're still open, aren't you?"

"For a pretty lady, the store never closes," he assured her with a wide smile.

Madison bit back a smile. At best, "Ol' Man Andrews" was all of thirty-five. She knew it was the owner from Granny Bert's description. Lamont Andrews was a towering six feet, seven inches tall, with broad shoulders and long legs, both of which had earned him a basketball scholarship to Howard University. That may have been over a decade ago, but he still looked every bit the athlete, even in business attire. She didn't see a single gray hair amid the dark, making her wonder why Monte referred to him as 'Old Man Andrews.'

"I won't stay long," she promised.

"Take your time. I'm running reports, so I'll be here for a while."

"Still, I'll try not to keep you."

"I love numbers," he assured her. "I can get lost in them for hours."

Madison glanced around. "I see you offer much more than just precious metal."

He flashed her another bright smile. "Diversifying is the key to staying in business, particularly in a small town."

A sparkling, circular item caught her eye from within one of the cases. "Is that a dog collar? With *jewels*?"

The smile turned slightly apologetic. "What can I say? Some people adore their pets."

It gave her the opening she needed. "What about you? Don't you have a dog at home who'd like to wear this gorgeous collar?"

"Even if I did," he hooted, "I wouldn't trust it to carry a thousand dollars' worth of jewels around its neck!"

Madison stole a peek at the price tag, which was more than twice that amount. *Okay, so Lamont Andrews was obviously a businessman. He was here to make money, after all.*

"I agree. At least, not without a tracker and a hefty insurance policy." Her expression was skeptical.

"No tracker, I'm afraid. And the insurance policy is the buyer's prerogative."

"So that price is for the collar, itself?"

"Certified cubic zirconia," he assured her, "and genuine sapphires and rubies. A very exquisite piece, wouldn't you agree?"

"Oh, it's gorgeous, but I don't even have a dog. And I doubt my nephew would want that for his precious Pup. I can't really see that around the neck of a long-haired brown and white dog that's part terrier, part Bassett hound, can you?" She watched for a reaction to the description of Monte's dog.

It was brief, but a flash of irritation crossed his face. "Probably not," he agreed.

Madison affected a sad face. "Apparently, I'm too late, anyway. I think his dog ran away or was run over. He's been missing for days," she said, adding a worried fret to her voice.

She thought he muttered 'good riddance' beneath his breath, but he looked sympathetic. "That's too bad," he murmured. "In that case, I take it you don't need me to unlock the display?"

"Not yet. But if the dog comes back—and if I win the lottery—I may change my mind."

"No problem. Can I assist you with something else?"

She tried to think of another line of questioning, something that would help explain Pup's fascination with his property. She tried to think of what a gold and silver exchange and a curious dog might have in common.

"Uhm, I don't suppose you sell live traps, do you?" The metal was shiny, much like coins and jewels, and the first thing to pop into her mind.

"Excuse me?" The look on his face was priceless, but she had already begun. Too late to back out now.

"You know, for catching pesky critters like rabbits, or possums, or... or mice."

"You want a live trap to catch *mice*?" Clearly, he thought she had an intelligence threshold. A very low one.

"Maybe not mice," she corrected, scrambling to say something that made sense. "Something's been getting into my garden, and I don't want to *kill* it. I just want to scare it away. Or catch it, so that my son can take it down a country road and release it. That's why people live in the country, right? To enjoy the wildlife and the furry critters."

"That's not why I live in the country," he told her, his expression only slightly less than horrified by her assumptions. "I don't like furry critters."

"Oh. So, you *don't* have a lot of rabbits or possums or gophers out where you live?"

"Not really."

Madison was clearly striking out. No dog, no infestation of furry critters, nothing of apparent interest to lure a dog a mile down the road. *Unless...*

"I guess your wife and children are glad about that."

Lamont shook his head. "No wife. No kids." He dropped his head down and peered at her practically through his eyebrows. "You flirting with me? Because if you are—"

"I'm not!" she cried, fully aghast.

"No offense, but I'm just not into white chicks. Especially ones that are newly married to the chief of police."

"You—You know who I am?"

"Lady, everyone knows who you are. If they happened to miss your reality TV show last year, there was that business at your wedding, where your famous football player husband's All-Pro buddy was accused of killing one of your guests. And then there was the thing with your husband without his shirt o—"

Mortified, Madison held up her hand to stop him. She hardly needed a reminder of recent events.

Before she could apologize, he asked, "Do you want to tell me what this is really about?"

"My... nephew's dog." Monte Applegate may have been just a child, but he was still her client, and she valued her confidentiality policy. "It really is missing, and he thinks you may have had something to do with it."

"Are you talking about that chubby little redhead kid that keeps bugging me?"

"Probably."

He raised his eyebrows. "That's *probably* what your nephew looks like? You don't even know?"

"I mean he's probably been bugging you. He's really attached to his dog."

"I'll tell you the same thing I told the kid's father. I've seen the dog a time or two, and I always run it off." An unpleasant look crossed his face. Madison would best describe it as chilling. He leaned across the glass case to make certain she heard his threat.

"I don't have a dog, I don't want a dog, I don't even *like* a dog. And the next time I catch it digging up my property, I'm either calling the law or getting out my shotgun. So, tell your nephew or whoever the kid is to keep his furry little mutt off my property, or I'll take care of it myself, once and for all." He stood up to his full height, towering over her with his menacing glare. "And by the way," he snapped. "We're. Closed."

Madison stormed from the store, vowing to never darken its door again. She remembered, now, what else Granny Bert had said about Lamont Andrews. He was kicked out of the basketball program for fighting with another player. He was known to have a violent temper, and there was a rumor he had done jail time, but no one could confirm that fact. Upon his return to The Sisters several years later, he became manager of *The Gold and Silver Exchange* and was in the process of buying it before Gerald Adams ever went to prison. Maturity, Granny Bert claimed, seemed to have mellowed him.

After today, Madison begged to differ.

4

The next afternoon, Madison called her grandmother outside to her garage. With a rolling hand gesture, she made the presentation. “I present to you—” stepping aside, she revealed the item behind her “—the chair.”

Granny Bert examined the red throne with a critical eye. Bending at the waist, she stepped in to get a closer view. She circled the antique twice, viewing it from all angles. Kicked at the ornate wooden legs. Rattled the curved back with a veined hand, listening for a telltale creak. Trailed a finger over the faded velvet fabric.

Nodding slowly, she eventually stood back. “Seems sturdy enough for that hunk of a man you married,” she allowed. “How’s it sit?”

“See for yourself,” Madison invited.

Her grandmother settled upon its generous berth to conclude her official assessment. She braced her elbows on the padded arms and rocked against the upholstered backrest, wiggling to find the most comfortable position. After a moment, she shifted to the left. Pursing her lips, she moved to the right. Next, she scooted back. Realigned herself yet again, shifting more of her weight to the rear of the seat. She stayed that way for all of ten seconds before a frown added its worth to her already heavily lined forehead.

"This has to be the lumpiest cushion I have ever sat on," the old woman snorted. "I swear, someone must have put lumps of coal under the fabric. Don't get me wrong. The bones of the chair are good. It's sturdy, plenty wide, and has a good height, especially for a man as long legged as Brash. But this cushion has to go!"

"I agree. Obviously, the material is in bad condition and has seen years of wear and tear. Not to mention, there's that long gash across the back of it, almost like someone slashed it with a knife."

Her grandmother's eyes sparkled with sudden interest. "Maybe someone was murdered in it!"

"Granny! What a thing to say!" Madison shook her head in exasperation.

With a spryness that defied her eighty-one years of age, Granny Bert sprang from the chair to re-analyze the gash. "You sit down," she instructed the younger woman as she moved around behind the chair.

A bit warily, Madison seated herself in the chair.

"It definitely looks like the damage could have been done by a knife." Granny Bert's voice came out muffled as she bent to examine the cut with a cynical eye. "A long, thin, sharp blade. Perfect for slicing and dicing and stabbing your enemy in the back."

Madison was unprepared for the abrupt jar as Granny Bert rammed her fist into the back of the chair mid-sentence.

"Ow! What did you do that for?" she grumbled.

"Proving my point. Someone could have been murdered in this chair." She came back around to face her granddaughter, her eyes sparkling with excitement. "Maybe this can be your next case!"

"This is a birthday gift for my new husband, not a search for a new mystery to solve," Madison pointed out. "Besides, I've had more than my fill of murder, mayhem, and dead bodies in the past year and a half, thank you very much."

Her mind flashed back to the string of mysteries she had been involved in since returning home and opening her own temporary agency. Many of her clients seemed to have *In a Pinch* confused with a private detective service; that, or they knew a good deal when they saw one. Her rates for temporary employment were much lower than those charged by a private investigator, and yet the results were virtually as effective.

For that very reason, she often thought about pursuing her own PI license. Brash, however, wasn't keen on the idea, and being as they were newlyweds, now might not be the best time to create friction.

"*You* may not be looking for a mystery to solve, but maybe the mystery is looking for you. Admit it. You're a magnet for dead bodies and danger."

Madison couldn't control the shudder that slid across her shoulders. "I wouldn't say I was a *magnet*..." she murmured, the denial weak and tepid upon her tongue.

"I beg to differ. Ronny Gleason. Caress Worthington. The skeletal remains of Clarence Ford. An organized gambling ring. A drug smuggling operation." Bony fingers ticked off the count. "Shall I continue?"

"No, thank you." The words were polite, but the tone was dry.

The older woman didn't give up so easily. "You have to admit, the location of the slash is perfect for stabbing an unsuspecting victim."

"If you're using a sword," Madison pointed out. "This has a thick back. I'm not sure an ordinary knife would be long enough to penetrate the cushion *and* a person's chest cavity. Not enough for a mortal wound."

As she spoke, she ran her fingers along the cushion beneath her.

This murderous seat, on the other hand, might just do the trick. She didn't recall the seat being this lumpy before. Perhaps something had shifted during transportation.

"You could be right," her grandmother agreed reluctantly.

Madison continued to worm her fingers through a tiny rip along a seam in the cushion. "I just hope I can get this recovered in time for Brash's birthday."

"You have three weeks. How long can it take?"

"Seeing as this is my first solo project, probably about six." Her mouth twisted with the rueful admission. "It looked simple enough while I was working with Ralph, but I'm not feeling quite so confident now. But I appreciate you letting me use your garage. Even with my huge house and four empty bedrooms, I could never hide this project from Brash at home."

"The motor home is too tall to fit in here, and it won't hurt the Buick to get a shower now and then. You may as well use the space to do your work."

Madison looked down at the chair where she rested. "I can't believe Ralph gave me such a good deal. Between the employee discount he offered me and the fact I have no idea of what else to buy the man who has absolutely everything, I couldn't pass it up."

Her grandmother was still scrutinizing the bargain in question. "Why does this chair look so familiar to me?" she wondered aloud.

"Other than the fabric, it's almost a perfect match to the one already in my bedroom. I guess this was a popular style back in the day." Madison continued to work the cushion's hole with her finger, knowing she would soon inflict even more damage.

"I thought that fancy designer had all your bedroom furniture custom made."

"She did. Kiki designed the settee in the turret and all the tables from wrought iron to match the custom headboard Nick designed, but the upholstered chair beside the bed was original to the house. She initially planned to have two chairs, but for whatever reason, I just ended up with one. Which was fine, until Brash and I married. I thought having his own chair might make him feel more comfortable in the space designed for a single woman."

To an outsider, Madison's talk of custom-made furniture and renowned interior designer Kiki Paretta might sound as if she had money to spare. Nothing could be further from the truth. Desperation and a sad lack of funds were the very things that had driven her to accept last year's outrageous proposal made by HOME TV and her conniving grandmother. Granny Bert had hornswoggled celebrity carpenter Nick Vilardi into remodeling the stately old Victorian mansion Madison now lived in, and it hadn't cost the destitute young widow a dime.

Not that it meant Madison and her twins hadn't paid, because they had. Dearly. Appearing on a nationally televised reality show had cost them their privacy and quite often their pride, but it had given them a forever home.

"What fabric are you using?" Granny Bert asked.

"That charcoal-gray tweed over there. I thought it would be a nice balance to all the creams and whites Kiki used in the room. She accented with mossy green and hints of charcoal, but I don't think a green chair would look right. The charcoal gray will be more masculine and offer the right balance."

Her grandmother nodded, but she still eyed the chair with a glimmer of suspicion. "If you can pull this off, I think you'll have yourself a winner."

"Those are the magic words," Madison acknowledged. "*If I can pull it off.*"

"You know what I've always told you. There's only one way you'll ever know if you can do something, and that's to try."

"I'm certainly going to give it my best shot."

"Say it with more conviction, child," her grandmother chided.

Madison pulled her fingers from worrying the cushion. Folding both hands in her lap, she squared her shoulders back and spoke with determination, just as her grandmother had taught her. "I'm giving this my best shot. And when I'm done, it's going to knock Brash's socks off."

The new show of confidence pleased her grandmother, but she couldn't resist a chuckle before returning to the house. "Being a newlywed, you might want to knock off more than his socks, but that's the spirit."

Granny Bert returned an hour later, waving something in her hand with a triumphant smile.

"Found it!" she beamed.

Madison straightened and arched her back. Her muscles cramped from bending so long at a time.

Ripping the covering away was faster, but Ralph taught her to remove the old material as meticulously as possible. When kept intact, the discarded fabric could be used as a pattern for new coverings. With that in mind, she ripped seams and gently tugged fabric free from the threads, careful to do the job as Ralph had shown her.

"What'd you find?" Madison turned to retrieve her water bottle and take a long draw of refreshment.

"The proof I was looking for. *That chair* came from the Big House!" She pointed an accusing finger at the chair now minus its back fabric.

"From my house?" Madison questioned. "How?"

"Beats me, but I knew it looked familiar. That's because I remembered it as part of a set. They used to be in the formal library. Just look."

Madison peered down at the photo in her grandmother's fingers. "Could be," she acknowledged. "I see two chairs. But it's hard to know if this is one of them, especially since the photo is in black and white."

"Of course it's in black and white."

Madison held up a hand before the older woman could get started. "I know, I know. Times were hard back then. Barefoot in the snow. Only running water was what you tossed out the back door to run downhill. Walked five miles to school, uphill each way. Yada, yada, yada."

"Hard times had nothing to do with it, Miss Sassybritches. Colored film hadn't been invented when this photograph was taken."

"Then I can hardly see how it's proof that this red velvet chair and the monochromatic one in the picture are one and the same. I can't even be certain that one of them is the chair from my bedroom."

"If you would give me a minute to explain, you would realize I'm right. As usual."

Madison rolled her eyes. Granny was in a *mood.*

"Roll those eyeballs to the back of the picture, Missy, and just read Juliet's documentation."

Holding in a huff just begging for release, Madison took the snapshot from her grandmother and did as instructed. The pencil writing was faint, but she could read it easily enough. *'Pair of handcrafted chairs given as wedding present from Herman and Amelia Yank.'*

"Nice wedding present," she allowed. She still didn't

understand how this explained anything.

"Now let's look at the bottom of that chair."

"Do you know how heavy that thing is? It was all Derron and I could do to get it unloaded and in here."

"You and Derron are wimps."

Despite her bold claim, even with Madison's help, Granny Bert had trouble turning the chair upright. Careful not to put pressure on the antique legs and snap them off, together they managed to tip the chair over so that the underside was exposed.

"What are we looking for?" Madison asked.

"The masters always signed their work," the elder woman informed her. "It was a sign of quality workmanship and pride, something that's sadly missing in today's culture."

Madison spotted a deep scrape along the bottom of the seat frame. "Is this it?"

"Nah. Too jagged. That looks more like something gouged into it, maybe by accident. No, more like... this! See this?"

She saw what her grandmother pointed to, but she couldn't make out the details. Fishing her cell phone from her pocket, she used the flashlight feature to illuminate the spot.

Carved neatly into the wood were the words 'Yank & Son, Brenham, TX. 1918.'

"You see? I told you!" Granny Bert gloated. "This chair originally belonged to Juliet Randolph Blakely and once sat in the house you now own."

Madison was duly impressed. "You were right, Granny. This chair was part of a set." She pulled back in wonder, letting the irony sink in. "How weird is that? I go to an antique store in another town and buy a chair that not just looks like the one I own, but is, in fact, part of an original set!" She shook her head in amazement.

"It is ironic, I'll give you that."

"I wonder how they got separated in the first place. Wonder if Miss Juliet got rid of the second chair when her husband died in that tragic accident? Maybe it was too difficult, seeing his empty chair there beside hers."

"No," Granny Bert said thoughtfully. "I remember these chairs. That's why I went looking for the picture to begin with. Both chairs used to sit in the formal library. Your Uncle Jubal and I used to slip in there by way of the secret passage, and we would hide under the chairs when we heard someone coming. I remember banging my head on one of them hard enough to see stars." She rubbed the offended spot, as if she could still feel the pain after seventy-five-plus years. "If you look real close, you may see some of my hair stuck in the joints."

"Maybe that's what caused the gouge," Madison teased. "Your head is certainly hard enough."

"It had to be, to raise first your father, and then you," the older woman retorted.

"Do you remember if both chairs were in the house when you inherited it?"

Granny Bert searched her memory banks. "You know, I think they were. I know they were there shortly before Juliet died, because I remember sitting in them when I came to visit. But I didn't sell the chair, so how in tarnation did it wind up at a resale shop in Navasota?"

"I have no idea. Help me turn it back upright."

Her grandmother grumbled as they manhandled the bulky load. "I declare! Forget coal. This thing must be filled with rocks!"

"It certainly felt like it to my back side," Madison said with a grin. "You're right. This seat cushion *has* to be replaced."

Something fell as they returned the chair to its proper position, clanking against the concrete floor like a lead brick.

"I think we were right!" Madison giggled. "It sounded like a rock just fell out." She swooped down to retrieve the fallen object, snatching it up in her hand.

When she opened her fist to inspect the rock, a gasp escaped her lips.

"Granny!" Her voice came out in a shocked whisper. "Is—Is this what I think it is?"

"If you think it's a gold nugget, then, yes. I'd say that's exactly what it is."

5

With enormous eyes, they stared at the golden chunk in Madison's palm.

"This—This is incredible," she murmured.

Her grandmother's hand wasn't quite steady as she reached for the golf-ball-sized nugget.

When she lifted it to her mouth and tested it with her teeth, Madison cried out, "What are you doing?"

"Beats me, but they always do that in the old westerns."

Ignoring her grandmother's antics, Madison was still in shock. Her mouth hinged slightly ajar. She finally stated the obvious. "This is actually *gold*."

"It appears that way."

It took a full moment to process, but the thought came to them at the same time. "Let's see if there's more!"

"Wait!" When her grandmother would have clawed her way through, Madison cautioned, "Don't tear the fabric!"

"How do you propose we get inside, without ripping it open?"

"There's a little hole right here." Madison slipped her finger into the rip she had found earlier. "Let me see if I can feel anythi... yes! I feel something!" Holding her mouth just right, she worked her finger back and forth to enlarge the ripped seam. When her crooked finger snagged something cold, she carefully extricated a long, golden chain. A crudely formed heart-shaped nugget swung at its end, its surface naturally rugged and irregular in its raw state. Embedded into the crevices, several small diamonds and rubies twinkled in the light. It was the oddest piece of jewelry either had ever seen.

"I—I don't believe this," she breathed.

"Believe it!" Granny Bert said. "And work faster, or I'm taking a pair of cutting shears to this chair."

"I need the fabric in one piece for a pattern. Let's turn it back over and go at it from underneath."

The previous weight seemed to disappear. With new energy, they easily had the chair upside down again in no time.

"Gently pull the fabric away from the wood frame."

"When it comes to gold, I don't do gentle," her grandmother snorted impatiently. "You'd better do it."

"Give me a minute. I just need to loosen this part here... and this side..."

While Madison proceeded with care, Granny Bert mused, "Just think. All the times I've sat on this very chair, I never dreamed I was sitting on a fortune!"

Continuing to work the fabric free, Madison said, "Which begs the question, '*why* were you sitting on a fortune?' Why would someone—presumably Miss Juliet—hide gold inside a chair cushion?"

"Times were different back then. People didn't trust banks like they do nowadays. It wasn't unusual to bury money in your yard or hide valuables inside your house. The more common the hiding spot, the more sense it made."

"But a chair?"

"Why not? Obviously, it worked!"

Freeing the fabric from around the wooden bracing, Madison dug her fingers into the cushion's dense cotton batting. As her nails scraped against something hard, her eyes lit up and she smiled. "There's something more inside."

In all, there were three more golden nuggets of varying sizes. One was almost large enough to cover the palm of Madison's hand.

Staring down at their discovery, Madison once more shook her head in awe. "This is insane. I still can't believe it."

"I can't believe she left it there all those years, untouched!"

"Do you think she forgot about it?"

Granny Bert snorted. "Look at that glitter, girl! Would *you* forget something like that?"

"No, but as an heiress to the Randolph Estate, apparently Juliet Blakely was financially set for life. Maybe this was insignificant compared to the rest of her fortune."

"You forget. I was the benefactor of her estate. There was no grand fortune." Her tone was dry. "Don't misunderstand me," Granny Bert was quick to add, lest she sound ungrateful. "I was nothing but her cook's daughter, and yet she left most everything to me, including the mansion, the town, and about sixty thousand dollars in cash. But that was hardly enough to make her forget she had half a million dollars or so stuffed inside a chair cushion!"

Madison couldn't let the first part of her grandmother's statement go unchecked. "You were also her friend, and the one person she hadn't alienated with her bitterness." That settled, she added, "But if Juliet didn't hide it in there, who did?"

"I have no idea. She lived alone in that big old house, rattling around with only a handful of staff.

Believe me, if any one of them had a fortune like that, they wouldn't have been working for her in the first place."

"I guess I should call Brash. He'll know what to do."

"What do you mean, know what to do?" Granny Bert demanded sharply. "Are you calling him as your husband, or as the law?"

"Both, I guess. But as the law, he'll know the proper channels for reporting the gold."

When she reached for her phone, she found her arm snagged by her grandmother's steady grip. "Not so fast. Why would you report the gold? And to whom?"

"I—I have no idea," she admitted. "But I'm sure Brash will know. He's dealt with found items before."

"That's because they're most often lost or stolen. Neither one seems to apply in this case."

"But... But... But..." She sputtered like an old-time percolator.

"Who originally owned the chair?" the older woman demanded.

"Miss Juliet."

"Who owned the chair as late as '83?"

"Miss Juliet."

"In 1983, who did she leave the house and all of its contents to?"

"You."

"And who did I sell the house and all of its contents to?"

A groove appeared between her brows. "Me."

"Who purchased the chair from *New Again*?"

"Me."

"We're not sure how the chair came to be at *New Again*, and I can't swear to its whereabouts from 1983 until just now, but I do know that fabric is old. Older than forty years. So, given the fact the chair was original to the Big House, and not only do you now own the Big House, but you also purchased the chair from a legitimate and reputable business, who do you think is the rightful owner of said chair?"

"M—Me?"

Granny Bert poked a gnarled finger into Madison's arm. "You. So why would you report a lost and found item, when you're already the rightful owner?"

"Because it's full of gold! It must be worth a fortune!"

"A fortune that is now yours, child. Don't look a gift horse in the mouth."

"No." Madison shook her arm free. "No, that gold is not mine."

"Then whose is it?"

"I have no idea. That's why I need to report it!"

They had reached an impasse, staring at the other with determination shining in their eyes.

"Do you still have Juliet's old journals?" her grandmother suddenly asked.

"Yes, of course. I would never get rid of those. They're a piece of this town's history."

"Let's go through the journals and see if they make any mention of having or hiding something valuable, or of any strange happenings in the house."

"I think having someone slip into her room and watch her sleep qualifies as strange." She referred to Juliet's friend and secret admirer slipping into her room by way of a hidden staircase and gazing at her with unrequited love.

"But we already know about that," Granny Bert reasoned. "I'm talking about something new. If you find something in the journals, you'll know the gold belonged to her and now reverts to you, so reporting it would be pointless."

"We've already read most of the journals," Madison reminded her, "when we were trying to find the person the skeleton belonged to."

"But we only skimmed through them, looking for names of people who may have frequented the house. At any rate, before he died in the cellar, Clarence could have hidden his fortune in the mansion for safekeeping. Juliet may or may not have known about it. Either way, they're long dead, so they have no claim to it. Either way, it belongs to you now."

"I—I don't know about this..."

"Have I ever steered you wrong?" At her granddaughter's incredulous look, Granny Bert quickly amended the question. "Have I ever had anything but your best interests in mind?"

The concession was reluctant, if not cautious. "Well... no."

"So, trust me on this. Let's not mention this to anyone, not until we have a better idea of who hid the gold, and why."

Frantic eyes flew to meet hers. "Not even Brash?" Madison cried.

"Your husband is the ultimate Boy Scout. If he thinks there's an inkling of suspicion concerning the legality of the stash, you know he's going straight to a higher authority, most likely the Treasury Department. And what do you think the government would do with that gold?"

"Take it?" she speculated.

"Exactly! It wouldn't matter if you could prove it was part of Juliet's estate or not, because by then, it would be theirs. Unless you're prepared to hand it over to them right now, I strongly suggest we sit on this for a while longer." Granny Bert darted a glance to the upturned chair and smirked. "No pun intended."

"I still don't like keeping something from Brash..."

"You told him about the chair?"

"Of course not! But that's different. That was a

birthday present."

"Think of what a birthday present a few pounds of solid gold would be!"

Madison pursed her lips, contemplating the situation. She still found it mind boggling.

Sensing she was weakening, Granny Bert suggested, "What about this? You were planning to keep the chair a secret for another three weeks. Let's give ourselves three weeks to find out who hid the gold. If we don't know by then, we'll tell Brash about it and let him help decide what to do. Fair enough?"

"I—I guess."

"Then we have a deal? Three weeks to find the truth, or we go to Brash."

Madison took the hand extended to her and shook. "Deal."

After a moment, a new worry occurred to her. "In the meantime, what do we do with the gold?"

"Let's split it up. Not because we don't trust one another, but because of its value. And because," Granny Bert added in a cautious tone, "like it or not, it could come with a potential for danger."

"I suppose you're right. If anyone should find out we have this... Oh, Granny, you're right! This could put us in danger! We should just tell Brash and be done with it."

A crooked finger waved in Madison's face. "Three weeks. You promised me three weeks."

"But..."

"A deal is a deal. We shook on it, Madison Josephine Cessna. You can't back out on me now."

With a defeated sigh, Madison nodded her head.

Granny Bert was right. A Cessna never reneged on a deal.

6

Madison stuffed the necklace and two of the nuggets into her purse. She wasn't sure what was heaviest—the gold or her guilty conscience.

She sneaked into her own house and hurried to hide the items in a safe location. But where? Even in a house sprawled across three stories, she couldn't seem to find a secure hiding place. She eventually stashed the contraband in the hidden panel where she had discovered Juliet Blakely's personal journals. If the overhead cache in her private library was good enough for the original owner of the house, it was good enough for Madison.

Before leaving her bedroom to start dinner, Madison tested the weight of her bedside chair. Heavy because of its solid frame and size, it nonetheless seemed lighter than the chair she recently purchased, giving her no reason to suspect it harbored its own gold. Even if it had, she reasoned, the secret would most likely have been exposed when Kiki recovered it to match the stylish new suite of rooms.

The thought gave her pause. How trustworthy was the designer? Being famous didn't automatically make her honorable. In fact, so often the exact opposite was true. What if Kiki had, indeed, found a hidden trove of gold and kept the discovery to herself? For that matter, had Kiki even done the work? She could have easily handed it off to one of her staff. Their integrity was just as questionable.

Madison bit her bottom lip, imagining how *that* conversation would go.

Excuse me. You did some work at my house almost a year ago now. Did you by chance discover some hidden gold while recovering an old chair? By the way, that's a stunning diamond tiara you're wearing with your cashmere work shirt. And I love your new yacht.

"Earth to Mom. Come in, Mom."

The unexpected voice startled her, causing her to jump.

"Blake!" Nerves made her voice sharp. "What do you mean, sneaking up on me like that?"

"I called your name like five times. Hardly sneaking." The sixteen-year-old frowned as he pulled a jug of orange juice from the refrigerator and poured himself a generous portion. "What's for supper?"

"Something with ground turkey."

"Spaghetti squash?" he suggested in a hopeful voice. "With some of that garlic bread you make?"

"See if we have enough squash. You can eat one all by yourself. Do you know if Megan will be here for supper?" Brash's daughter split her time between parents. The vivacious teen also happened to be best friends with Bethani, Blake's twin, and had been a permanent fixture in the Big House long before her father was.

"I think she and Beth are up in their rooms doing 'homework.' So, you know, talking on the phone."

"Then we'll count her in for supper. How was baseball practice?"

"Good. Coach says I should make All-District

without a problem."

"That's nice," Madison murmured, her mind distracted by a certain stockpile of gold.

"Mom? Can I ask you a question?"

"Sure, honey. What is it?"

"Why did you just put the turkey, package and all, in the oven? I thought you browned it in a skillet. Without the plastic and Styrofoam."

"Oh, my word! Look what I did!" She jerked open the oven, thankful she hadn't turned it on.

"Mom, are you okay? You seem... stressed."

"What? You think I'm hiding something?" she all but shrieked.

"Nooo," Blake said, drawing the word out. "That never occurred to me." He flashed a wide smile. "Until now. But you are, aren't you? You're hiding something." His blue eyes lit with intrigue. "Is it for me?"

"No, it is *not* for you!"

"But you *are* hiding something."

"Go upstairs and do your homework."

"I don't have any homework."

"Then go upstairs and help your sisters do theirs."

"I'm pretty sure they don't need my help doing the kind of work they're doing." His blue eyes sparkled again. "They're trying to waggle invitations to Prom."

"In that case, they *do* need your help. Be a good brother and scare the boys away. Remind them that Brash is the chief of police and not someone to be crossed."

"Mo-om," he started, stretching the protest into a two-syllable word.

"If you don't want me wrecking the entire meal, you need to give me a few minutes. It's... been a long day."

If there was one thing her son took seriously, it was his food. Without another word, he turned and vacated the kitchen.

Five minutes later, the conversation reincarnated itself. This time, with Brash.

"Hello, my gorgeous wife."

Madison jumped, banging her head against his nose as he nuzzled her neck.

"You scared me to death!" she accused. "I didn't hear you come in."

"I called your name twice. And you may have broken my nose."

"I'm sorry, sweetheart. Does it need ice?"

"I'll survive."

"What are you doing home so early?"

"It's thirty minutes past my usual time. Is supper ready, or do I have time for a quick shower?"

"You have time."

He peered over her shoulder, to the uncooked meat in the skillet. "It helps if you turn the burner on," he suggested.

"Very funny." Madison discreetly turned off the empty back burner, instead engaging the one beneath the skillet.

"Honey? Why is the spaghetti squash in the microwave still whole? Don't you usually cut them in half and scoop out the seeds before you cook them?"

"Uhm, well, you weren't here to cut them in half for me," she offered lamely. *Darn it! She had done it again.*

Brash casually stopped the dual microwaves and pulled the squash from their plates. "I'll let these cool before I cut them. In fact, I'll go take my shower and come back to help you cook. Maybe then you'll tell me what's bothering you."

She attempted a look of innocence. "Who says something is bothering me?"

Brash dropped a kiss onto the end of her nose. "I

know you too well, sweetheart. Something is definitely bothering you." He walked to the refrigerator, took out an opened bottle of wine, and splashed some into a glass. "Here," he said, pushing the goblet into her hands. "Drink this and try to relax. I'll be back in ten minutes."

Madison accepted the offer with a sigh.

It would be a very long three weeks.

With Brash's help, Madison managed to get dinner on the table. She considered it a bonus when she neither served the meal raw nor caught the kitchen on fire. While the teenagers washed the dishes, Brash led her out to the back-porch swing. It was a sad commentary on her state of mind that she followed him like a calf to slaughter, lured there by another glass of wine.

"Talk to me."

She didn't quite meet his eyes as she hedged, "We talked all through dinner."

"We listened to the kids talk," her husband corrected. "I now know more than I want to know about who's taking who to prom, who broke up and who's hoping to get back together, and why Stephanie Havlicek can't wear a white dress. Which, by the way, I thought only applied to wedding gowns, but obviously, high school has changed from when we were there. And in a big way, if that's now considered appropriate conversation at the dinner table." With a heaved sigh, Brash shook his head in sad reflection.

"Amen to that. Remember when we only wore long evening gowns to Prom? Now they wear these short little dresses and stiletto heels. I remember when—"

"You can continue this trip down memory lane if you like, but don't think I'll forget that you have artfully changed the subject and owe me a full explanation of what's eating at you tonight."

"You keep saying something is bothering me, but it's not."

"Maddy, we both know that's not true. Just tell me. Maybe I can help."

If only she could tell him! But she had made Granny Bert a promise, and she intended to honor it.

"Is it something at work? Something with the kids? Something *I've* done?" He leaned in close to ask the latter, nudging her with his arm.

She nudged him back, a smile hovering on her lips. He was too irresistible for her own good. "None of the above."

"But there *is* something."

She knew he would continue to needle her. She finally blurted out, "It's your birthday! I don't know what to get you for your birthday."

"Is that all?" Brash stretched his arm out along the back of the swing and pulled her in close. "Sweetheart, I have everything I've ever wanted, and everything I'll ever need. I have you. I have Megan, and Bethani, and Blake. That's more than enough for any man."

After accepting his kiss, Madison leaned her head against the steady thump of his heart and soaked in the goodness that was Brash deCordova. How she loved this man!

"I understand that, and I know how you feel," she told him. "I also know you won't let me get by with that same answer when my birthday rolls around. This is the first birthday we're celebrating together, and I want it to be special."

"It will be. I'm spending it with you."

"And I'll be buying you a gift, so you may as well as give me some ideas."

"I honestly can't think of a thing I need."

"Then tell me something you want."

"You."

"You have me. You gotta do better than that."

"There *is* nothing better than that," he murmured, nuzzling her neck.

"See? This is exactly why I'm in a frenzy, trying to decide what to get you and what to do for your party!"

"I'm having a party?" A look of concern crossed his face.

"We always celebrate birthdays with a party. Don't you?"

"Sure. For Megan. Or when someone turns a memorable age, like fifty, or seventy-five. I'm turning forty-three. Just an ordinary old birthday."

"There's nothing ordinary about celebrating the day you were born. I, for one, think it should be a national holiday." She ran her fingers through the dark, auburn fringes of his hair, tugging his face down for a kiss.

"A national holiday, huh?" His mouth hovered over hers.

"Absolutely."

A holiday called for fireworks. When Brash rained kisses down upon her, a shower of sparkling lights danced through Madison's head. His lips trailed over her cheek, along her jaw, and into the curve of her long, graceful neck. Maddy obliged by moving her head and giving him better access.

"Sweetheart?" Brash murmured between kisses.

"Yeah?"

"Why were you out on Sawyer Road yesterday?"

She pulled away, swatting at his chest. "No fair!" she accused. "You're trying to take unfair advantage of my distraction."

"On the contrary," he countered smoothly. "I'm asking before *I* got too distracted."

"Nice try, Mr. D."

"You didn't answer my question."

"What? You're spying on me now?"

"Of course not. In a town as small as The Sisters, I don't need to. Nosy neighbors do the work for me." He wiggled his eyebrows in a jest before explaining, "Burl Evans called and said he saw you out his way. He wanted to let us know he sold his watermelon patch to his daughter and son-in-law so they could build a house, but that he'll still have plenty of melons when summer rolls around. He's moving the patch out to his other property off County Road 451."

"I saw that. Looks like a nice house. Does his daughter live here?"

"Not yet. His son-in-law is a professor at A&M but will commute once the house is ready and they move in. He said College Station was growing too fast, and they wanted to raise their children in a small town. What took you out that way? Do you have a new client?"

"As a matter of fact, I do. Monte Applegate has me on retainer."

Brash ran the name through his mind. "Applegate. I know Herman Applegate and his wife Jean. She's a big-time artist and has showrooms in Austin, Dallas, New Orleans, and a couple of other places. Remember? She gave us that painting of bluebonnets for our wedding."

"Yes, I love that painting."

Brash tried to place her new client. "I know their son Troy, but I don't think I know a Monte."

"He's Troy's son. And before you ask, he's all of eleven or twelve, and he's paid me a very generous sum of twenty-two dollars to find his lost dog."

A smile hovering on his lips, Brash nodded. "Ah, now I know who you're talking about. Officer Schimanski mentioned a boy came in, wanting us to help find his dog. He promised to keep an eye out for the pup but explained we couldn't dedicate any resources to searching for a lost pet."

"Hence, my latest gig."

"Any luck?"

"I made a preliminary drive-by of the yard he escaped from and the area Monte says the dog likes to roam. It's about a mile down the road, but he prowls around Lamont Andrews' house sometimes. Which is unfortunate, because Lamont doesn't like dogs."

"I'm not sure there's many things Lamont Andrews likes, other than money, flashy cars, and flashy women."

"Yeah, I sort of got that vibe."

"Just from driving by his house?"

"Not... exactly."

Brash gave her his infamous smirk. "How, exactly?"

"On my way home, I dropped by the *Gold and Silver Exchange*. I'd never been there before, so I thought I'd look around and maybe ask a few questions."

"And?"

"And it's nothing more than a glorified pawn shop, if you ask me."

"Was Andrews there? Did you get to ask your questions?"

Her sigh was heavy. "Oh, yeah." She felt her husband's gaze boring into her, even though she studied the night sky. "He made his dislike for dogs very clear. He said if he found it there again, he would shoot it. Then he kicked me out of the store."

Beside her, Brash bristled. "He kicked you out of the store?"

"He told me they were closed, totally opposite of what he had said when I first came in. By that time, he knew I wasn't a paying customer, and he didn't want to waste his time on me."

"I don't want you going back there again."

Hearing the growl in his voice, she quickly assured him, "Don't worry. I don't intend to! But why, by the way, do you say that?"

"There's something about the man. I can't put my finger on it, but I don't trust him. He's known to have a volatile temper and, if you ask me, he's a bit paranoid. He's always claiming there's someone lurking around his shop, trying to break in. I can't tell you how many false alarms I've answered over there."

"Doesn't he have an alarm system?"

"Yes, and plenty of locks to back it up. But we all know a lock is only designed to keep an honest man out. If a criminal wants in, he'll find a way."

7

The man fumbled in the dark. Clumsy without the aid of overhead lighting, his fingers at last connected with the lantern. He twisted the button, cranking it to its full extension.

Two thousand lumens of bright, white light flooded the old barn, washing it with the harsh brilliance of LED illumination.

He looked around with satisfaction, taking stock of his treasures. The shelves were full, piled high with valuables. A meticulous inventory list accompanied each set of shelving, detailing the precious items and separating them into distinct collections.

Some were treasures the man had collected in his travels. The more he had to scour for them, the more he treasured them.

Many were investments. Sure bets for a profitable return.

Others were insurance for the future. Their value would only increase over time.

Still others were short term. Disposable items he could sell as the need arose.

The light glinted off the neatly aligned items, winking back at him with hues of shimmering gold, warm copper, and shining, dancing silver. It was a rainbow of metallic color, and it was his. All his.

Together, the items on these shelves were his kingdom. His destiny.

As an afterthought, the man remembered the dog.

"Where are you, mutt?" he grumbled. He whistled, but the dog didn't come.

"Some watchdog you are! I put you here to guard my treasures, and you're off chasing a rat!" He grumbled again but pulled something from his pocket. "No matter. I brought you kibble. You can have it for dessert."

The man took a final survey of the barn, a smile lingering on his face.

All his.

8

On her last day of work at *New Again Upholstery*, Madison tried to soak up as much knowledge as possible. She was full of questions, including those about her recent acquisition.

"Do you keep records on where your furniture pieces come from?" she asked.

"As much as possible, but often times, we acquire items from unknown origins."

"I don't understand."

"Sometimes, we purchase a piece at auction or off the internet. We go to garage sales and flea markets, and, yes, we even do a little dumpster diving from time to time," Ralph Musa acknowledged without apology. "People bring things in to sell or trade. Sometimes, they ask us to recover a piece and then never return to pick it up. After six months, it goes out on the floor to sell. We try to learn the history of a piece, but sometimes we never know its background."

"I don't suppose you remember how you acquired the chair I bought?"

"The red velvet?"

"Yes. The one I'm recovering for Brash." *The one with a fortune stuffed inside its cushions.*

"I'll check the records to be sure, but if I'm not

mistaken, we got that one on a trade. A few months ago, a man came in looking for a locker-type cabinet with a lock. Said he needed it to store valuables in. He offered the chair as a trade, and I liked its bones. I thought it seemed like a fair trade, so we made the deal, and he took the cabinet with him."

"I don't suppose you remember his name?"

"I certainly do. There's no need to check the records; it's all coming back to me now. A few days after the transaction, I wondered if he thought to secure the cabinet to the floor. As light as it was, it wouldn't be a secure location for anything of great value. A thief could easily make off with lock, stock, and cabinet. I decided to give him a call, so I looked up his contact information. The guy called himself Paul. Paul Revere."

"How original."

"He was an odd one, all right, but seemed harmless enough."

"Do you remember what he looked like?"

"Gray hair. Maybe some sort of beard. About my height. A few years my senior, I would guess."

The description was so vague, it could be anyone over the age of seventy. It didn't give Madison much to go on.

"If you need help recovering the chair, just let me know," he continued. "It's a good, solid piece. I'll be happy to lend you a hand."

"Thanks, Mr. Musa. I appreciate that. And I may just take you up on your offer."

"It would be my pleasure."

On her way home that afternoon, Madison stopped by *New Beginnings* to grab a cup of coffee with her best friend. She could use the jolt of caffeine to prepare herself for the evening ahead. Brash had the late shift, so she could spend the time pouring through Juliet Blakely's old journals.

Genny gladly took a break and joined Madison at the back booth.

"You have a smudge of frosting right here," Madison advised, touching the correlating spot on her own face.

"Oops. Hazards of the job." With a giggle, Genny brushed a hand across her cheek. Touching her finger to her tongue, she nodded. "Buttercream frosting like what's going on Virgie Adams' birthday cake. Mr. Hank is throwing her a party for her eightieth birthday."

Blowing on her coffee to cool it, Madison nodded. "Granny Bert is looking forward to going. It's a surprise, right?"

"Supposedly, but Miss Virgie was in here the other day, dropping hints on her favorite cake flavor and talking about buying a new dress."

"Busted."

"It seems that way," Genny agreed. "But it's sweet of him to try. I know she's been down in the dumps lately, what with the trial and all."

"It must be hard, knowing your son and grandson are going to prison for what will no doubt be the rest of *her* life, at any rate. I testified when called, but I didn't stay for the full trial; living through it the first time was enough for me, thank you very much. I heard Gerald got twenty years. Paul was sentenced to an extra four, because of the hidden mics."

Genny clucked with disapproval. "Greed," she all but spat. "Just because they thought *their* family should have inherited the old house, instead of Granny Bert."

"Exactly. But it was Miss Juliet's house to do with as she pleased. *I* had absolutely nothing to do with it."

Back in the day, Truman Ford had been butler at

the old estate, and Rose Hamilton had served as cook. Their children and grandchildren, including Hank Adams and Bertha Cessna, practically grew up in the house and had quite naturally developed an emotional attachment to the property, even though any sense of ownership stopped well short of a legal claim. There was a long-held assumption that the butler's offspring would be named heirs, so when Juliet Blakely left everything to her cook's daughter, the news hadn't settled well.

Gerald Adams and his son had nursed the grudge until it became a sickness. They turned the old family business of "bootlegged" liquor into a modern-day meth lab and refused to let the old rivalries between the towns die. More because of her family name than the fact she now owned the old mansion, Madison had been caught up in their madness.

"Yes, but karma won out in the end." Genny flashed her trademark dimpled smile. "Each of you is now living in your respective Big House. Theirs is run by the state, yours is run by love." The dimples deepened. "Karma."

After a mock toast with their coffee cups and a shared chuckle, Madison moved to a new subject. "Your friend Mr. Pruett seemed in rare form the other day. Has he had any more midnight callers?" Her hazel eyes danced with amusement.

"Not that I'm aware of. He came back the next day with some other tall tale, but I haven't seen him yet today. He normally comes in at least every other day, always to order the very same thing. You would think he would grow tired of chicken-fried steak, but he eats it at least three times a week."

"My guess is that the man likes order with little variation. Just look at his wardrobe. I've never seen him in anything but khaki work clothes."

"You have a point," the restaurateur agreed. "The only thing he ever changes are his stories. According to him, he's had 'a long and distinguished career' in either the Army or the Navy, he's been the band leader for an all-female orchestra, he's a retired helicopter pilot, done a jaunt with the Secret Service, served on the Board of Directors at the Smithsonian, spent eight years designing and building a helicopter that will make him a millionaire many times over, and done undercover work for the nation's top security agencies and at least two administrations. For my own safety, he can't be more specific. With so much classified information that can't be revealed, he's worried the documentary about his life will have too many holes in it." Genny flashed her dimpled smile. "By my best estimate, the man should be about a hundred and twelve, give or take a year or so."

"That could make for a long documentary," Madison mused with a smile. "Maybe they should consider turning it into a mini-series."

Genny rolled her eyes. "Don't give him any ideas. According to him, the producer is either his daughter or his niece, depending on the day he tells it. I'm afraid to call him on the oversight, in case it turns out to be one of the situations where she's actually both."

"Sounds like the Havlicek family," Madison murmured, unable to keep the grimace off her face.

"That's what I'm afraid of. But in this case, I think he just forgets which story he made up last."

"You seem to know him as well as anyone. Some people say he makes up these stories because he's lonely and doesn't have a life outside his imagination. Others say he's delusional or even borderline psychotic. Which do you think it is?"

Genny pursed her lips, thinking before she answered. "I don't think he's dangerous, if that's what you're asking. I want to think it's nothing more than an overactive imagination. I want to think he's just a lonely old man, with no wife, few friends, and a housekeeper who only comes twice a month. I *don't* want to think he's just out-and-out lying. Nor do I want to think he's that detached from reality."

Madison heard the lingering doubt in her friend's voice. "But?" she prodded her.

Genny's sigh was heavy. "But I just don't know. Some of his stories..." She shook her head, reluctant to repeat some of the outrageous claims he had made. "He's big on conspiracy theories and top-secret investigations that, and I quote, 'will rock this community when the truth is discovered.' According to him, there's some sort of scandal currently underway at *Juliet Bank and Trust*, an investigation of questionable practices at the Naomi Post Office, and," she lowered her voice in imitation of the older man, "'strange goings-on' at *The Gold and Silver Exchange*."

Madison didn't share her friend's laughter. Instead, her brows puckered together.

Genny was quick to notice. "What's wrong?" she asked.

"I recently made my first trip to the *Exchange*. By mutual agreement, I won't be going back."

Genny's gasp was audible. "Lamont Andrews threw you *out*?"

Madison's shrug was casual. "More or less."

"How does one 'more or less' throw another someone out of a place of business? On the few and rare times I've had to ask a customer to leave and never come back, there was nothing 'more or less' about my request. Believe me. They *knew* they were being thrown out!"

"Lamont Andrews told me, in no uncertain terms, that he was *closed*." Seeing her friend's look of confusion, Madison waved her hand in airy explanation. "It was in his tone."

Genny chose to nod in agreement, even though a frown still puckered her forehead. "What, exactly, prompted such a reaction from the store owner?"

"I was questioning him about my latest case."

"You have a new client? That's great. Who is it?"

Client confidentiality aside, Genny was her best friend. Plus, she often helped Madison solve some of her more perplexing problems. Madison had no qualms about sharing. "Monte Applegate."

"As in ten-year-old Monte Applegate? About yay high—" Genny held her hand up to indicate his height "—with red hair and rosy cheeks? *That* Monte Applegate?"

"He's paying me the very respectable amount of twenty-two dollars to find his dog," Madison explained.

"Ah, that's what he was doing in here talking to you the other day. We got so busy after that, I never had a chance to ask you about it."

"Pup is fond of wandering and often visits Lamont Andrews' house, which is about a mile down the road. Mr. Andrews made it abundantly clear that he does not like dogs."

Genny wrinkled her nose in distaste. "From what I understand, Lamont is known for his temper."

A shudder worked through Madison's shoulders. "I only got a glimpse of it, but what I saw wasn't pretty."

"Have you found the dog yet?"

"Not yet. I haven't told Monte, but it's not looking too favorable. Pup's already been gone almost a week."

"I saw the posters around town."

"And on your bulletin board," Madison pointed out.

Genny shrugged. "It seemed the least I could do."

"Well, not the *least*," Madison said pointedly, looking at her friend with hopeful eyes.

"Uh-oh. I know that look. And doesn't Lamont Andrews live out on Sawyer Road? The same road where we did reconnaissance at the old Muehler place?"

"So we already know the area," Madison was quick to say.

Genny was still skeptical. "If I recall, that adventure didn't end so well."

"But last year, we were dealing with illegal cockfights and a gambling ring. This time, we're merely searching for a lost dog."

"I seem to remember dogs in that location, as well."

Madison made one very important distinction. "Unlike the Rottweilers, this is a friendly dog."

"I assume you plan to go, with or without my help," Genny surmised.

"How can I not? He's my client."

With a resigned sigh, Genny asked, "Do I need anything special? Running shoes? Black clothing? A supply of pork chops?"

Madison looked at her friend in confusion. "Pork chops?"

"It's a dog. I thought you might try to lure him out with food."

"That's not a bad idea, but no, you don't have to sacrifice tomorrow's lunch special."

"You wanted to go tonight?" Genny asked in dismay. "The hubby and I have plans."

It was still odd, thinking of Genny as a married woman, but Madison had never seen her friend happier than she was now.

"I don't want to ruin any plans you and Cutter have," Madison replied. "I know it means waiting all weekend, but I was thinking Monday afternoon. Before five o'clock." When Genny merely studied her with narrowed eyes, Madison scowled. "Stop looking at me like that. I don't plan to break into his house and barn. I just want to look around."

"While he's at the store," Genny clarified.

"You know it's ingrained in our Southern hospitality to invite visitors in for refreshments. This way, I'm saving him the bother."

Her friend wasn't buying it. "I don't think Lamont Andrews is the sort of man who's concerned with the rules of hospitality."

"But why put him to the test?" Madison reasoned. "I'll just have a look while he's not around and save us both an unpleasant confrontation."

Genny frowned. "In an odd way, that almost makes sense."

"Then you'll go with me?"

"Sure. We haven't had much excitement in the last couple of weeks."

"And with any luck, we won't have any then, either. Just a simple recon mission."

Genny's dimple showed again when she grinned. "When are any of our schemes simple?"

Over the course of their twenty-five-year friendship, the two had freely schemed and plotted, always knowing the other had her back. Explanations and excuses weren't necessary; if one asked for help, the other agreed, no questions asked. Things didn't always go quite as planned, but they never faced the situation alone. Whether it was getting stuck on the water tower while writing 'Seniors 95' in hot-pink letters, fleeing across a field in the dark while chased by dangerous men, startled goats and angry Rottweilers, being trapped in a burning house after 'letting themselves in' to snoop, stealing away to Ft. Hood to see a boyfriend deploy only to discover he was a three-time cheater, or dozens of other antics that ranged from hilarious to harrowing, the friends came through the trials and triumphs. Together.

"So, maybe we get off track some of the time..." Madison agreed with an innocent shrug.

"More like *most* of the time!" The bell on the door jangled, drawing Genny's attention. "Oh, look. Speak of the devil."

Mr. Pruett shuffled into the diner, clad in his customary khaki outfit. He seated himself at his favorite table, not far from where the two women sat. They could easily hear him place his order for chicken-fried steak and a glass of sweet tea.

"Told you." Genny grinned.

"If only his tales were as dependable."

Before the after-school waitress had an opportunity to escape, Mr. Pruett started on one of his stories. Genny made a mental note to commend her girl later; to her credit, the teenager bit back a grimace and managed to look semi-interested in what he had to say. She politely listened as he rambled on with his latest rant.

Today, he obsessed on another conspiracy theory. One word piqued Madison's interest.

Gold.

Sitting up straighter, she strained to hear his words. Laughter from another table made the rant difficult to hear. Catching only a word here and there, she frowned over at her friend. "What's he saying about gold and some government conspiracy?"

"Ooh! I know this one!" Genny's eyes twinkled with animated glee. She bounced in her seat and patted the table like a game contestant ringing a bell. "It's his latest and greatest obsession. Something about the government confiscating all the gold. Something about Teddy Roosevelt and the urgent need to hide all gold and silver from the 'prying eyes of Big Brother.' He gets really worked up over this one."

Still acting as if it were all a game, Genny missed Madison's audible gulp.

"Hiding... gold?" she squeaked. For thirty glorious moments, she had forgotten about her own quandary over hidden gold. It came back now with a sickening rush.

Genny still hadn't noticed her discomfort. She was too busy mimicking the older man's voice, repeating the words she heard often enough. "It's the only way to preserve our constitutional rights. We have a duty to our forefathers to—"

The laughter from the other table died down. They could hear Mr. Pruett again, his voice ringing loud and clear. Genny yielded to the words from the man himself, almost in perfect sync with her own.

"—to our forefathers to resist the call to turn in our gold. The certificates they'll give in exchange aren't worth the paper they're written on! It's Roosevelt's way of seizing what's rightfully ours so the government has total control of the gold market. That way, they can make us or break us at will. Mark my words, you'd better hide every ounce of gold and precious metals you possess. Do *not* hand them over to the government!"

"That should be easy enough," the young waitress said with a sad sigh. "I don't own any." She generously overlooked the fact that Roosevelt was simply a name from her history books. All she knew about him was that he was once president.

"Believe me, I have mine stored in a secure location. I've acquired an impressive collection of jewels and precious metals over the years, but I swear on the grave of my beloved wife, Big Brother will never find them and take them from me!" He pounded the table for emphasis, his usually colorless cheeks taking on a blush of anger.

"Big Brother?" Latricia was clearly confused by the

term.

"Uh-oh," Genny said, all traces of her former humor gone. "Looks like it's time for me step in and save the girl from a totally different rant, this one on the internet and the invasion of our privacy. It's the infamous book *1980* come to life, he claims." With a roll of her eyes, Genny slid from the booth and bid her friend farewell.

9

It was a rare occurrence, but Madison had the evening to herself. Being Friday, Bethani was spending the night with Megan at the Aikman household. Blake would go home with Jamal after their out-of-town baseball game. Madison usually attended his games, but this one was two hours away and a rare miss for her.

With the kids gone and Brash at work, it left Madison free to peruse the old journals in leisure.

As fascinating as the entries were, she didn't have time to read every one of them. There were twenty-six journals in all, spanning seven decades.

Instead, she concentrated on searching the flowing script for key words and references to anything hidden. Given the fact Miss Juliet was unaware of the illegal moonshine still in the basement or the hidden spiral staircase that secreted from her bedroom to the crude room in the sub-basement, Madison didn't hold much hope for such insight.

The entries were like a time capsule into the past, detailing the growth of the area and the slow and withering death of the author's most cherished dreams. Juliet Randolph began the journals as a young woman, full of hopes and ambitions. She had grand plans for the future and for the newly established town bearing her name. The pages chronicled the path of her life, which started with such sweet promise, but slowly soured with time.

The turning point in her life hinged upon one fateful summer. Those few months held the happiest moments of Juliet's time on Earth, as well as the most devastating.

In the spring of 1919, cotton king Bertram Randolph's illness exceeded the knowledge of local doctors. A specialist came in from Boston, a handsome young man who promptly stole the heart of both of Randolph's daughters. Though by all accounts a brilliant physician, he couldn't save the man's life, but his arrival changed the towns forever.

The story was a staple in local lore, about how Darwin Blakely couldn't decide between the prim and proper Juliet, and the vivacious and daring Naomi. His indecision cemented the rivalry between the bickering sisters and their prospective towns. Dallying with both women's affections, he finally made his choice, but the damage was done. Soon after he and Juliet returned from their honeymoon trip, word came that Naomi was expecting his child, and the downward spiral began.

Madison didn't bother reading the entries from that time. Having read them before, she knew they were filled with alternating bouts of fury, hatred, betrayal, and humiliation. She remembered that, ironically, most of the rage was directed solely at the sister, and not the man responsible for her pregnancy. Many people believed Darwin Blakely took the coward's way out when he died in a freak accident mere weeks after the discovery. It was no wonder his widow turned bitter after that, valuing her pride and her standing in the community more than she valued her own flesh and blood. The entries immediately following Darwin's death were even more difficult to read, so Madison chose not to. She skimmed the pages, at best, hoping a single key word would pop out at her.

When she finally came across the word *treasure*, she snapped to attention and pulled the leather-bound book in for closer inspection.

Despite the gaping hole left in my soul, despite the pain that seems too heavy for one heart to bear, I cherish the brief time I had with my beloved husband. He made my life richer for being in it. The treasures he gave me go beyond the weight of gold and the sparkle of jewels; Darwin gave to me his heart. He shared with me his dreams. He shared his hopes for making a difference in the medical field, not just here but worldwide. He wanted to one day travel the world and introduce modern medicine to foreign lands. My dearest husband possessed a generous heart; his inheritance was destined for something greater than himself, he claimed. His was a golden dream. A golden life tarnished too soon by the cruel hand of fate.

Madison read the words a second time, trying desperately to read between the lines. Was there a hidden meaning among the prose? Why had she chosen those particular words? Words like *weight of gold*, *sparkle of jewels*, and *golden*? What was this inheritance she mentioned?

Though no one had ever said as much, Madison always had the impression that Darwin had been a bit of a fortune seeker. Apparently, Granny Bert didn't share that impression, however, as she had named one of her sons after the man. No doubt, she had chosen the name out of respect for her friend and the warm memories the older woman shared of him.

Not being privy to those memories, Madison knew very little about the man, other than he was some fancy doctor from up North and considered a specialist, something that was still rare in those days. She knew an advanced education came at a cost, which suggested he was a man of means. Having heard the stories of how he toyed with the two sisters' hearts, she always thought it had more to do with money than it did love. She suspected he chose the woman most likely to advance his career: Naomi was too unpredictable and outspoken for most social circles, after all, whereas Juliet was the epitome of good manners and the perfect hostess for a distinguished doctor's climb up the ladder of success.

She had drawn her conclusions, in part, from a conversation she and Granny Bert had not so long ago. The first time Madison read the journals, she ran across an entry referring to Darwin's grandchildren. Sadly, Love, the daughter he had with Naomi, died as she gave birth to her second child. More than once, Love's drunken, widowed husband had come to Miss Juliet, demanding money he felt his family was entitled to. According to her grandmother, Juliet's lawyer insisted the illegitimate heirs had no legal claim to her fortune, primarily because Darwin Blakely did not contribute to her wealth. In her mind, that equated to him mooching off the cotton baroness, but what if she were wrong? They were hardly married long enough for the ink to dry on their marriage certificate, much less their bank statements. Just because Darwin was a two-timing scoundrel didn't mean he had no money.

Maybe she had been wrong about him. She knew being a cad had nothing to do with what was in a man's wallet, and everything to do with what was in his heart. What if they each had their independent fortunes, left to them by wealthy parents? What if Darwin's inheritance included four sizable gold nuggets and a unique necklace?

Still, why would that inheritance be stuffed inside a

chair cushion? It made no sense.

Madison made herself a note to learn more about Darwin Blakely. She jotted down a few thoughts before returning to the journal. Flipping back to entries first mentioning him, she read word for word. Considering the physician quickly became the enamored writer's favorite subject, she realized it might take a while. Miss Juliet penned page after page about the man, extolling his endless virtues and recalling every moment they spent together. Why mention something as mundane as a metallic rock when she could write endlessly about the light in his tender eyes or the strength in his arm when he escorted her to and from his prized automobile?

Madison gave special attention to the entries around Darwin's proposal and their brief engagement. There was no hint of a dowry or an extravagant wedding present from her bridegroom. Instead, her husband gifted her something much more personal—a built-in bookcase for the bedroom, where she could keep her most treasured trove of books. Madison already knew he had commissioned the piece to be built while they visited his family in Philadelphia, even though, unbeknownst to them, the carpenter added special details of his own. Their month-long absence offered plenty of time to construct the secret staircase and dugout room, hidden deftly behind the new bookcase.

Considering the possibility that they may have brought the inheritance home with them when they returned to Texas, Maddy searched for mention of added baggage or perhaps the generosity of his family. There was nothing to hint at either. Growing frustrated, she spent the rest of the evening pouring through the journals until her back ached and her eyes threatened to cross. Worst of all, she was barely through the decade in which the couple married. Another five or so decades loomed ahead, waiting for her in yet more journals.

Feeling defeated, Madison returned the books to the secret cubbyhole in the second-floor library. In the future, she would pull the volumes out one by one as she read them. Climbing up and down to retrieve and replace two dozen books was hard on her back, and perhaps part of the reason for its protest. Plus, removing the leather-bound journals left her newly added box exposed and unprotected. If she wanted to keep the box's golden contents a secret, she couldn't risk having it seen.

On impulse, Madison opened the box, just to make certain the items were still safely tucked inside.

It felt wrong, somehow, leaving such a valuable necklace to tangle there in a box otherwise filled with rocks. Even if those rocks were made of gold, wasn't it possible they might crush the chain? Somehow rub against the pendant and knock a jewel loose? She had no idea of the necklace's actual worth, but it had to be in the hundreds of thousands; even without the diamonds and rubies, the nugget was quite large and quite valuable. It seemed almost sacrilegious to leave it there, unprotected, to languish in a simple cardboard box.

"I suppose it's better than being stuffed inside cotton batting, crushed by who knows how many tooshes over the years," she murmured aloud. "It's a wonder it's still in one piece!"

She pulled the necklace out to examine it. She hadn't decided yet if she thought it was exquisite or atrocious. The only thing she knew for certain was that it was one of a kind. The nugget itself was in its natural state, leaving her to suspect the irregular heart-like shape of the stone was compliments of Mother Nature, rather than a jeweler. Left unpolished, it was rough and jagged in places. In those crevices and cracks, jewels had been added. Madison was hardly a diamond expert, but she had no doubt these were the real thing. The only question was *why* someone would stud a raw nugget of gold with such precious stones. Surely, the jewels would have more value if they were set in a traditional form of jewelry. She could envision the diamonds and rubies swirled into a magnificent ring. Imagined them fashioned into a proper pendant, secured in place by delicate white-gold prongs.

How were these jewels even attached? If she didn't know better, she would think this was an amateur job. But who kept a collection of precious stones laying around for a craft project? And who used a gold nugget worth hundreds of thousands of dollars as a blank canvas? Something was *off* about this piece of jewelry. It was too unusual to be ignored, yet too odd to be admired.

Still undecided on how she felt about the piece, Madison returned it to the box, but not before wrapping it in a tissue. It seemed the least she could do to protect it. At the last minute, she snapped a photo of it with her phone, marking the picture *Hidden.*

Tucking the box back behind the journals, another piece of jewelry flashed through her mind. The jewels from the *Gold and Silver Exchange* were as out of place on the dog collar as they were on this crude gold nugget.

"Obviously, some people have far more money than I do," she reasoned with a sigh, "if they can place precious stones so frivolously. If *I* had a dozen or so extra diamonds laying around..."

She never finished her sentence.

"And what would you do, wife of mine, with a dozen or so extra diamonds?" Brash's voice asked from the doorway. The sound startled her so badly, she almost fell from her perch as she slid the hidden panel back in place.

"Watch it, Maddy!" he warned sharply, rushing across the room to act as a safety net. His handsome face pulled into a scowl. "What are you doing up there to begin with?"

"I—I—" She stumbled over an answer, the same way her feet stumbled over a steady foothold. She waited to reply until she was once more on solid ground. "Your birthday is coming up. Don't ask questions, and don't go snooping around." As an afterthought, she added in an irritated tone, "And don't be sneaking up on me like that!"

"Didn't you hear the tone when I disarmed the alarm? And again, when I armed it?"

"Obviously I didn't, or I wouldn't have almost fallen off the stool!" she all but snapped.

"Why are you using a stool, anyway? That's what the library ladder is for. Remember how cool you thought that was the first time you used it?"

"It's also way over there, and I'm over here. The stool was quicker."

"But the ladder is safer," he pointed out. His dark eyes twinkled as he lifted them to the secret panel. "So, you're hiding my gift, huh? What is it?"

"I'm not telling you!"

"Will I like it?"

"No, I bought you something I knew you would hate." Madison rolled her eyes, not yet ready to be charmed by his smile or the playful light in his eyes.

"If you're thinking jewelry, I'm not really a diamond sort of guy," he advised. "Even if other people are frivolous with their jewels, I can't really see me in a diamond tiara. I'd rather have a new fishing pole or tackle box."

"How long were you standing there?" she asked with suspicion.

"I came in on 'more money than I do' and the sound of the sliding panel." He shook his head in pretend remorse. "Didn't get to see a thing."

"Good. Stop being so nosy."

"I didn't know I was." He pulled the belt from his waist and loosened the buttons of his uniform. "But since I apparently am, I'll be deliberately nosy and ask who has so much more money than you that they can be frivolous with their jewels?"

"Uhm, I saw a ridiculously extravagant dog collar the other day." At least this much was true. "It had diamonds, rubies, and sapphires, of all things!"

"Diamonds? On a dog collar?"

"Okay, so the diamonds were actually cubic zirconia, but the rubies and sapphires were real."

When Brash walked into the adjacent bedroom, Madison trailed behind, eager to put distance between them and her hidden secret. He sat on the edge of the bed to tug the cowboy boots off his feet.

Exactly why he needs a chair, she noted with satisfaction.

"Where did you see something as crazy as that?" he asked with a chuckle. "Some city slicker with a pet poodle who wears booties and a mink-lined coat?"

"That may have been where it came from originally, but I saw it right here in town. At the *Gold and Silver Exchange*."

Brash released a small groan. "That's exactly where I've been for the past hour."

"Really? Did they have another suspicious person lurking around?" It had happened several times over the past few months. In fact, she recalled Brash mentioning a similar complaint when she first came back to town. That was over a year ago.

"No. The cleaning crew accidentally set off the alarm. Even though Sandy Henry admitted her mistake and apologized repeatedly, Lamont Andrews insisted I search every inch of the place."

Madison glanced up at the clock, surprised to see the late hour. She had spent more time reading the journals than she realized. "What was the cleaning crew doing there at this time of night?" she asked, opening the double doors of the walk-in closet.

When she first saw the design for her newly remodeled suite of rooms and extravagant closet, she thought it was overkill. What was Nick Vilardi thinking, putting double doors on a closet? Now, just a few months later, she couldn't imagine squeezing through a standard doorway carrying an armful of laundry.

Shrugging out of his shirt, Brash said, "I asked the same thing. She said business has picked up, and she has to work all kinds of crazy hours to fit everyone in. Since most of her jobs are businesses who want the work done after hours, it means working well into the night."

"If business is that good," Madison reasoned, stepping from the closet with her gown in hand, "she should consider hiring more help."

Brash flashed her a smile. "I told her that, too. She asked if *In a Pinch* washed windows."

Distracted by the sight of her husband's bare chest, she of all people understood the sensation it created during their homebound honeymoon several weeks ago. The man—*her* man—was sculpted of muscle, and very finely so. She still saw occasional pictures floating around social media sites, despite Brash's desperate plea for the madness to stop. They tried getting an injunction against the media outlets who released the photos, but multiple photographers had snapped the pictures and the images had gone viral. Recalling the pictures was like recalling words spoken into the wind.

"Windows?" she murmured, losing the thread of the conversation.

Bending to take off his socks, Brash shrugged. "I guess even cleaning services outsource their least favorable jobs. Everyone wants sparkling windows, right? But no one wants the job making them sparkle." Despite his easy banter, his voice betrayed his tiredness. Standing to unfasten his jeans, he turned in time to see the sparkle in his wife's eyes.

The lines of exhaustion vanished from his face.

"Maddy, darlin'?" he drawled slowly.

"Yeah?"

"You don't need that gown."

10

The man moved along the uneven floor of the old barn, his feet shuffling across the warped and weakened boards. He carried a clipboard in his hand as he counted, recounted, and confirmed the inventory of the shelf.

"Copper collection. Check."

Satisfied, he hung the checklist back in place and moved to the next set of shelves. He repeated the same process.

"Jewel collection. Check."

He paused long enough to pat the dog on the head. Reared up on its hind legs, Pup rested his furry paws on the man's knee.

"There's a good boy," the man cooed. "There's my watchdog. You'll guard my treasures, won't you, boy?"

Pup wagged a shaggy tail in reply, and the man moved along, returning to his work.

"Silver all accounted for. Check."

Another shelf, another inventory.

"Ancient artifacts. Check."

He crossed to the far side of the old structure.

"Modern art. Check."

He moved in front of the next set of shelving, a frown marring his face. "Vases. All here. Except...

where is that Chinese vase? No, not the Nippon Jade. The... ah, yes. There." The frown gave way to a look of serenity. "All accounted for. Check."

There was one last shelf.

"Ah, the gold."

He lingered here, carefully inspecting each piece. Counting. Recounting. Counting again. The repetition brought him comfort. He had always liked numbers, particularly if they pertained to his wealth. There was safety in numbers. Security.

Numbers were finite. They never changed. Even when everything else in life changed, numbers never did. Numbers didn't evoke his anger. Numbers didn't taunt him. Numbers didn't confuse him. Numbers comforted him. He liked numbers.

"Gold. Check."

He enjoyed counting so much, he liked numbers so well, that he started over again.

"Copper collection. Check."

11

As soon as Monday's lunch crowd thinned, Madison and Genny left for their recognizance mission.

"This brings back *way* too many memories," Genny moaned as they took the blacktopped road out of town. She peered out the front windshield, scanning the sky. "Is it getting cloudy outside? I swear it's getting darker by the minute. Oh, wait. That's just the memories of that night."

Madison ignored her theatrics. "Or maybe it's the shadows from the trees. It really is a lovely drive with all the trees edging the road, creating those lacy patterns on the pavement."

Genny merely grunted. A few miles down the road, she muttered, "That little clump of trees isn't so lovely. That's where we parked our getaway car. And that's the fence we had to crawl through to escape the goats, the dogs, and the men with guns."

"Technically, the fence would have only stopped the goats," Madison pointed out. "Had they not been distracted, the dogs and the men would have kept coming. If we look closely, we may see traces of my clothes still snagged in the barbed wire."

"Thanks for the reminder. And for the record, that burned-out shell of the Muehler farm *definitely* isn't so lovely."

"It gets prettier as we go," Madison was quick to assure her. "See? A nice big hayfield, with all that tall grass, just blowing in the wind, waiting to be cut and bailed. Oh, and look. Deer."

"I enjoy a drive in the country as much as the next person, Maddy. In fact, I live down a road very similar to this one, in case you've forgotten."

"Is something wrong, Genny? You seem... a bit testy."

"I'm fine. It's nothing."

"Really? Because it feels like something. We've gone on a hundred of these goose chases, you and me. One of us says frog and the other jumps, no questions asked. But this time, you're asking questions. So, I know it's something."

"I guess you're going to point out that, normally, it's me who says frog, you who jumps."

Madison couldn't help but smile. "That's true. You're usually the leader of our shenanigans. I've always been the one to play it safe."

"Until last year, when you came back to The Sisters," Genny pointed out. "I've seen a definite change in you, girlfriend. You have a new confidence about you. A new strength. New leadership abilities."

"Is that your eloquent way of saying I've taken over and rooted you out?"

"Not at all. I couldn't be prouder of you! I've always known you were a strong woman, but since Gray's death, you've really come into your own."

"Trial by fire," Madison mumbled. "But we weren't talking about me. We're talking about you."

Genny studied the passing scenery. "I'm not accusing you of taking over," she assured her friend. "But feel free to do so at any point. Lord knows, you've followed me on some wild and crazy stunts." She chuckled in memory before continuing, "If I'm finally stopping to ask questions, maybe I'm just finally catching up to you. Maybe I'm finally growing up, myself. Maybe I see the importance of becoming more responsible, less reckless."

Madison gasped aloud. "Genesis Baker Montgomery!" she gushed. "Are you *pregnant*?"

She glanced over in time to see her friend blush. "We're trying," Genny admitted.

Madison all but squealed. "This is so exciting! My best friend is going to be a mother! I'll finally be an aunt!"

"It's too soon to say, but I'm hoping..." Genny cupped her belly with a protective hand. Her blue eyes shone with excitement. "But, please. No one knows we're even trying."

"I won't say a word," Madison was quick to assure her. She almost bounced in her seat. "But a *baby*! It's been so long since I held a tiny baby in my arms. My babies are almost grown. It seems like only yesterday, our roles were reversed. Gray and I were trying to get pregnant, and you were already picking out names."

"Little did I know you'd need two names!" Genny laughed. "And as much as I love the twins, I sincerely hope I don't follow suit. I'm terrified enough over the thought of one baby, much less two!"

"Terrified? What's there to be terrified of?"

"Ha! Listen to you, putting up such a brave front. I've been right there beside you, sister. All the times you cried, wondering if you were up to the task of raising children. The first time you spanked Blake and you called me, second-guessing yourself while bawling your eyes out. The first time—"

She interrupted her friend with a firm but gentle voice. "You're right, Genny. You were always there for me. Just like I'll be there for you. But you already have an advantage. You've always been such a huge presence in Blake and Bethani's lives. You've helped raise them, so you already have experience. And I can't think of a single soul who will be a better mother than you." Madison reached out her hand to squeeze her friend's fingers.

"Thanks, Maddy. That means a lot to me." Genny returned the squeeze.

"If you want me to turn around, I will. I'll drop you back at the café. No hard feelings."

"There certainly will be!" Genny huffed, drawing her hand away. "If you take me back and make me sit on the sidelines while you have all the fun, there will *definitely* be hard feelings! Don't you dare leave me out, girlfriend. Not until I'm too big to waddle to the car or until I've gone into labor."

This was the Genny she knew and loved. Madison laughed, promising, "I wouldn't dream of it."

Five minutes later, they parked the car just down from Lamont Andrew's house and casually walked into his yard. If someone happened to be home—a girlfriend, for instance, or for some reason Lamont, himself—their cover story would be car trouble.

When no one came to the door, they took it as an invitation to look around.

"I don't get it. What does Pup find so fascinating about this place?" Genny asked.

"Beats me. Lamont doesn't have kids, doesn't have a dog, doesn't even have a cat Pup can torment. He certainly doesn't offer treats and belly rubs when Pup shows up, but *something* is fascinating enough for the dog to keep coming back."

Genny motioned with her blonde head. "What's in the shed?"

"Fort Knox, judging from the padlocks."

"Hmm. It looks like a hard wind could blow it over."

Madison nodded. "That's exactly what I said." They

stood back to ponder the barn's stability. "Does anything strike you odd about that barn? Besides the locks, of course."

"Not really. Looks like a typical old hay barn to me."

"But, look at Lamont's house and how neat the yard is. Then, look at the grass around the barn. It doesn't look like it's been cut all year."

"Obviously, he uses the driveway as a dividing point. Left side neat and trim, right side wild and woolly. What's so strange about that? He probably seldom uses the barn."

"Then why the overkill on locks and chains? And why are there tire tracks leading up to the door? Someone has been here recently."

Genny flashed a smile. "That's part of the beauty of living in the country. No city ordinances on keeping yards mowed. I know we have a *huge* yard around the farmhouse. Cutter started putting up a fence, but until it's finished, he uses an imaginary line to determine where the yard ends. He mows up to the edge of it and not an inch more. Looks like Lamont Andrews does the same thing."

Madison shrugged in agreement as they crossed the gravel driveway and approached the barn. Picking their way forward through the unkempt grass, they edged up to the barn and peered through the cracks of the weathered boards. The interior of the old structure was dark, offering no hint as to what laid inside. Maddy pushed on a few of the boards, testing their strength. One rattled in place. Another swayed inward with applied force. None gave way completely.

"I guess it's sturdier than it looks," she decided.

They circled the old barn, realizing it was larger than they first thought. It sat in the far-right corner of the property, backing up to the edge of the neighbor's high game fence. Only a thin strip of grass separated the two properties.

"Sure. Back here, the grass is controlled," Madison muttered.

"Makes sense," Genny reasoned. "I imagine the game ranch sprays around the perimeter to keep the fence free of grass and briers."

"Look." Maddy pointed. "I think something's been digging back here."

"Pup?"

"Maybe."

Madison found a missing knothole large enough to peer through. She engaged the flashlight feature on her phone and aimed it into the abyss. There was just enough light, and just enough eyeball space, to make out a row of shelving along one wall. She could tell that most of the shelves were full but couldn't see well enough to determine what they held.

"This isn't working."

Madison concluded with a sigh, stepping away from the building.

"At least we tried."

"I guess. And I don't see any signs of Pup having been here recently." Reluctantly, Madison turned to leave. "I'll just have to break the news to Monte that—"

"Wait." Genny held up a restraining hand. "Do you hear something?"

"I hope it's not Lamont coming home."

"No, it sounds more like... whining. Maddy, I think it's a dog!"

"Pup! Here, Pup!" Maddy called.

From inside the barn, a dog barked. The sound came from the front of the structure, but the more they called, the closer the sound came. It was now mingled with excited whimpers, yaps, and the steady thump of a wagging tail.

"We hear you, boy. And we're going to get you out

of here," Maddy promised.

"And how do you propose that?" Genny demanded. "These boards are more solid than they look. Remember?"

"There's got to be something around here we can use to pry a board loose. It only needs to be a small opening." She looked around, hoping a pry bar would magically appear. When that didn't happen, she took matters into her own hands. "You stay here while I go find something."

Mission accomplished, Madison returned a few minutes later. She found Genny crouched down at the dog's level, visiting through the boards. The blonde woman had found another knothole to stick her finger through, and Pup was busily licking her fingers, bringing laughter with his exuberance.

The laughter died when she saw her friend lugging a large, heavy ax. Her eyes widened in surprise.

"You aren't seriously going to use that thing, are you?"

"I most certainly am!"

"B—But... that's breaking and entering, " Genny sputtered. "Destruction of property. It's bad enough that we're trespassing. Lamont Andrews will throw every accusation he can against us, until one of them sticks." Her eyes widened even more. "I don't want to have this baby in prison!"

"Okay, you are definitely pregnant; the Genny I know doesn't panic like this." Madison rolled her eyes, all the while secretly thrilled for her friend. "First of all, I have no intention of entering. I'm just trying to get Pup to exit. Second, we might be doing him a favor, tearing down a decrepit old barn like this one. However, there's no reason to get that wild look in your eye. I don't want to tear it down. I just want to loosen one board. As for trespassing..." Madison looked over at her friend and grinned. "It only counts if you get caught."

"Madison Josephine! When did you become so cavalier about breaking the law? And you, the wife of the chief of police! What's happened to you?"

"Like you said. I've had a year and a half of personal growth. Desperate times have called for desperate measures, and if I've been anything since Gray died, I've been desperate. I think I finally realized what you and Granny Bert have been telling me all along." She lifted the ax with determination. "Sometimes you gotta do what you gotta do."

As Pup licked her fingers again and whined in what she was certain was a plea for help, Genny heaved out a resigned sigh. "I think Pup is desperate in there. And I think there's some sort of animal cruelty law that says you can rescue a trapped animal." She stood and brushed off her hands. "Let's do this."

In Madison's mind, the feat was easy enough. All she had to do was lift the ax over her shoulder, swing it a time or two, the board would splinter into a dozen pieces, and Pup would be free.

In reality, the ax weighed a ton. She couldn't get it above her elbow, much less swing it with gusto. How did Brash make this look so easy? She had watched him cut wood for bonfires and his parents' fireplace a dozen times, and he never had a moment's hesitation when wielding the tool.

Maybe that's how he gets those killer abs, she mused, momentarily distracted by thoughts of her husband.

When she did finally manage to get in a good, hard swing, the blade bounced off the weathered wood as if it were made of rubber.

"I think it's so old it's petrified!" she panted, already exhausted with her meager efforts.

"Let me take a swing," Genny offered.

"No! If you *are* pregnant, I plan to keep you that way. No ax, my friend."

"Then I better stand back. You look a little dangerous with that thing. I'm afraid you might chop off my leg or something."

"I don't have the strength. Just like I don't have the strength to break through one of these boards."

"Maybe we could pry one loose. Just enough to let him out."

It took far longer than it should have, but after ten minutes of grunts, groans, two broken fingernails, a gallon of sweat, and more strained muscles than either cared to acknowledge, they were successful. Wedging the ax between two boards, they wiggled and coaxed until a few nails pulled loose. With a loud creak, one of the boards gave way and slowly scraped against the dirt. It was a tight fit, but with coos of encouragement from his rescuers, Pup squeezed through the narrow opening and scampered to freedom.

Exhausted, the women fell back onto the ground to rest. Pup ran circles around them, happily yapping and licking, professing his undying gratitude.

After a brief respite, Madison was still panting when she said, "We—We need to get out of here."

"You may have to help me up. I'm not sure I can move."

Pup danced around their feet as they walked back to the car. "School's out by now," Maddy said, glancing at her watch. "I hope Monte is home."

"I saw the school bus go by while you were putting the ax back."

"Can you imagine how happy he'll be when he sees his dog?" Madison was already smiling, envisioning the happy reunion. She opened the door to the backseat. "Get in, boy. Let's take you home."

12

Knowing she had reunited the boy and his dog gave Madison a warm feeling of accomplishment and satisfaction. No money on earth could equal the reward of seeing the youth's happiness over having his beloved pet back.

She was vague on details when telling Brash the good news. She admitted little more than finding the dog near Lamont Andrews' house, 'about the same place he had gone missing.' Offering her husband a second helping of his favorite dish and quickly changing the subject, Madison narrowly avoided an inquisition by the lawman. It helped that all three teens were home tonight, all vying for a chance to talk about themselves. With a grateful smile, Madison gave them the floor.

With one case down, the next morning, Madison turned her attention to another problem: finding out more about the gold.

Immediately after starting her online research, ads popped up on her browser and social media sites with offers of gold coins, fine jewelry, and the best price for an ounce of gold.

"But searching the internet is anonymous, right?" she muttered in aggravation. "No one is tracking my history. And I'd love to sell you a prime piece of mountain property down in Galveston, too." She sighed, thinking Mr. Pruett was right. Big Brother was always watching, and he had been reincarnated as the World Wide Web.

Madison decided to walk over to the public library and contaminate their browsers, instead of her own.

The fact that the library was directly across the street from the Big House was hardly by accident. When drawing up the city plat, Juliet Randolph (later Blakely), insisted the library be adjacent to the mansion. She funded the project herself and set up a generous trust fund for decades to come. Despite the current decline of libraries worldwide, the Juliet Municipal Library was ensured a long and prosperous future.

Even with such easy access to the thousands of books inside the public library, the Big House sustained two libraries of its own. The formal library on the first floor, filled with many first-edition treasures and literary greats, now served double duty as the official office for *In a Pinch*, superseding Madison's previous space at *New Beginnings'* back booth. Juliet's upstairs personal library, filled with books curated to fit her precise tastes and whimsy, was now Madison's personal office and sanctuary. Despite her offer, Brash had yet to set up his own desk inside.

With a nod to the library's benefactor, Madison researched Darwin Blakely first. She wasn't surprised to see an entire section dedicated to Juliet's true love. There were artifacts from his life and times, quite a few of his medical books, photographs of the man and of the couple on their wedding day, and various volumes of literature and reference books tying back, however loosely, to the handsome physician. The section was a literary shrine to the man Juliet had loved and lost.

Madison soon learned that her earlier assumptions about the doctor had been wrong. He hadn't been an opportunist, taking advantage of Miss Juliet's wealth. He had plenty of his own. From everything she read, he came from a very rich and upstanding family in Philadelphia. Old money, even back then.

Hope flared within her when she read that his uncle, Hiram Blakely, amassed even greater fortunes when he struck it rich in the Alaska Gold Rush. Maybe the gold had belonged to Darwin! It was too soon to say if he was the one to hide it in the chair, or if Miss Juliet had done so after his death, but it offered a new possibility.

Her hopes sank when she realized that Hiram was ostracized from the family for his chronic sense of wanderlust. He died during a mining accident, never to be reunited with the loved ones left behind.

After spending the morning with her nose in books, by noon, Madison's head swirled. She felt as if she had taken a crash course on that elusive element called *gold.*

While Alaska and California were known for their gold rushes, Madison learned that gold could be found in most any state and any country. Even Texas had seen a few small claims over the years. She was certain, however, that the gold in the chair wasn't native to her state; nuggets that size would be considered a major find, she was sure.

Her research revealed inconsequential information on how to mine for gold, the best places to find, buy, or sell the commodity, the differences in quality and grade, the history of mining, and the world's largest claims. But after hours of research, however, she never found a hint of how the four nuggets came to be inside the chair.

"Are you still finding everything you needed, hon?"

the librarian asked.

Puffing out her cheeks, Madison spoke more to herself than the older woman. “A secret gold rush here in River County would be nice. We have so many caves around here, some of them could have held gold, right? Even better, a listing of unclaimed gold would be nice. Sort of like a lost and found for gold nuggets.”

Sadie Bealls propped her hands upon her generous hips and beamed with pleasure. “Is Mr. Jenkins still using that in his science class? We cooked up that assignment thirty years ago! I didn’t know he still used it.” She misread the confusion on Madison’s face for worry. “Oh, don’t you worry, hon. I won’t spill the beans about you helping your young ‘uns with the assignment. As long as you send them in at least once or twice to gather information, I’ll play along with you. The whole idea of the assignment was to not only make science fun, but to hone library and research skills, as well.”

Madison quickly recovered. “Uhm, yes. It sounds like a brilliant plan.”

“Why, thank you, hon. Like I say, I helped develop the assignment *years* ago. Come to think of it, it may have been closer to forty years ago. I’ve been retired as school librarian for over twenty years now.”

The elderly woman was roughly Granny Bert’s age and, like her grandmother, still active in mind and spirit. She led Madison on a brisk march to the rear of the library.

They entered a room lined with old tomes. A woman was cleaning, running a feather duster along the higher shelves by way of a ladder.

“I’m almost done in here,” she assured Madison. “If my dusting won’t bother you, I’ll finish this shelf and be done.”

“You’re fine. Don’t let me rush you.”

With a demure smile, the woman turned away and went back to work.

"So," Sadie Bealls told Madison with a sweep of her hands, "this is where you'll find most of what you're looking for. Local prospecting claims, assayer notes, and surveys are right here in the reference section. One aisle over, you'll find photos of local claims and the biggest nuggets found in each state. Another aisle over is lost and found."

Madison shook her head as if to clear it. "Wait. Two things. One, are you saying there have actually been claims of gold strikes here in the area?" Her mouth hung slightly agape.

Miss Sadie smiled indulgently. "I suppose that depends on how you clarify the word 'strike.' The truth is, hon, that every river in the world has traces of gold in it. Rain erodes rock walls containing the gold, and it naturally flows downhill, entering rivers and streams. Gravity pulls it downward where the current is slower. Eventually, deposits are formed. As the riverbeds dry up or shift, the deposits remain, either as flakes or nuggets. As you know, caves are formed when underground water cuts through rock formations, so it stands to reason there's gold in most caves, as well. Whether or not there's enough to bother mining is another matter, entirely."

Madison stared at her in fascination. "But people have tried. Right here in our area."

"Some people always try to strike it rich, hon. It's human nature." The librarian's smile looked sad. "What was your other question?"

"Pardon me?"

"You said you had two questions. That was only one."

It took a moment for Madison to collect her senses and retrace her line of thought. "Oh, yes," she recalled.

"The lost and found. There's truly a file for that? It was just wishful thinking on my part!"

"Well, now, why don't you just send your kids in and let them find that out for themselves?" With an ambiguous smile, the elderly woman sashayed away.

Madison stared after her in surprise. It took a solid moment to realize she had an audience. The woman dusting the shelves had listened to her exchange with the librarian in open curiosity, and still studied Madison's dumbfounded look.

With a sheepish smile, Madison lifted her hands in a helpless expression. "Who knew?"

As the rhetorical question needed no reply, the woman simply turned away.

13

"Granny? Granny Bert, are you home?"

"In the kitchen."

Madison made her way back to the heart of the old home. It was here that she had learned to cook. Here on the scarred countertops that her grandmother showed her how to measure ingredients for cookies and cakes and light, fluffy biscuits. Here she had learned to roll out piecrust, even though hers never quite came out like Granny's. Here at the old scrubbed pine table, she had done her homework and had late-night talks with her grandparents.

Here, that she had created a heart full of cherished memories. The laminate may have been old, and the appliances outdated, but in Maddy's eyes, the kitchen was perfect just the way it was.

"What's that?" she asked, peering into the massive pot as she dropped a kiss on her grandmother's wrinkled cheek.

"Jambalaya. Larry was down at the coast this weekend doing a little fishing and brought me back a whole mess of fresh seafood. I figured the best way to cook it was all at once. There should be plenty, if you and Brash want to join us."

"Who else is coming?"

"I invited Larry, but you know your cousin. Other

than business, he's been a bit of a loner since his divorce, but his parents will be here. Since Joe Bert and Trudy are coming, I invited Glen and Daisy. Might as well have two of my four boys together, even if the other two are scattered to the ends of the world."

Madison didn't point out the fact that neither her uncle's home in West Texas nor her father's missionary assignment in Africa were the ends of the world.

"What about Sticker? Is he coming?"

Her grandmother gave a disapproving sniff. "I haven't spoken to Mr. Pierce in the past few days."

"Uh-oh. Trouble in paradise again?" she guessed.

For over sixty some-odd years, her grandmother had been toying with rodeo legend Sticker Pierce's heartstrings. They had taken time out for marriages—a long, happy one for Bertha and Joe Cessna until his death eight years ago, and six or so marriages to various women, none of them particularly long nor happy, for Cutter's grandfather—but the two had become reacquainted last year when Sticker returned to The Sisters. Old flames still stirred between them, but both were too stubborn and too set in their ways to commit to anything beyond an on-again/off-again courtship. Granny Bert spent most of her time miffed at the older gentleman for still being so attractive and flirtatious toward other women, particularly those she had a long-standing feud with. More than once, Madison had compared the octogenarians' romance to that of teenagers.

"Paradise? Is that the name of that new club in Snook, the one where Mr. Pierce may or may not have been seen cutting the rug with none other than Dolly Mac Crowder?"

A smile hovered around Madison's lips at the outdated expression 'cutting the rug.' She doubted her twins even knew what that meant. They did know, however, that any sentence including Dolly Mac Crowder was a negative one.

"I think it's called *The Armadillo Hole*."

"Which is exactly where I'd like to stuff that old biddy. Her and her new pearly white false teeth. I'd send them both right down an armadillo hole!"

Madison knew when to change the subject. Her grandmother and Dolly Mac Crowder shared such a long and ancient history, no one was certain when or why their feud began. Everyone, however, knew it was still ongoing.

"Alrighty, then." Madison pushed away from the stove, but not before a last appreciative sniff. "I'll let you know if we can come for supper. I haven't seen any of the family since my wedding."

"That's the problem with folks these days," Granny Bert grumbled. "Always busy, busy, busy! Never take time for the important things in life, like visiting with kinfolk and strengthening family ties. No time for loyalty."

Madison hastily changed the subject, yet again. "Hey, I've got some good news. I found Monte Applegate's dog!"

"Really? Good for you." She looked genuinely pleased. "Where did you find it?"

"Believe it or not, he was locked up inside Lamont Andrews' old barn."

"On purpose?"

"I don't know. I hope not."

"You didn't ask Lamont?" Granny Bert propped one fist upon her hip and glared at her granddaughter. "You didn't demand to know if the man all but trapped that poor little boy's dog and left it for dead?"

"No, I didn't. And for good reason, so stop glaring at me."

"It'd better be good, girl. Let's hear it."

Madison hesitated before admitting, "I... may have been on his property without an official invitation."

Granny Bert leveled her gaze on her. "So, you were trespassing," she surmised.

"Sort of. And I may have sort of... broken into his barn. Actually, what I did was break the dog *out*." When Granny Bert didn't say anything, Madison hurried on, "What's important here is that the boy and the dog are reunited, and Lamont Andrews never has to know of my involvement in what is essentially a happy ending."

Granny Bert waggled a gnarled finger. "What's important here is that there's hope for you yet, girl! I swear, every day you're getting more and more like your old Granny!"

Unsure whether that was a good thing, Madison merely offered a wan smile. Genny had said as much yesterday. *Should she be concerned?*

"Did you come to work on the chair?"

Thrown by the question, Madison pursed her lips in worry. "No, even though I guess I should. Hey. If we do come for supper tonight, we'll have to keep Brash out of the garage."

"No problem. I'll tell him it looked like rain, so I hung my underwear on the indoor clothesline. No man wants to see his grandmother's unmentionables."

Blake hadn't wanted to see them, either, particularly while the older woman was wearing them, but according to her son, his young eyes had been scarred for life. And that was *before* the debacle with Granny Bert's geriatric exercise class with several of her friends.

"Actually, I came by to pick your brain," she informed her grandmother. She made herself a glass of tea and took a seat at the table.

"I'll gladly share my wisdom with you, child. What is it you'd like to know?"

"This wasn't it, but before I forget, you still have it hidden, right?" There was no need to call the gold by name. They both knew exactly what she meant.

"Girl, I once hid an expectant nanny goat in the house, and your grandfather didn't know about it for a week. Please don't insult my intelligence."

"Sorry. No offense."

"Your question?"

"What can you tell me about Joe Don Peavey and Hugh Jenkins' little scheme of panning for gold?"

"It wasn't a scheme. They had a nice little business going for a few years. The summer tourists especially enjoyed it."

"Did anyone ever truly find any gold?" Madison challenged.

"Doesn't matter. It was all in fun, and they had signs everywhere, warning folks they might not find a thing. But the fun was in the challenge, you know? That one chance in a million that you might actually find a little color." Her grandmother smiled at the memories. "Being the science teacher over at Sisters High, Hugh always threw in a little geology lesson with every try. And if you chose to take the big expedition, there was rock climbing, and hiking, and good, physical exercise for the kids. It was a shame, really, when they had a falling out and decided to close down."

"Actually," Madison had to admit, "that does sound fun. It sounds like something Blake would have enjoyed."

"You should book a trip to Mason this summer," her grandmother advised. "They have several topaz mining operations up there. It's the only place you'll find a blue topaz."

"Hmm. That sounds like fun, too. I may check into that."

"That's also where they filmed your grandfather's

favorite John Wayne movie."

"*The Searchers*?" Madison had fond memories of watching the old western classic, curled up at Joe Cessna's side.

"Sure is." Her grandmother nodded. "But I suspect we're getting sidetracked. Why the questions about *Muehler Creek Mining*?"

"I spent the morning at the library. Sadie Bealls says hello, by the way. I'll be honest. I was shocked to learn there were trace bits of gold found in our own backyard. Nothing the size of those nuggets, mind you, but gold, nonetheless."

"One or two folks found more than trace bits, but you're right. Nothing like what we found."

"There's something else I want to ask you about. I forgot to look it up at the library. I heard Mr. Pruett mention something about the government confiscating people's gold. I think it has something to do with Teddy Roosevelt."

"Close. It was Franklin D. Roosevelt, and it was Executive Order 6102."

"You mean it was real? I didn't bother looking it up at the library because I thought it was just another of his fantastical stories!"

"Nope. For once, he's telling the truth. Back in '33, the government decided they needed to take control of the nation's gold. Because of the Great Depression, folks lucky enough to have it were hoarding theirs, and it put the government in a pickle. They decided to make it illegal to own more than a small amount of the precious metal. They paid the people for turning it in, of course, but with paper. Then they turned around and upped the value of gold, which immediately devalued the dollar. It also made the government a handy little profit."

"*Our* government?" Madison clarified. "You're

telling me the United States government confiscated personal property from the American people?"

"Sure am. The very same people who took control of the liquor industry and made booze illegal. And you know how well *that* turned out."

Granny Bert was just getting started, tuning up to stand on her soapbox.

"These are the same folks who want to take our firearms and leave us defenseless. Mark my words, girl. Control a man's money, control a man's liquor, control a man's ability to defend himself and his family, and you control the man." She pounded her fist on the tabletop for emphasis. "That's not how the United States was meant to be, controlled at every turn by our government."

Madison appreciated her grandmother's passion, but her own mind moved in other directions.

She stood and paced around the table in thought.

"So, if someone was afraid their gold could be confiscated, it makes sense that they would hide it."

"You wouldn't believe some of the crazy things folks did, trying to hold onto their gold!" Granny Bert slapped her leg with a laugh, her earlier ire all but forgotten. "That was before my day, mind you, and the law was soon revoked, but I've heard the tales."

"So, hiding their gold in a chair wouldn't be at all unusual."

Granny Bert bobbed her gray head up and down. "I see what you're getting at. And a chair makes perfect sense. In fact, I don't know why I didn't think of that sooner! Even the necklace makes sense now."

"It does?" Madison questioned, her tone somewhat skeptical. "Because I've been having a heck of a time making sense of that piece. I can't decide if it's artistic or atrocious."

"There were clauses in the Order to allow for

personal jewelry, professional jewelers, dentists, and the like. It makes sense that someone tried to disguise a hunk of raw gold into passing as a piece of jewelry. And my vote, by the way, is on atrocious."

"Either they realized it would never pass scrutiny, or they were too embarrassed to wear it in public, hence its life amid the cushions." Madison's posture slumped. "Miss Sadie put me on a ton of information, but I didn't see a single neon sign that pointed to our chair."

"Of course not. That would be too easy, now wouldn't it?"

There was a definite whine in Madison's voice. "Just this once, I was hoping for easy."

"What have I always told you? Anything worth having is worth working for."

"Does that include finding a fortune you didn't work for and, therefore, probably don't deserve?" she asked in an artificially sweet voice.

"If you work hard enough to keep, it counts as earning it."

"You just made that one up," Madison accused.

"Doesn't mean it's not true."

"Tell me. *Why* am I the only one doing all this research? I feel like my head is going to explode!"

"Because if it were up to me, we'd sell the gold outright and be done with it," Granny Bert reminded her. "You're the one who's so worried about following the proper channels."

"Yeah, well, those proper channels have given me a major headache." Madison rubbed at her temples. "Did you know there's a lost and found for gold? Back in the day, if a prospector suspected someone swiped some of this gold, he could list it with the assayer's office. Assuming he had bothered to have it weighed to begin with, he could report the exact weight and a general description of it. If anyone found unclaimed gold, or if someone came in with a claim that matched it, officials were supposed to check it out before they were paid."

Granny Bert cackled at the absurdity of such an endeavor. "And I reckon it was never once enforced! What yahoo would turn in gold to the lost and found, instead of claiming it for themselves?"

While the older woman laughed and carried on about who would be such an idiot, Madison watched her with an unamused expression. When Granny Bert finally noticed, she sobered.

"Oh, right. You're one of those yahoos, aren't you?" she mumbled, only half under her breath. A snicker burst out again, but Madison wanted to believe it was the result of her further observations. "And how does one 'describe' gold? A lumpy rock? A bag full of dust? Anyone with a lick of sense would just pour a little out of the bag or knock a chunk off the rock so it wouldn't weigh the same thing. Sounds to me like they had some politician in charge of the operation, instead of someone with a lick of common sense in their head."

Madison let out an exasperated sigh. "Well, I'm running out of ideas here. I thought I was onto something when I read that Darwin Blakely's uncle hit it rich in Alaska, but it turns out he was the black sheep of the family and never returned from the Yukon. He died in the mines that made him a fortune, many times over. I can't find anything else—in the journals or in the library or even on the web—that offers insight into the gold we found stuffed in that chair. I don't know where else to look!"

"Try the journals again," her grandmother advised. "Especially around the time the Executive Order was in place. And maybe do one of those image searches on the internet. Ugly or not, someone may have taken a photograph of that necklace."

14

"Good morning, dollface," Derron Mullins greeted his employer. "Imagine seeing you here."

Madison looked anything but amused. "Very funny. Shall I point out that this is my office?"

Derron tossed his perfectly manicured blond head. "Shall I point out that today's Wednesday, and it's the first time you've set foot inside all week?"

Madison wrinkled her nose, knowing he had a point. Still, she needed to assert her authority, what little she had. "Shall I point out the fact that I could fire you for your insolence?"

"Shall I point out the fact that you love me and need me too much to ever do such a foolish thing? Especially since I just got us a new client?" He waved a piece of paper in the air, his look smug.

Giving up all pretense of making good on her threat, she brightened. "Really? Who, what, when, and where?"

"I'll give you one clue. It doesn't involve the world of journalism, even though you just hit the Big Five, minus the how." When she looked at him in confusion, he elaborated, "You know, the Five W's. Who, what, when, where, and how. The cornerstone of newspapers everywhere and the key to every good story."

"That's old school, my friend. These days, it's all about public opinion, not facts. No one cares anymore about—" She stopped herself mid-sentence, thumping a hand to her forehead. "Oh. My. Gosh. They're right. I'm turning into my grandmother!"

Derron looked horrified. "Heaven help us. One Granny Bert is more than enough!"

"You can see the kind of week I'm having," Madison complained. "And now I have to go back to the library and do another mind-numbing search, before I go back to Granny Bert's to work on Brash's birthday present. I need coffee."

"You have a cup in your hand."

She looked down, almost in surprise. Swallowing the remaining contents in a single gulp, she corrected, "I need more coffee."

"Let me get that for you, dollface." Derron jumped up from behind his desk and came to take her cup. "What was it you said you got your hunky husband for his birthday?"

Madison waited until he had pressed the button on the coffee maker before she waggled her finger in reprimand and gave him an *I'm-onto-you* smile. "Nice try, but I'm not telling you."

Pouting prettily, he accused, "You did that on purpose. You let me make you coffee before you shot me down."

"In some offices, it's customary for the employee to make coffee for his or her boss."

"But we always strive to be different, now don't we?" He smiled brightly. "That's what sets us apart."

"What sets us apart is that we're the only temporary service in River County. You never told me what our new job was."

"You never told me what your gift was."

"Because I know you. Brash will give you one of his

best smiles or be wearing that shirt you like so well on him, and you'll spill the beans. So, nope. Not going to happen." She motioned for him to bring her coffee. "Now, tell me about this new client."

"Marvin Combs needs us for a week at *Marvin Gardens*. He said he had heard such good things about us from *Lewis Insurance Company* and *Lone Star Law*, that he was willing to give us a try. He wants us to start as soon as possible."

"What's the job? I don't know a thing about irrigation systems and landscaping!"

"No worries. He wants you to set up a new filing system for him. Apparently, Shawn Bryant was so impressed with the system you set up for him, he's telling everyone you're an organizational specialist."

"Wow. Word travels at the speed of a snail." Her voice dripped with sarcasm. "That job was almost a full year ago."

"Considering there aren't that many offices in The Sisters, it could be worse," Derron reasoned.

"True."

"What brilliant system did you use?" he wanted to know. "Why haven't you incorporated it here in our office?"

"I have. It's called the alphabet. Not to speak ill of the dead, but apparently Gloria Jeffers used something completely different when filing. What Shawn Bryant called brilliant, I called the only logical choice."

"Well, don't tell Mr. Combs. Just cruise over to *Marvin Gardens*, pass go, and collect our two hundred dollars."

Madison curled her lip at his *Monopoly* reference. "Cute, Derron. Real cute."

Overlooking her dry tone, the petite man ran his hands over tailored khaki slacks and tugged at the collar of his starched, button-down shirt. "Thanks," he said. “I try.”

Once more, she was reminded that the man dressed better than she did. Touching a hand to her necklace, she consoled herself with the thought that at least today, she had remembered to embellish.

With her thoughts on another necklace, Madison left the office in Derron’s capable hands. Despite his theatrics, the man was an excellent assistant. He had impeccable telephone skills, a warm, easy way with people, and a social grace that Madison often envied. Not only was he perfect in an office setting, but he also did an excellent job when in the field. Whether performing clerical duties or carpentry skills, the man was a natural, and she knew she was lucky to have him in her corner.

For all his attributes, however, her one and only employee wasn’t without his faults. Despite his professionalism when working with clients, the man could be downright nosy. Fearful of being left out, he often overstepped the bounds of propriety and butted in, even when and if he wasn’t invited. Madison considered him a good friend and a sounding board and normally didn’t mind his overzealous curiosity, but this wasn’t something she wanted to share with Derron.

Keeping secrets from the man was almost as hard as keeping them from her husband, so she chose to do her research at the public library.

Contrary to what the younger generation might believe, the internet wasn’t the only source of information. Much of what she obtained yesterday, for instance, couldn’t be found online. Older publications and local concerns weren’t always transcribed and uploaded to the web, which was why libraries were still so important. Now more than ever, educating the public on how to utilize a library was crucial; Sadie

Bealls' research assignment truly sounded brilliant.

Besides, using the library was quieter than working from the office, where Derron was prone to break out in conversation, song and dance, or, worse, all three at once. Here at the library, she had the entire place to herself. Other than Sadie Bealls, there was no one in sight.

Uploading the picture she had taken of the necklace, Madison waited while the engines ran a search to match images. Opening another window, she researched jewelers, both past and present, known for their unusual creations.

"If this doesn't count as unusual, I don't know what does!" she muttered to herself.

She ran searches on the general availability of loose rubies and diamonds, the cost of such, the tools required to make simple jewelry pieces, and even watched a YouTube video on making gem-studded creations. All the while, the image search ran in the background.

"If it's having this much trouble finding a match," she reasoned aloud, "at least there's a certain level of comfort in knowing there are no other pieces out there like it."

By now, she had firmly decided the piece fell into the 'atrocious' category.

"Hon?" The librarian's voice preceded her into the research room where Madison ran her inquiries. "You still in there?"

"Yes, ma'am. Still working."

"Oh, that's no problem, hon. I was wondering if you could do me a big favor."

"I'll try."

"I need to run some books over to Arlene Kopetsky. She fell and broke her leg and can't make it into the library today. Every Wednesday, just like clockwork, she checks out three books for the week. She wants me to run them over to her real quick. Would you mind holding down the fort while I'm gone?"

"It's not that I mind, but I'm afraid I don't know anything about the library system," Madison confessed.

"Oh, that's okay, hon." The librarian used a hushed, conspiratorial tone, even though no one else was around. "I doubt anyone will come in, anyway." She smiled as if letting Madison in on a big secret.

Madison replied in kind. Smiling, she said in a loud whisper, "I'll stall them if they do."

"I won't be but a minute. A chime sounds when someone opens the door, so you can just pop your head around the corner and let them know I'll be right back."

"No problem, Miss Sadie. I'll be here."

"Perfect!"

Before she turned away, Madison got a glimpse of the paperback titles she held in her hands. "*Those* are for Miss Arlene?" she questioned. "The organist at First Baptist?"

The librarian looked down with a giggle. "She calls them her dirty indulgence. She claims if the worst thing she ever does is have a paper boyfriend and a steamy romp between the pages, she can still go to Heaven with a clean conscience." She held up a book entitled *Mary Ann's Italian Stud*. "This one is actually pretty good. She's reading it on my recommendation."

Madison waited until the elderly woman was out of earshot before she burst into giggles.

Turning back to the computer, she saw her image search still wasn't complete. Could there have been an error uploading the original?

She was debating the merits of starting over, versus giving it another five minutes, versus giving up altogether, when the lights above her flickered.

"What is that about?" she muttered.

It didn't affect the computer, so she decided to give the search another five minutes. She had already invested this much time in the effort.

A minute or so later, the lights flickered again.

"The power better not go out on me now!" she wailed. "If it does, I'll take it as a sign I should call it quits for the day." She rolled her head around her shoulders, working the kinks out of her neck. "I'll wait for Miss Sadie to return and then I'll go. I may even treat myself to lunch with my best friend."

With thoughts of having lunch at *New Beginnings*, she found herself almost *hoping* the power would go out.

She didn't anticipate, however, how dark the library would be without lights. Or how large and empty it would seem. As the lights flickered a third time before shuttering completely, even the computers went dark.

"Ooo-kay," she said aloud, trying to sound positive. It was as black as pitch in the massive space. "Well, I guess that's decided. No more search. Definitely lunch."

She used the light on her cell phone to gather her papers and push her chair back in place. She had intended to erase all history on the computer once she was done; she hoped a power failure served the same purpose.

Madison gingerly made her way toward the front, guided by the faithful light of her phone.

She also hadn't anticipated how empty the place would feel. How her footsteps would echo. It almost sounded as if they came from another direction, but she knew it was simply a trick of sound. She was the only person inside the big, old, suddenly spooky-feeling library.

Wasn't she?

Or was that a swish of material she heard somewhere off to the right?

Wasn't that a noise? A soft bump against objects unknown?

"M—Miss Sadie? Is that you?"

There! That was definitely a noise!

Madison swung her flashlight to the right, but there was nothing to see. Nothing but a long, blackened hallway and another huge, empty room, filled with row after row of books.

All dark. All silent. Millions of words. Thousands of authors' voices. All mute. All taunting her with their eerie emptiness.

Before Madison could work herself into a full-blown panic attack, another noise, this one loud and bumbling, drew her attention. The front door opened, and light tumbled inside, silhouetting the elderly librarian as she returned.

"Heavens! Why are the lights out?" she gasped.

Relief made Madison's voice weak. "I—I have no idea."

"I forgot how dark it is in here without power. And how stifling the air can get."

"Does this happen often?"

The older woman worked to keep the door propped open and sunshine pouring in. "Occasionally, but usually it's weather related. Hurricane, tornado, bad thunderstorm." She waved toward the blue sky beyond. "But there's not a cloud in the sky today!"

"Is there an emergency generator?"

"Yes, but it's a tonic to get started. I told the board of directors we need to have it upgraded. It's not like we can't afford it."

"Maybe the power will come back soon," Madison offered.

As if conjured by her words, light suddenly filled the

library again. Motors hummed, electronics beeped, and the space was no longer silent.

"Ah, there we go!" Sadie Bealls beamed. "I suppose there was a glitch in the system somewhere."

"I guess," Madison murmured. If so, it hadn't affected the old mansion across the street. She received text message alerts whenever the power went off at the Big House, and her phone showed none.

"Thank you for library sitting. Arlene was delighted to get her books."

"No problem. You'll be okay here if I go? What if the lights go out again?"

"Don't worry about me. I know the layout like I know my own face, with or without the lights. I'll be fine, hon."

Still feeling a bit rattled, Madison looked around to see if someone had come in without her knowing. She still couldn't shake the feeling that someone had been there in the dark with her.

"You run on along, hon. I'll be fine," the librarian insisted.

Taking her at her word, Madison texted Genny once she was across the street. The power hadn't blinked at the Big House, or on the Naomi side of the tracks. It seemed the glitch had only been at the library.

"Too bad I had to be inside when it happened," she sighed aloud. "All the more reason to treat myself to lunch."

"We may have to rethink our *Snoop and Soup* empire," Genny informed her best friend, sliding into the back booth across from her. She had been busy when Madison arrived, but was able to join her for dessert.

Madison pretended dismay. "Ah, and it had such

promise! One-stop shopping, right here in The Sisters. A bite of lunch, a bite out of crime. Win/Win." She shook her head with exaggerated gloom. "What toppled our empire, before it was even built?"

"My nerves! Apparently, I'm not cut out for this cloak and dagger stuff. Lamont Andrews came in for lunch, and I swear, the man looked straight through me! I know he knows. He's just biding his time, before he sics the law on us for trespassing, destruction of property, breaking and entering, and who knows what else."

"You forget. I'm married to the law, and I honestly don't think he can make a single one of those charges stick, even if he tries. Which I sincerely doubt he does. He kept a poor, defenseless dog in captivity, you know. One that didn't belong to him."

"He could easily say he locked the barn, not knowing the dog was inside," Genny reasoned. "Which could very well be true, I might add."

"Whose side are you on, anyway?" Madison frowned.

"Definitely not his. But you didn't see the way he glared at me!"

"Probably because he knows you're my best friend and was afraid you might poison his food."

"Then why did he risk his life by coming in for lunch?" Genny shot back.

Madison picked up a cookie from the plate Genny had delivered, her hazel eyes twinkling. "For a Gennydoodle cookie, obviously. You know they're to die for."

Not seeing the humor in her friend's smart comeback, Genny wrinkled her pert nose before sipping her coffee.

"Is that still settling on your stomach?" Madison asked in a low voice, her subtle nod indicating the cup of caffeine.

"So far. Although this morning..." A grimace touched Genny's face, gone as quickly as the bout of nausea had vanished.

"This is so exciting!" Madison said in a hushed whisper. "I can't wait for the official confirmation!"

"Shh! No one can know."

She made a show of locking her lips and throwing away the key, deliberating not uttering a word.

The problem came when she started to take a sip of her coffee. After the episode at the library, her nerves were still on edge, and she needed the caffeine.

With an apologetic shrug, she told her friend, "Sorry. I guess the lock wasn't waterproof."

15

"I hear good things about you, young lady," the owner of the landscaping business told Madison when she arrived for work. "Shawn Bryant says you're a whiz with a filing cabinet."

Madison felt she had to be honest with the man. "I'm afraid he may have exaggerated a bit. His former secretary had a very... unique filing system. I simply set it up the proper way."

"That may be all it takes here, but I reckon I'm not sharp enough to do it. You'll find the filing cabinets there on the left. I'll be out of the office today on a job, so you can use the drafting table to make as big a mess as you need. The coffee is around the corner, next to the restroom. Can you think of anything else you'll need?"

"Uhm, not at the moment."

"If anyone calls, just take a message and write it down on that yellow tablet. I haven't replaced Sandy yet. She had already cut back to part-time before she quit altogether a couple of months ago. I'm trying to hold the position open till summer, when my granddaughter Danni Jo wants to work. I thought if we got the files in order now, it would make things easier when she takes over. That's our busiest time, and I don't want to overwhelm the kid. This will be her first job."

"I know Danni Jo," Madison smiled. "She goes to school with my twins, Blake and Bethani."

"And I know Blake! A very impressive young man. Not only is he a cracker jack ball player, he's quite enterprising. He's already been around, applying for a summer job."

"He has?" Madison asked in total surprise. He hadn't said a word to her. She wasn't certain if she should be upset that he hadn't talked to her about it or impressed that he had taken the task upon himself.

Marvin Combs nodded with a smile. "He even gave me a resume. Credited his athletic training as a reason he would be right for this job, carrying sod pallets and digging holes and exerting physical effort. Claimed he was strong as an ox."

"He *is* strong," Madison agreed. "But I feel I must warn you. All that strength requires fuel. He may need a snack break every hour or so. And by a snack, I mean a hamburger and fries, or anything you and I would consider a full meal."

Marvin laughed. "I remember that stage! Raised two boys of my own, so I know it well. And just between you and me, I believe in keeping my workers hydrated and energized. I don't supply anything as heavy as a hamburger, but I keep fresh fruit and energy bars in full supply."

"And for that, if you should hire him, you will have my son's undying loyalty," Madison predicted.

"He doesn't know it yet, but he has the job."

"He'll be thrilled." Madison knew he had hopes of saving up to buy a truck, something she still had mixed feelings about. Even though he and his sister were sixteen, to her, they were still her babies!

"I'll be in and out for the next little while, loading

the truck to take to the job site. If you come across something you don't understand, let me know. Otherwise, I'll let you get to work."

"Sounds good." She smiled, liking the gentleman already. If Blake was serious about getting a job, she didn't mind it being for this man.

Marvin left within the hour, but not before poking his head back inside the office and checking on her.

"Finding everything okay?" he asked.

Madison had to be honest. "I'm finding a mess! You're right. These files are all over the place."

Marvin hung his head. "I should have paid closer attention, but she was a good receptionist other than filing, so I let it slide."

"So far, I haven't been able to even see a pattern. I'll literally have to start from scratch." She nodded to the pile of files she had already pulled. "I hope you were serious about me making a big mess. I may have files lined up from here to Juliet."

Something sparked in his memory, and he snapped his fingers. "I seem to remember her saying something about that. Juliet, I mean. I think she used that in her system. She was big on the rivalry thing between the towns."

"Excuse me?"

"I didn't grow up here, myself, so I don't understand the big hoopla about which side of the tracks you live on," Marvin admitted. "To me, the two towns run together and should be considered one. They share the same school, same police department, same water system, so I don't know why they can't make nice and share everything else. But Sandy didn't see it that way."

"That's your former receptionist?" she guessed, vaguely remembering him mention the name before.

"That's right. She's a hometown girl, so she grew up with the thing between the sisters. The two old women,

I mean. From what I understand, they never could get along."

"Unfortunately, that's true," Madison agreed. "The only solution their father could think of was to give each daughter her own town."

"And in my opinion, that was the problem. He gave them everything they ever wanted and didn't make them work for what they had. Same problem many parents have these days."

The more the man talked, the more Madison liked him. He would be a fine role model for her son.

He shook his head, continuing, "Tearing apart the family was bad enough. But tearing apart the towns and making folks choose sides was just flat-out wrong. I'm afraid Sandy was one of those people who still held a grudge. Crazy thing is, she wasn't even born when the sisters had their falling out, so she shouldn't have had a dog in that fight to begin with."

The landscaper's sigh was heavy. "But I remember, now, that Sandy separated the files according to which town people lived in. I told her from the very beginning, I would offer the same level of service and professionalism to people in Juliet as I did to those here in Naomi, and she knew I wouldn't stand for favoritism. But I reckon filing was one thing she could control. I don't know if that will help you any, but I suspect that's what she did. She kept the towns divided once again."

"For the record," Madison told him, "you probably know I have deep roots in the community, even though I haven't always lived here. But I agree with you. What happened back then is water under the bridge, and it flowed long ago. It's too bad that some people can't help but churn the waters and keep them muddy."

"You and I are going to get along just fine," Marvin Combs decided with a pleased smile. "Just fine."

By the end of the day, Madison had made considerable progress. *Marvin Gardens* had a large clientele, which translated into many folders that required shuffling and refiling. By the time she found a good stopping point and left the office in respectable order, it was much later than Madison realized. She called Brash to tell him she was running late, and then headed out the door.

She promptly collided with another body.

"Are you following me?" a voice demanded.

"Ex—Excuse me?" Dismayed, Madison stared up into the angry face of Lamont Andrews. The *Gold and Silver Exchange* sat next door to her temporary employment.

"You heard me. Are you following me? This is the parking lot for employees only. You have no business being back here, unless you're stalking me."

"I am hardly stalking you!" she cried in outrage.

"Then what are you doing back here?"

"Judging from all the bags of fertilizer and mulch, it looks to me like my car is parked on Marvin Combs' property. I hardly see how that concerns you."

"I know you were at my house the other night, lady. I know you've been snooping around." Lamont Andrews stepped closer, moving into her personal space. He loomed over her with a menacing glare. "I already told you. I don't know where that mutt is, I don't care where that mutt is. I would just as soon shoot it as I would look at it." His face contorted with something frighteningly close to rage. "Stay. Away. From. Me."

He swept past her, storming out to a dark vehicle. He paused before opening its door, jabbing his finger into the air. "Understand me? Stay away!"

Long after a cloud of exhaust swallowed the sight of it, Madison stood in the same position, her mouth agape. Anger made her body tremble. Thoughts made her mind swirl in splintered directions.

If he knew the dog had been rescued, he wasn't letting on. He still pretended he was innocent, even though she had found the dog behind his locked door.

She had been at his house during the daytime, not at night.

If he saw him again, she had no doubt he would kill that poor little dog.

She wasn't following him. In fact, she made a point to avoid him by going to his house while he was at work.

Lamont Andrews was a volatile man.

Lamont Andrews was not a man to cross.

16

The moon ducked behind a cloud, hiding its face from the slumbering world below.

He made his move in the darkness. Sidling up to the barn, he inserted a key into the first lock. Twisted the dial and listened for the tumbling clicks on the back-up combination lock. Eased the thick, heavy chains down to the ground, careful not to make a racket.

As the moon revealed its face again, he slipped inside the barn and went to work.

The man was agitated tonight. He moved about the old barn with tense, jerked moves.

For once, the numbers didn't bring him comfort.

Something wasn't right. He couldn't put his finger on it, but something was missing.

He had forgotten something.

He circled the barn, counting and recounting. Checking his lists. Taking his inventory.

It all added up, and yet it didn't. Whatever was missing, it wasn't on his list.

Perhaps if he started over.

Again.

17

The three-week deadline until Brash's birthday was shorter by half, and Madison had made little progress on the chair. Other than removing the ancient red fabric and securing a pattern for the new charcoal tweed, she hadn't done a thing. If nothing else, today she planned to replace the stuffing and the seat cushions.

As she inserted the padding the way Ralph had shown her and secured it in all the crucial places, Madison thought about the gold. It still made her nervous, having that kind of fortune in the house. Most of all, it bothered her that she kept it a secret from her husband. But she had promised Granny Bert, and a promise was a promise, particularly to one's grandmother.

Especially to *her* grandmother. Granny Bert didn't take betrayal well.

Nor had Miss Juliet. Thoughts of the town's founder filled Madison's mind as she worked. She understood how the woman came to be so aloof and obsessed with appearances.

It had been painful enough for Madison, knowing Gray had cheated on her and forsaken their marriage vows. But Miss Juliet! Knowing that her own sister carried Darwin's child. Betrayed by both her sister and her husband, even if it was before their wedding. It was no wonder she kept people at arm's length after that, not wishing to be hurt again. With her pride in tatters, she probably controlled the things she could, including whatever air of dignity she could muster. If she became obsessed with outward appearances, it was no wonder. She had to have been devastated, not only by the betrayal, but also by Darwin's sudden death.

It explained the shell of a woman she became, but it didn't explain why she might have hidden gold in her library chair. And it certainly didn't explain why she left it there for all those years.

But if Juliet hadn't hidden it there, who had?

The first time her phone rang, and the caller hung up, Madison thought nothing of it. Misdials happened. But when it happened again five minutes later, she stopped her work to look for her phone. Caller ID didn't recognize the number. Slipping the phone into her back pocket, she returned to her work. Another tuck here, binding there, and the back should be in place.

She stood back to survey the job as her phone rang a third time.

"Hello? Is anyone there?"

Silence greeted her.

"If this is a telemarketer, I'm not interested."

The caller was still on the line, but not speaking.

"I'm hanging up now. If you can't talk to me, please don't call back."

Five minutes later, her phone buzzed again. Madison hit the *Ignore* button.

They repeated the cycle twice more. Every five minutes, the phone rang. Every time, Madison ignored the call.

By the sixth call, she had reached the end of her patience.

"What do you want?" she demanded by way of greeting.

"I, uh, wanted to invite you to lunch. But never mind."

Madison pushed an unsteady hand through her hair. "I'm sorry, sweetheart. I thought you were someone else."

"I hope so," Brash chuckled. "I hope the honeymoon's not over already."

"Never," she assured him. "You mentioned lunch? I could definitely use a break."

"Good. As much as I love *New Beginnings*, that jambalaya the other night was so good, it has me craving seafood again. Today is Fish Taco Friday at *Montelongo's*. Meet me there in thirty minutes?"

"Best offer I've had all day!" she quipped.

She had just enough time to clean up her mess, go home, freshen up, and meet her husband at their favorite Mexican food restaurant.

As she headed out to the car, her phone rang again. Distracted, Madison answered, forgetting about the earlier hang-ups.

A mechanical voice, surely altered by one of those computerized gadgets, finally spoke.

"This advice is golden. Back. Off."

Startled, Madison instead dropped her phone. It clattered noisily to the pavement and gave a healthy bounce, coming to a stop beneath her car. By the time she crawled under the carriage, fished out the phone, and put it to her ear again, the caller was long gone.

The mechanical echo of the threat—and a black vehicle—followed her home.

"You seem a bit on edge. What's wrong with my beautiful wife today?" Brash wanted to know, less than three minutes after they were seated.

"Why—Why do you think something's wrong?"

"For one thing, that forced little laugh you just did. For another, you avoided my question. And the reason I asked the question in the first place"—he leaned in close to whisper— "I just know."

"It's nothing. Really."

"Is that why you're adding salt to your water?"

Trying not to look startled, she fibbed, "I—I heard it was good for digestion."

"Talk to me, sweetheart. What's wrong?"

She couldn't tell him the whole truth, not without breaking her promise to Granny Bert. Vowing to have a talk with her grandmother that very afternoon and call off their ridiculous agreement, Madison went with a half-truth.

"I had a few irritating calls earlier. Telemarketers, I'm sure. That's why I answered so testily when you called. I was in the middle of... something," she caught herself just in time, "and didn't have time for such nonsense."

"What were you in the middle of that demanded such close attention?"

"No questions, remember? It's too close to your birthday. Same rules as Christmas."

Brash nuzzled his face against her ear. "I really liked that nightgown you didn't wear the other night. You can just give me that again, and I'll be a happy man."

"You'll get that, but you'll also get a present. One you can unwrap in public. Which is where we are now, so behave yourself." She gave him a gentle shove.

"We're married," he protested.

"And we're being watched by half the town."

He glanced up and saw several patrons of the restaurant looking their way, most of whom wore amused smiles. With a playful wave of his fingers,

Brash reluctantly pulled away and sat straighter in his chair.

"I'll motion Juanita over for a fresh water while you tell me what else is bothering you. Telemarketers don't usually rattle you."

"This one was persistent."

Brash allowed her to leave it at that as they ordered and ate their lunch.

"Why did you only work at *Marvin Gardens* for about an hour this morning?" he asked, scooping a bite of shrimp queso onto a tortilla chip.

"He had a client coming in, and they were going over designs. We couldn't both use the drafting board."

"He has you working on the drafting board?" her husband asked in surprise.

"No, no. I just use it to spread the files out," she was quick to explain. "His former receptionist left a *huge* mess. Get this. Apparently, she was one of those small minds who still subscribes to the old Juliet vs. Naomi mentality. She segregated her files according to which town their clients lived in."

Brash shook his dark auburn head in disgust. "There are all kinds of prejudices in the world. Unfortunately, there's no cure for small minds."

"And small minds don't just live in small towns."

"Very true."

Madison looked around the restaurant, noting how crowded it was. "I didn't realize how popular Fish Taco Fridays were."

"Could be because it's also Fried Catfish Friday."

"Come to think of it, that is what's on most people's plates," Madison noted. "Oh, look. There's Hank and Virgie Adams getting up from that table. Now don't forget and say something about the party. It's a surprise."

"You're not going to try to pull that same trick on

me, are you?" Brash grumbled.

"Why? You don't like surprises?"

"Not the kind that involve people jumping out at me, making loud noises. Makes my trigger finger itch."

A smile twisted his wife's lips. "I will definitely keep that in mind."

The Adamses stopped to exchange greetings, but no mention was made of the upcoming birthdays for either the older woman or the lawman. As the couple bid them goodbye and turned to leave, they stopped to speak to Tom Pruett, who Madison hadn't noticed until that moment. He sat at the next booth, but with his back to her.

If nothing else, the khaki shirt should have been a clue to his identity, but her attention was fragmented today, torn between the disturbing phone calls and her handsome but observant husband.

Their tacos came, and Madison turned her attention to the meal, until something Virgie said caught her ear. Hearing the word 'chair,' she tuned in to the conversation taking place at the adjacent booth.

"Are you still enjoying it?" the woman inquired.

"I'm afraid I no longer have the chair," Tom Pruett replied. "For reasons I can't go into, I had to dispose of the item." As usual, the man made it sound like something of grave importance. Another of his top-secret missions that would 'rock this community when the truth was discovered,' no doubt.

"Oh, dear!" Virgie Adams seemed genuinely distraught. "You... destroyed it?"

Did Madison imagine it, or did Miss Virgie dart her eyes toward her?

Madison blinked and sat up straighter. Why would Miss Virgie look her way? Could it be they were discussing *her* chair? The one originally part of Juliet and Darwin's gifted set? But... why? How?

"No," Mr. Pruett answered. "To my knowledge, the chair is still intact. I... can't recall the specifics—or rather, can't *reveal* the specifics—but there was a reason I had to relocate the item. Something quite urgent. A matter of national concern."

"Over *that* chair?" By now, Virgie Adams' distress had turned to absolute confusion. "The red velvet? But how on earth..."

Understanding dawned in her husband's eyes, and he shifted on his feet, subtly stepping away from the man at the booth. "I don't mean to rush you, Mother, but we really need to go," he said, taking his wife's elbow. "Good to see you again, Tom."

"But... But... I don't..."

Virgie was still sputtering her confusion when her husband hustled her away. Tom Pruett continued to speak, even though he had lost his audience.

"Yes, it was quite urgent. As much as I liked that chair, I could no longer keep it. But it worked well in my negotiations, so things worked out for the best." Madison saw him bend his head, presumably to take a bite of his meal, but she could hear him still muttering. His voice was much lower now, but occasional words floated back to her. *Government. Secure. Narrowly avoided a major conspiracy.*

"Madison?" Brash asked. He watched her face in concern. "Are you okay? You have a very strange look on your face."

"I—uh—I... Would you excuse me for one minute? I just remembered a message I'm supposed to give Miss Virgie." She jumped up from her seat, knowing how lame she must sound. "It's to throw her off track about the party," she fibbed. "I'll just be a moment."

She hurried to catch up with the older couple, reaching them as they walked to their car.

"Excuse me. Mrs. Adams?"

"Oh, hello again, dear."

"I know this must sound a little out of left field," Madison began.

"After the conversation I just had, nothing will strike me as strange," the woman assured her.

"That's just it. I couldn't help but overhear your conversation with Mr. Pruett."

"The old goat has gone soft in the head!" Hank Adams harrumphed. "That's not the first time I've heard him say something off the wall. He likes to think he was once in the Secret Service, but I say it was more like a secret asylum for the insane."

"Hank!" his wife cautioned.

"It's true. When he's not going on about one of his conspiracy theories, he's taking about his wealth. According to him, he's some big-time collector. One of these days, someone's going to take him seriously and knock him in the head, hoping to steal from him. If it doesn't kill him, maybe it will knock some sense into his head."

Hank Adams sounded just like Granny Bert. No wonder they had been friends for so many years.

"Again," she said, "I know this will sound like a strange question, but were you by any chance talking about a chair that came from the Big House?" Madison ventured to ask. "A red velvet with curvy, graceful lines?"

The older couple exchanged an uncomfortable look before Virgie admitted on a sigh, "Yes. Yes, that's the one."

"But... how did it get from the Big House?"

"I didn't steal it, if that's what you're thinking." There was a touch of offense in Hank's tone.

"No, of course not. I'm just trying to make sense of something. You see, I just bought that chair from an upholstery shop in Navasota. It's a surprise birthday gift for Brash. I plan to recover it, but Granny recognized it as part of a set that once sat in Miss Juliet's formal library. I'm just trying to put the pieces together." She didn't dare mention the biggest mystery of all, of how a fortune in gold came to be hidden inside.

"Navasota?" While Virgie made noises of surprise, her husband spoke over her words.

"It's true. The chair was part of a set. But one of the legs had loosened, and I was afraid it wasn't safe to sit in. Years ago, I took it home with me to repair, but before I got around to it, Miss Juliet took ill and died. Somehow, I just never took it back. It sat in my workshop for the longest time, until just a few years ago. Virgie made me clean out the shop, and we decided to sell the chair in a yard sale."

"I know it wasn't rightfully ours to sell," his wife added in a worried voice. "But no one was living in the Big House anymore, and we had had it for so long, it seemed strange to take it back after all that time. We didn't make a lot of money on it. We only charged twenty-five dollars. But—But I'll be happy to give it to you, seeing as you're the rightful owner. Hank, get out your wallet."

"No, no. I'm not asking you to pay me. I just couldn't imagine how the chair wound up in Navasota."

"I'm afraid I can't tell you that. After what Tom just said, I wouldn't even try."

Madison took a few more moments to assure the couple she wasn't upset with them over the chair. On the contrary, she told them, she was thrilled to have solved at least one piece of the puzzle.

Tom Pruett, of course, was another matter.

By the time she hurried back to the table, the man was already gone, but her husband was waiting for her with patient but inquisitive eyes.

"I'm sorry about that, sweetheart," she said,

offering what she hoped was an appeasing smile. "But you know how birthdays are. Full of secrets."

Brash merely raised a skeptical brow. Later, as he walked her to the car, he commented again on her strange behavior during lunch and her earlier preoccupation.

"You keep glancing around. Afraid that telemarketer is going to jump out at you?" Despite the tease in his voice, his eyes reflected his concern.

"Something like that." She attempted a smile.

A frown moved across Brash's face. "Lamont Andrews hasn't said anything to you, has he?"

"Why—Why would Lamont Andrews say something to me?" She willed the guilt out of her voice.

"You said he practically threw you out of the store last week. I thought maybe he had said something more."

"I told you. I don't plan to ever set foot in his business again."

Which was true, but not the whole truth. She hadn't told Brash about the confrontation in the parking lot.

Her evasive answer seemed to satisfy him. "You let me know if he gives you any more trouble."

"I'm sure he won't." She saw the argument building on his lips. "But if he does, you'll be the first to know." She stretched upward to press a kiss on his lips, worrying that Brash would, indeed, be the first to know. He'd know the very moment that Lamont insisted he file charges against her.

Brash held the door open while she slid behind the wheel. "What's your plan for the afternoon, my love?" he inquired.

"I need to run back over to Granny Bert's and help her finish something."

"Ah, so you moved my present over there. Didn't trust me not to search the cubbyhole, huh?" He teased her with waggled brows.

"I told you. No questions."

But as she drove back to her grandmother's, constantly scanning her mirrors for signs of the dark sedan, Madison knew that excuse would only hold for so long.

18

"Granny? It's me. Are you home?" Madison let herself in, thinking it odd that the door was locked. No matter how many times she cautioned her grandmother, Granny Bert usually left the locks free. The older woman claimed she didn't know what the world was coming to, if she had to lock her doors here in The Sisters. She said she wasn't sure what was worse: locking herself inside a home she had lived in for sixty years or locking her friends out.

Granny Bert's voice came from somewhere in the dark interior. "If I wasn't home, I wouldn't be answering you, now would I?"

"Where are you?"

"Over here by the window. Trying to decide what that woman and that car are doing out there."

"What woman? What car?" Madison hurried to the window to peek out alongside her grandmother.

"I never could get a good look at the woman's face," Granny Bert complained. "She had some sort of scarf tied around her head."

"What was she doing? Where is she now? Who was she?" She shot out the questions in rapid repetition.

"Walking down the sidewalk."

Madison craned her neck to see. "Where? I don't see

her."

"She's already gone. This was a good five minutes ago."

"Then why are you still at the window?" Madison asked, stepping back. "What's so strange about a woman walking down the sidewalk?"

"Nothing. *If* she had stayed on the sidewalk. But she nosied herself up to the door. Didn't ring the bell, but she was sniffing around. Before I could ask her what she wanted, she sidled over to the windows and peered inside."

"Granny, you shouldn't open the door to strangers," Madison cautioned.

"Am I five?" her grandmother demanded. "I've been around the block a time or two, young lady. Do I need to remind you that *I'm* the one who taught *you* about safety?"

"If I remember correctly, Uncle Homer wasn't too thrilled with some of the lessons I learned." Madison grimaced in memory.

"Served him right for not coming around more often. He was your grandfather's oldest brother, but you barely knew him because he stayed in his fancy house in the city all the time. It wasn't your fault that you mistook him for a stranger offering kisses and candy. You kicked him where it mattered, just like I taught you," Granny Bert said with satisfaction.

"It didn't hurt your feelings any, since he was your least favorite brother-in-law. But I'm pretty sure it hurt his. In more ways than one!"

"That's okay. He had no business divorcing his wife of forty years and marrying someone half his age. And don't blame yourself for the second divorce, either. It may have been a coincidence that it happened shortly after his visit."

Her tone exasperated, Madison prompted, "What

did the woman do after that?"

"How should I know? That was a good thirty-five years ago."

"Not the second wife. The woman at your window! Did you call Brash?"

"Why would I call the law? I handled things on my own."

"I'm almost afraid to ask."

"I've been working in my flowerbeds, soaking it down to get ready to put in some new plants. The sprinkler was still hooked up, so I eased over to the side of the house and cranked the water hose up on high. I still don't know who the woman was, but she can sure run!"

Madison laughed, until it occurred to her that her grandmother had locked the doors and was hiding behind the drapes. "I think you mentioned a car?"

"I'd already noticed it once, before the sprinkler lady came by. It came by again after that. I'm trying to see if it comes by a third time. The windows are tinted, though, so I can't see who's inside."

"What color is the car?"

"Black or a very dark gray."

Madison drew in a sharp breath. "I saw it when I left earlier." She assumed the worst. "I think someone knows about the gold," she said breathlessly.

"How? I haven't blabbed. Have you?"

"No! Not even to Genny. Or to my husband."

"Then there's no reason to think someone knows our secret. You're just letting your nerves get the best of you, girl. Don't get skittish on me now."

"But someone is following me! And now they're stalking your house. You even have your door locked!" Madison pointed out, as if that fact alone were definitive proof.

"The woman seemed a little too bold for my liking,"

Granny Bert admitted. "I just locked my doors to be on the safe side."

"You'll come home with me tonight." It wasn't an invitation.

"I'll do no such thing!" Granny Bert dropped the curtain and faced her granddaughter with indignation. "I refuse to be run out of my own house."

"But Granny, this is getting serious. Someone called me earlier."

"What did they say?"

Madison relayed the message, but her grandmother wasn't convinced.

"I think there's another explanation. I think that car out there belongs to Lamont Andrews."

"Lamont? Why?"

"The man has a temper. And a mean streak, to boot. After your little confrontation in the parking lot yesterday, I had Sybil check out his story. She called her friend over in Temple, whose nephew went to college with Lamont at Howard. He confirmed that Lamont was kicked out of school for violently beating another player unconscious. The rumors about him were true. He served four months in jail."

"*Now* you tell me!" Madison wailed. "I knew the man was ornery, but I didn't know he was dangerous. I'd have never broken into his barn if I'd known *that*!"

"Well, now you know. And apparently, *he* knows, too. That you were there, I mean. And I assume he also knows I was checking up on him, a fact he doesn't seem to view too favorably, judging from the way he keeps circling the block."

"It might not be him. It might be whoever called me earlier. They specifically mentioned the gold."

"Not necessarily. They used the word *golden*. It could have been an unfortunate choice of words. A coincidence. Or," her grandmother pointed out, "it could have been Lamont's attempt at being clever. He does own the *Gold and Silver Exchange.*" She emphasized the word gold.

"Either way, we have to tell Brash about this. This is getting out of hand."

Granny Bert waved a bony finger in her face. "You promised me, girl. You agreed to three weeks, and it's only been one."

"One and a half. And that was before the phone calls, and before the dark car."

"It was also before you waltzed onto Lamont Andrews' property and chopped down his barn!"

"I didn't chop anything. To be honest, I could hardly lift the ax. The best we could do was pry a board loose, which I'm certain can't even be proved. For all he knows, the dog got loose on his own."

"Unless he has one of those fancy surveillance systems in place. He may have watched the whole thing unfold from the comfort of his store's easy chair."

"I hadn't thought about that," Madison admitted, her mouth turning downward. "He has an elaborate enough one at the store.... And all those locks and chains around that old barn. I swear, the locks are worth more than the lumber!"

"So, I see no need in tipping our hand about the gold, not until we know for sure who hid it in that chair."

"But... what about the woman?"

"Could have been an over-zealous Jehovah's Witness, come to save my soul. Or could have been Lamont's girlfriend."

"I... guess," Madison reluctantly agreed. "I suppose we can give a little while longer. Or until we know for certain who's behind the calls and the windshield. But I'm warning you. If it's not Lamont, I'm going straight to Brash and telling him everything. Agreed?"

"You drive a hard bargain, but... agreed." To seal the deal, her grandmother offered her hand.

"You'll still come home with me tonight, right?"

"Not tonight." Bertha Cessna shook her gray head.

"Why not? The kids will love having you there."

"First of all, I'm not going to let some punk run me out of my house, just because he's got his nose out of joint. I suspect he's just throwing a little temper tantrum and will run out of steam soon enough."

"And second?"

"I have two servings of jambalaya left, so Sticker's coming over for supper tonight."

"Ah. The two of you are speaking again."

"If the man wants to talk about his shenanigans and explain this latest lapse in good sense, I'm willing to listen. I got nothing better to do while I'm eating my supper."

"That's generous of you."

She seemed not to notice the dry note in her granddaughter's voice. "I'm not about to throw that jambalaya out. I don't want it a third time, and it's not enough to even tease your son with. May as well give it to the old fella while he's groveling."

"You don't want Sticker seeing other women, but you won't commit to a real relationship with him. One of these days, he's going to get tired of waiting on you, you know," Madison predicted.

"And one day, pigs may fly." Granny Bert peered out to scan the sky again. "But that's not happening today, so why worry about it? Today, I'm offering to help you with the chair. Come on, girl. Let's work on your man's birthday present."

"Oh! I can't believe I forgot what I came to tell you. I know how the chair disappeared from the Big House."

She relayed the story to her grandmother, who, after hearing it, shook her head and snorted. "That sounds like Hank. He was always doing odd jobs for Juliet. It would have been noble of him, but I couldn't shake the feeling he only did it because he thought he would one day own the whole kit and caboodle. I guess when she passed, he assumed the chair was his, and there was no need to take it back."

"And when you were named heir, instead of him? Why didn't he return it then?"

"I told you. We went through a rough patch there for a while, but we'd been friends for too long to let it come between us. I imagine he was miffed at first. Probably kept the chair out of spite. I have no doubt he forgot he had it after that. Like he said, after all those years, he probably felt silly returning a chair no one even realized was missing. I certainly never thought about it again."

"That makes sense," Madison agreed. "But it still leaves a gaping hole in explaining the gold, and it doesn't answer the biggest question of all. Who put it there, and did they do it before or after it left the Big House?"

"I reckon you need to read those journals and find out."

Madison arrived home before Brash. Hurrying up to the second floor, she climbed onto the stool and leafed through the journals until she found the one dated 1933. Pulling the book free and sliding the panel back in place, she hoped to manage time for reading later that evening.

She was in the kitchen, the journal hidden beneath an opened cookbook, when the twins came in.

"This is a surprise. I didn't expect you two home so early." She smiled, accepting the kisses they dropped onto her cheek.

"Since we didn't have a game this week, Coach let us out of practice early and told us we were free," Blake said, going to the refrigerator.

"We're done with our cheer project," Bethani offered, "so there wasn't much to do after school."

"Since we all have a free night, we wanted to know if we could have a few friends over," her brother added.

"A party? On such late notice?" Madison asked with dismay.

"Not a party," Bethani assured her quickly. "Just some of our friends. We could order pizza and watch a few movies. Please, Mom? We hardly ever have friends over."

"Megan—"

"Is our sister and doesn't count."

"Where is she, by the way?"

"Helping her mom make brownies for tonight. But I see you have your cookbook out. You wouldn't, by chance, be in the mood to make cookies, now would you?"

Despite her daughter's charming smile, Madison was able to resist. "Sorry, kiddo. Not tonight."

"Not tonight about the cookies, or the friends?"

"Before you answer," Blake broke in, "I volunteer to wash your car tomorrow if you say yes."

"Hand wash here in the yard, or take it to the car wash in Riverton?"

This time, Blake offered the charming smile. "The car wash does such a better job than me, don't you think? Fewer streaks."

"And gives you a chance to drive my car," his mother pointed out. "Not to mention offers an opportunity to see Tasha."

"Yeah, I don't think Danni Jo would like that very much," Bethani teased, her blue eyes sparkling with laughter.

"Danni Jo?" their mother asked. "Since when?"

"Since Blake asked her to the dance."

Madison had trouble keeping up with the conversation. "Hold on. You're just a sophomore. Since when are you going to the Jr.-Sr. Prom?" she asked her son.

"Since I was voted doorman. They always invite two underclassmen to do the honors, and we can bring a date. I sort of invited Danni Jo." He spoke around a mouthful of apple.

Madison raised her eyebrows. "Sort of?"

The youth shrugged. "I invited her. Oh, and I'll need a tux."

"And I need a dress. Drew Baines asked me to be his date!" Bethani squealed, twirling around the room in a happy dance.

"Madam, may I have this dance?" Blake approached his sister with an air of formality, offering his hand like a grand gentleman. As the twins waltzed around the kitchen, Madison smiled at their antics. It did her heart good, seeing the two of them exchanging laughter instead of insults. She suspected it was all part of their plan.

"So, can we, Mom?" Blake asked, sashaying their way to where she stood. "Can we go to Prom, and can we have a get together tonight?"

Dipped low over his arm, Bethani offered an upside-down smile. "Please? Pretty please?"

Wavering, their mother asked, "Who did you want to invite?"

Sensing she was softening, the twins stopped dancing and propped themselves against the bar to tag team her.

"Not a lot of people."

"And we'll clean up before and after!"

"We won't need a lot of food. Just a couple of large

pizzas and the brownies. Maybe some chips and dips."

"I'll make the dip, Mom."

"I'll pick up the pizzas."

"We could get enough for you and Daddy D, and you wouldn't have to cook tonight. You work so hard as it is."

At that, Madison sent her daughter a sharp look. "Don't overdo it. And you still haven't told me the guest list."

"Not a lot. Just Danni Jo, Drew, Megan. Maybe Connor Evans."

"Hmm. That sounds suspiciously like a triple date. Let me guess. Connor Evans invited Megan to Prom. He's a junior, right?"

Bethani sidestepped the question. "He hasn't exactly asked her yet. But maybe after tonight..."

"What about Jamal?"

"He's the other doorman, and he's taking Latricia," Blake offered. "They've been going out for a couple of months now."

"I know that. I meant aren't you going to invite your best friend over for your party?"

"It's not a party. And Latricia has to work. She has that job at Aunt Genny's now."

"If it's a girl/boy thing, you can't have it upstairs. You'll have to stay down here in the family room."

"Mo-om!" they wailed in unison.

"You know the rules."

"What's the point in having the whole third floor to yourself, with a huge old ballroom turned game room, if you can't even have a party up there?" Bethani grumbled.

Madison offered no explanation. She gave them both the *Mom Look*.

"Fine," Blake huffed. "But do you and Daddy D have to be in there the whole time?"

"No, but just know we reserve the right to walk in at any given moment. Hands and buttons should remain in their proper location at all times."

"Eww!" Bethani pulled back with a horrified expression on her pretty face. "Mom, that's disgusting. Parents aren't supposed to say things like that!"

"Then how else are we supposed to remind you to behave yourselves?" Madison smiled sweetly. "Those are the rules. Take 'em or leave 'em."

Rolling her blue eyes, Bethani realized it was the best they would get. "I'll call Megan and tell her to call Connor."

"You must have been pretty sure of yourself, if Shannon is already making brownies."

"We know what a fantastic mom you are."

Madison accepted another kiss to the cheek before pointing out, "You don't have to butter me up, Beth. I already agreed."

"Yeah, but you really are the best!"

As the girl bounded out of the room, Madison looked at her son. "Speaking of Latricia and her new job... I hear you put in an application with Danni Jo's grandfather."

"I promise, that's got nothing to do with me asking her to Prom," the boy was quick to say. "I'm not trying to be sneaky and use her to get to him."

"The thought never crossed my mind. I was just curious why you didn't mention it to me first."

Blake shrugged. "I talked to Daddy D about it. He thought it was a good idea."

"Oh," Madison said in surprise. "Okay."

He heard the halting tone. "Mom? You're not mad at me, are you?"

"For taking it upon yourself to apply for a job? No, of course not. I think that shows real maturity."

"Thanks, but... that's not what I meant. I meant

because I talked to Daddy D, and not you."

"No. No, honey, I'm not mad. I guess I'm just not used to you talking to someone else about something before you come to me."

"I dunno," Blake said with another shrug. "It just seemed like a father/son thing, you know?"

Madison was touched, knowing Blake considered Brash his father. The two males had developed a strong bond, long before last month's wedding. Even before his unexpected death, Gray had begun to alienate their son. But the teenage years could be difficult to navigate, and Blake still needed a strong male role model in his life. Madison was more than delighted that Brash could be that role model and father figure for him, but she also couldn't deny the tiny sting that pricked her heart. It had more to do with the fact that her son was growing up than it did the fact he had turned to Brash first.

She couldn't think of a better example for her son than Brash deCordova. Trying not to turn mushy for the teen's sake, she blinked away unbidden tears and kept her tone light.

"Then I hope you and your father have worked out a way to get you back and forth to your new job."

"I haven't gotten it yet, Mom. And it won't start until summer."

"I doubt you have anything to worry about. You're a fine young man, Blake."

As she folded him into her arms, he accepted the hug. "You're not going to cry, are you, Mom?"

Madison sniffed away the tears. "No. No, of course not."

19

The teenagers were having a loud and boisterous time. After pizza and brownies, they started a movie, but it soon gave way to a board game.

"I never knew a board game could be so noisy!" Brash commented. He and Madison were in the formal library, close enough to keep an eye and ear on the teens, yet far enough away to give them a modicum of privacy.

"It's one of those new ones. Interactive, they call it."

"A far cry from *Monopoly*," Brash mused. "Although, my family could get rough and rowdy, particularly considering we were playing for cardboard real estate and fake money. We boys would gang up on poor Laura and bankrupt her before she even turned around."

"You meanies," Madison teased. "I never had brothers and sisters to play with, but my cousins and I liked to play games whenever we were together."

"Speaking of *Monopoly*, when are you scheduled to go back to *Marvin Gardens*?"

"Monday. I don't think it will take me but one more day. Two, at the most. All in all, it's been a pretty easy job."

"No encounters with your neighbor?"

"Uhm, neighbor?"

"Surely you've noticed you're working next door to the *Gold and Silver Exchange*."

"Of course I've noticed."

"And since you're avoiding my question, I take it you've seen Lamont."

"Maybe once, on our way to the parking lot," she admitted.

"You've only worked there twice."

"So, it could have been worse. I could have seen him going in *and* out, so a total of four times. One out of four ain't bad," she quipped.

"What were you doing with Miss Juliet's journal? I saw it in the kitchen earlier."

There was a reason the man was an excellent lawman and investigator, and an excellent football coach before that. He missed nothing. Madison decided she was tired of hiding so many secrets from her husband and decided to go with a partial truth.

"Someone told me something I found hard to believe, but it turned out to be true. I was curious if Miss Juliet ever mentioned it in her journals. Have you ever heard of Executive Order 6102?"

"Is that the one where the government confiscated all the gold so they could manipulate the economy?"

"Does everyone know about this but me? Yes, that's the one. I had never heard of it before Mr. Pruett went on a rant in front of poor Latricia Jefferson the other day."

"I saw the girl was working there after school now."

"She and Jamal are a couple, so that's why they're not here tonight, hooting it up with the others in there. The poor girl looked confused by Mr. Pruett's ramblings. But then again, he has that effect on most everybody."

Brash nodded in agreement. "I caught the tail end

of something about Nazi and Japanese warplanes the other day. I think he was really confused, thinking the year was 1941."

"I don't even know if he was born then. He has one of those colorless complexions that makes it impossible to guess his age."

"I'm not sure about his next of kin, but I think it's time someone intervened. The man needs to be in a home. He's not stable."

"You don't think he's dangerous, do you?"

"Only to himself and those within earshot of his ramblings," Brash assured her.

"You have to feel sorry for him, though. All alone, with just his crazy stories to amuse himself."

When a loud burst of laughter rattled from the other room, Brash grinned. "They're really having a good time in there. I have to drive Danni Jo home after this, so wine is out of the question, but why don't we have a glass of sweet tea out on the front porch swing? They won't even know we've stepped out."

"Good idea. I'll make the tea and meet you out there."

"I can get it."

"Nope. I'll make a sweep through the family room on the way, pretending to refill the chips."

"Hey, if there's any of Beth's dip left, bring me a little bowl. I think we have a budding chef on our hands."

Madison laughed, giving credit where credit was due. "Thanks to Genny. She's taught Bethani well. We all know who the real culinary genius is in the family."

"You do remember the two of you aren't blood related, right? I know the twins claim to inherit their blue eyes and blond hair from their Aunt Genny, but genetically speaking, that's not possible."

With a wide smile that he swore looked just like her

best friend's, Madison shrugged. "What's blood and genetics have to do with family?" She dropped a kiss on his nose. "I'll be right back."

Once she settled on the front porch swing amid colorful cushions and the crook of her husband's arm, Madison dared broach the subject of gold again.

"I keep thinking about that executive order. You don't suppose anyone here in The Sisters hid any of their gold to keep it out of government control, do you?"

"First, I'm not sure if there were many people around here who owned any gold. The Randolph sisters, maybe, if Daddy Bertram bothered with any commodity other than cotton and cattle. That's where his fortunes laid. I don't think Naomi was bankrolling her son-in-law at that time, so not even the Redmonds had much to spare. There may have been a few other well-to-do families, but even if they had gold, they probably would have turned it in. Which is my second point. There was a stiff fine and threats of prison if people were found hoarding gold. Most people needed the paper money they got in exchange. I doubt there were any serious hoarders here." He took a long draw of tea before adding with a shrug, "Then again, you never know."

They sat in contented silence, until Madison commented, "Town seems busy tonight. There's been more cars than usual passing the house."

"That black car has made several laps around the block. Eight, so far."

Madison sat up, away from the warm cocoon of his arm. "Black car? Where?"

"It went by just before you said that. I imagine it will come back around in a few minutes."

"Do you recognize it?"

"Not off hand."

"Do you think it's just kids, riding around on a Friday night?" She tried to sound casual.

"Could be, although most teenagers try to avoid making laps around the chief of police's house. Especially when he's sitting on the front porch watching them."

"Maybe it's someone who wanted to come to the kids' party."

"Non-party," he corrected with a crooked smile. "Blake was very clear that this was not a party. Now, sit back and relax, and tell me why the black car makes you so nervous."

"Who said it made me nervous?"

He gave her his trademark imperial smirk, the one known to make criminals spill all their secrets.

"Okay, okay. I saw one hanging around Granny Bert's earlier today. It seemed a little suspicious, especially since there was also an unknown woman trying to peek in her windows."

A concerned frown drew his dark brows together. "I've heard there's been a scam going around Riverton and some of the other nearby towns. Someone comes to the door, pretending to be with the utility company, or a lawn service, and or something that draws the homeowner outside. While one person keeps the homeowner distracted, their partner goes in and takes whatever they can carry out. They like to prey on single women, especially widows, and older citizens."

"That's terrible! I don't think Granny Bert would fall for a stunt like that, though."

"What did she do about the woman today? We didn't have any calls concerning a suspicious person."

"I asked her why she didn't call the law, and she seemed insulted. She took care of it herself by turning the sprinkler on. Granny didn't recognize the woman, but she said she was quite the runner!"

They both laughed at the visual and Granny Bert's quick thinking.

When the black vehicle came back around, a ripple of apprehension moved through Madison's shoulders. "I think I'm ready to go in now," she said, no longer enjoying their time on the swing.

"I think I might take a little cruise around town, myself."

While Brash was gone, Madison took out the journal and read.

There were entries she hadn't noticed before. Reading details about Darwin's love for medicine and his desire to help those less fortunate, she saw the young physician through a different lens. Even if it were rose colored and distorted by Juliet's undying love for her husband, it gave Madison a glimpse into the man's goals and ambitions. He wanted to make a difference in the world. He wanted to heal the sick and teach preventative medicine. He was a visionary for his time. It seemed truly a shame that his life ended so soon.

A few ambiguous entries piqued her curiosity. More references to his *golden life* and *golden ambitions.*

If my beloved Darwin had lived, we would perhaps be halfway across the world by now. Darwin had a golden vision of sharing his wisdom and talents with others. He wanted to heal the sick from all walks of life, all countries. We knew such a dream would come at a cost, but we were prepared to make sacrifices. Darwin set aside his inheritance to make his dream a reality. But, alas. Fate intervened, and our reality changed. Without the brilliant man and his sparkling vision, what did his golden inheritance matter? What does anything matter after that fateful day?

"Does she use those words literally, or figuratively?" Madison wondered aloud. "Did she forfeit his inheritance after that?"

There were a handful of similar entries, leaving Madison as confused as ever.

She leafed through the pages, looking for some reference to the new law forbidding the hoarding of gold. If Darwin's inheritance had been in the form of gold, how would Juliet have responded? Would she have kept the nuggets regardless of the order, ignoring the threat of fine and imprisonment for the sake of sentimentality? Or would she have complied, thinking his inheritance was pointless without the man?

Would Madison ever know the truth, or would it forever remain a mystery of how that gold came to be in the chair?

"Maybe I should just put them back and cover them up, once and for all!" she decided in exasperation. "Upholster right over them and leave them for the next person to find. A half-million-dollar time capsule for the next lucky finder." She shut the journal with more gusto than required. "Easy come, easy go."

But even as she made the brave proclamation, Madison knew she would never give up so easily.

She was too naturally curious—okay, too nosy, if she were being honest with herself—not to find the truth. The not knowing would drive her insane.

Plus, Granny Bert would never allow her to quit.

Like it or not, she knew the answers were out there. She just had to find them.

20

When the delivery service dropped the package off at *New Beginnings*, the driver had no idea the importance of what was inside.

Genny saw the uniformed driver hand the box off to her employee. One glimpse of the box marked with the 'Overnight' status, and her eyes lit up. It took great restraint not to turn away in the middle of Tom Pruett's explanation of how unmanned military drones operated. Even greater restraint not to take off running and rip the package from Louise's unsuspecting hands.

Her blue gaze kept darting to the package, even as Mr. Pruett carried on about drones. She listened for all of ten seconds, hoping for a stopping point in the story. He had to take a breath at some point.

Or not. Unable to take it another moment, Genny interrupted him mid-sentence.

"Excuse me, Mr. Pruett. But I see a package just arrived, and it's one I've been waiting on. I really do need to attend to this. Would you like me to send someone over with fresh coffee?"

"No, no. I've had my limit for the day. Too much caffeine isn't good for my training, you know."

Genny wasn't about to take the bait. She didn't dare ask what kind of training, knowing it would result in a long, bloated explanation. She made no comment at all, simply turned away and made a direct line to the front register. She didn't stop to linger when other customers turned her way in expectation, hoping to catch her eye and congratulate her on another fine meal. She murmured only a polite hello to those who spoke to her.

Louise had walked off and left the package on the counter. Unattended! As if its contents didn't have the power to change Genny's life forever. As if what snuggled inside couldn't determine the course of her and Cutter's new marriage.

They had only been wed since Valentine's Day. Less than a dozen short but blissful weeks. Most people wouldn't understand their decision, but it was theirs to make, wasn't it? This matter wasn't up for public debate or public ridicule. This was private.

That's why she couldn't very well march into any of the local stores and buy an over-the-counter pregnancy test. News of her purchase would be all over town before she even got home. Speculation would run rampant. Had she been pregnant when they said, 'I do?' Was that why the most handsome and eligible bachelor in town, thirty-two-year-old volunteer fireman Cutter Montgomery, had married the forty-year-old chef? Everyone knew he had a weakness for her apple turnovers, but why would a man like *him* want to be saddled with a woman like *her*? She had more curves and padding than most fashion models combined. Wagging tongues would twist the facts of their surprise courtship and taint it with vicious rumors, all before she had a chance to take the test! That's why she had to order the test off the internet and have it shipped overnight.

By the time Genny reached the overnighted box left so casually on the edge of the counter, she had worked herself into a frenzy. She snatched up the box and hugged it to her chest, needing to protect the precious white stick inside and the hope it held for her and her husband. Without meeting the eyes of any of her patrons or employees, Genny cradled the box to her and all but ran to her office. She didn't care what people thought or who was watching. She needed to be alone when she opened the package and saw for herself that the test had arrived safe and undamaged.

In truth, most of the diners weren't watching. They had no idea of the magnitude of the moment, or how Genny's heart had stuttered in her chest the moment the delivery driver stepped through the door. They were caught up in their conversations and their meals. Many were contemplating which one of Genny's fabulous desserts they would try after they polished their plates.

The woman at the table next to Tom Pruett caught his eye and smiled. "I couldn't help but overhear your conversation," she said. "What kind of training are you doing, if you don't mind me asking?"

"Not at all, not at all." The man loved any opportunity to talk about himself. "I'm doing continued training to keep my service certificate active. The doctor doesn't want me consuming too much caffeine."

"Oh? What kind of service?"

Tom Pruett darted his eyes around with caution, seeing who listened to their conversation. The man two tables over pretended interest in the menu, but Pruett had seen the way the man glanced his way earlier. He obviously had Pruett under surveillance.

"The kind I can't speak to at the moment," Pruett replied in an important-sounding voice. "Suffice it to say, I know my duty and am able to perform the tasks required of me."

The woman looked a bit confused, but she nodded in acceptance. Instead of escaping conversation with the older man like most people did, she encouraged him to keep talking. "Are you still collecting stamps?" she asked. "The last time we spoke, you were telling me about some of your rare finds."

"Er... yes." He barely missed a beat before brightening and picking up the conversation with enthusiasm. "Yes, I still dabble in rare stamps and coins. I've amassed quite an extensive collection through the years. Just last week, I picked up a nice little 1923 two-dollar Capitol US stamp. I had been looking for it for quite some time and ran across it in the most unlikely of places."

The woman nodded with real interest. "That sounds fascinating. How much is something like that worth?"

Pruett rattled on about the pricing structure for stamps like the '23 Capitol, comparing them to similar finds. He kept an eye on the man at the other table, knowing he still listened in. The chump wouldn't discover any national threats by eavesdropping on this conversation. Tom Pruett prided himself on being a trained professional. He wouldn't make a mindless slip that could compromise the security of his beloved nation.

"Why don't you join me?" Pruett offered, indicating the chair across from him. Their conversation would be more private that way and less likely to reach the ears of the spy two tables over.

"You wouldn't mind?" the woman all but gushed. "I would be delighted!"

Pruett shuffled from his chair to assist in seating her at his table. He pulled the chair a bit closer to his, so they wouldn't have to talk as loudly.

"I've been wanting to talk to you about your jewel collection." As soon as she took her seat, the woman continued their conversation. “Some of your designs sound fascinating! Is it difficult to make jewelry? I’m afraid I don’t know the first thing about fashioning fine gems and metals into fashion statements.”

Pruett was more than happy to tell her about his hobby. He soon forgot about the man from the other table and his suspicions of being under surveillance. He had the rare and undivided attention of a rapt audience. It didn’t hurt that his audience of one happened to be an attractive woman. She was too young for him, of course, but it was gratifying to know that someone appreciated his eye for detail and his voracious appetite for collecting. He was interested in all manner of arts and collectibles. He hadn’t even told her about his music collection yet, even though he didn’t recall seeing it lately. Where had he put those old 45s? It escaped him now, but she was asking about jewels, and those, he remembered.

“And you just keep an assortment on hand, waiting for inspiration to hit you?” she questioned in awe. “Why, that must be so expensive!”

“It’s difficult to put a price on art, you understand. Even more difficult to put a price on personal satisfaction. I find great pleasure in working with my hands and crafting unique pieces. If it means the cost of keeping a few diamonds and sapphires on hand, it’s a price I will gladly pay.”

The woman sat back with a look of fascination on her face. “You have led such a fascinating life! I can’t imagine seeing the things you’ve seen, traveling to all those countries and being involved in so many different projects and assignments. And to think, you live right here in our humble little community.”

“Traveling as much as I have, you learn to appreciate the simple things in life,” Tom Pruett assured her.

"I would *love* to see your collections some time! You should open a museum. Do you... Do you suppose I might come by some time? Would you consider showing me at least part of all you've collected through the years?"

Warning bells went off in Tom Pruett's befuzzled mind, but he couldn't tell where the danger came from. Was it from the earnest but eager look upon the woman's face? Was this some sort of trick to gain access to his fortunes? Was she playing him for a fool and only pretending interest in what he had to say?

Or was the danger from the man a couple of tables over? He couldn't remember what, but there was something about that man...

The man stood and threw his napkin upon his empty plate. As an afterthought, he dropped a couple of dollar bills on the table before turning toward the register. Tom watched as he approached, feeling increasingly uncomfortable as the man drew nearer to his table.

His breath caught in his throat when the man jostled into their table. It looked like a natural mistake. Clumsy, but natural. But Pruett knew better. It was a warning from the other man. A subtle reminder for Pruett to stay alert, to stay on guard of what he said and who he trusted.

"Pardon me," the man murmured, glancing down for only a moment as his lean thigh clipped the corner of the table. "My bad."

With the casual apology, Lamont Andrews continued on his way to the register.

Cutter swept into the café, his hazel eyes searching for his favorite blonde.

"She's in her office," someone offered.

"Thanks, Merle," he murmured, brushing past the two men seated near the door.

He bit back an uncharacteristic flash of irritation at the number of eyes following his progress through the artfully restored old space. When Genesis Baker came back to her hometown two years ago, she had bought and remodeled the old building in downtown Naomi. She had transformed the century-old structure, turning it into something fresh and trendy without compromising the landmark's spirit and integrity. She opened her café and bakery before the paint was even dry, and it had been an instant success. Cutter suspected he had fallen for the woman eight years his senior the moment he laid eyes on her dimpled smile and beautiful blue eyes. If that hadn't been the exact time, it was the moment he tasted her apple turnovers. He had been hopelessly in love with her ever since.

He knew he should be grateful for the devoted customers and thriving business she had grown and cultivated. And he was. He couldn't be prouder of her accomplishments, and her talents continued to amaze him. He wasn't one of those men who pounded his chest and insisted he be the breadwinner for the family; he was the first to admit, when and if his welding business hit a slow time, the income from the restaurant would be a godsend.

But sometimes, he regretted that they had so little privacy. The patrons of *New Beginnings Café and Bakery* were so devoted and so enthusiastic, they felt territorial about the business. He knew such dedication was hard to find in today's landscape, and he couldn't be prouder of the loyalty the townspeople showed to his wife. And to himself, as well. But often, the community thought of the café as theirs. They felt as if they had a stake in the business, and in the hours and days it should be open. If the public had a choice, those leaded glass doors would never close. Genny needed time off, however, and the two of them needed some time to themselves. They were still newlyweds!

Cutter knew the public felt vested in their relationship. They had watched it develop on national television, under the sharp and talented eye of Home Again producer Amanda Hooper. Somehow, the astute businesswoman was the first to notice their attraction to one another and she had turned it into reality television gold. She even gave them a celebrity couple hashtag. Gennecut.

It had taken weeks for Cutter to convince Genny to give him a chance. Yes, he was younger than she was. No, it didn't matter to him. No, he wasn't too young to know what true love was. He had only known it with her. Yes, he wanted to marry her.

In the end, it was Genny who proposed to him. Right here, in this very café. In a room full of diners and onlookers.

Intellectually, Cutter knew that was part of the reason the public felt like they were included in the romance. They had watched it from the beginning. From all the times he lingered there at the counter like a schoolboy with his first crush, from that dance on Valentine's Day when time stood still during their first slow dance, from the many hours of filming Amanda curated to tell their story, right up until the moment Genny went down on her knee and asked if she could marry him, they had had an audience.

But, sometimes, like now, that audience bothered him. As much as he appreciated their loyalty, there were times he couldn't help but resent their interference. Their watchful eyes.

He felt them on him now, as his cowboy boots thumped out a steady beat against the tiles. He wanted to jog the distance to the back. Wanted to run to his wife and fold her in his arms and forget the fact there were dozens of people in the dining room, speculating about the eager light in his eyes. He wanted privacy for this moment.

Instead, he nodded politely to those in his path, greeted the employee who scurried out of his way, and smiled as if this wasn't a huge moment in their lives.

"Genny darlin'?" he asked, rapping on the office door with his knuckles.

"Come in!"

He kissed his wife before asking anxiously, "Did it come in?"

"Yes." She nodded her head to the box behind her. "I opened it. It's all in one piece."

From the grave expressions on their faces, an onlooker might think it was a nuclear bomb. A precious vial of a rare and life-saving serum. Not a single stick of white plastic.

That plastic, however, had the power to proclaim their fondest dreams a reality.

"Have you... done it?"

She shook her head with regret. "It says I need to wait until morning."

"I'm not sure I can wait that long!" he confessed.

"If it comes out pink," Genny reminded him, "you'll have to wait eight months before we meet our creation." She giggled at the mere possibility of such magic.

Cutter cupped her face in both her hands. "I want you to know, darlin', that no matter the outcome, I'm dedicated to turning that test pink. I'll try every single day, if that's what it takes."

She allowed him to kiss her soundly before she came up for air and murmured, "You do know there are only a few days a month a woman can get pregnant."

He nibbled the side of her neck. "Practice," he

whispered in a husky voice. "We'll consider the other days practice." He gently nudged her backward, pressing her legs against the edge of her desk. "I'm willing to practice right this very minute."

"Cutter! Not... Not now," she said, but her voice was already losing its conviction.

"Give me five good reasons I shouldn't clear this desk and make love to my gorgeous wife, right this very minute."

"I can give you about thirty, and they all watched you come back here. Out of nothing but nosiness, they'll wait for you to come out, too."

Cutter growled in frustration. "Tonight, then," he told her. "You can let someone else close up, and we can spend another nice, quiet evening alone. A repeat of last night, Mrs. Gennecut."

"As tempting as that sounds..." She allowed him to kiss her neck as she spoke. "I can't. Tonight is Trey Hadley's birthday party, remember? You promised to wear your bunker gear and hand out plastic helmets and candy."

He frowned as he pulled away. "Is that tonight?"

"Yes. And next week is Virgie Adams' party, and right after that is Brash's."

Cutter threw up his hands in frustration. "How many birthdays can a town of two thousand residents have?"

Genny gave him a look. "Really? Surely, you're more than just a pretty face. You do the math."

"Okay, okay," he relented. "But I'm telling you right now. If Trey's great-grandmother pinches my butt again, I'm out of here."

"The senior Mrs. Hadley?" Genny gasped. "When was this?"

"The most *current* pinch was about three weeks ago. She called in a report about smelling gas. I took the call and when I bent over to check the pilots on her stove, the old broad pinched me!" Cutter's face revealed his indignation.

"This has happened before?"

"Only when I make the mistake of getting within two feet of her," the man with the dark-blond hair sulked.

Instead of being sympathetic, Genny laughed with glee.

"Oh, handsome husband of mine. You shouldn't be so irresistible!"

21

Madison was pleased with herself for finishing the job at *Marvin Gardens* by early afternoon Tuesday. Once she got the swing of it, refiling every single customer folder wasn't so difficult, after all. Just time consuming. It didn't require an elaborate organizational overhaul, simply an understanding and application of the alphabet.

Brash hadn't found the black car in town that night, nor had they seen it again. Not recognizing the car as local, he suggested it could have been someone from out of town, but Madison thought it looked like the one Lamont Andrews was driving when he roared out of the parking lot.

While her son and husband may have known details about every vehicle ever made and could easily identify one upon sight, Madison wasn't nearly as astute. To her, a car was a necessary tool to get from point A to point B. She was more interested in safety features and good gas mileage than she was classical style and RPMs. She only noticed vehicles when she needed to, but it was something she was trying to get better about. Times like these proved the need.

To her disappointment, Lamont didn't come to work on Monday. He arrived on Tuesday in a white little number that sat low to the ground and had a bold racing stripe down its side. It was only fitting that the stripe was deep, bright red, the same color as rage.

And blood, an inner voice whispered in her mind.

Her phone rang as she left the landscaping business.

“Maddy? Can you run by here on your way home this afternoon?” Genny asked.

“I’m headed home now. Is this a good time?”

“It’s fine.”

“Are you okay, Gen? Is something wrong?”

“I’ll tell you when you get here.”

Madison walked into *New Beginnings* less than two minutes later. Winking when she saw her friend, she said, “How’s that for jumping? You said frog not two minutes ago.”

“Can’t get much faster than that,” Genny agreed with a smile. The sparkle in her eyes, however, was lackluster.

“So? What’s up?”

“Let’s go to my office.”

Not liking the sound of her voice, Madison followed with a solemn expression.

Genny shut the door behind them and motioned for Madison to have a seat. “I wanted to talk to you about two things.”

“Okay.” She waited for her to continue in her own time.

“I’m not pregnant.”

“Oh, Gen. I’m sorry. I know how much you wanted to be.”

“We were both very disappointed, but we know it’s early still. We can keep trying.”

“Absolutely. Sometimes it takes months.”

Genny managed a wry smile. “Dedicated man that he is, my husband vows to try every single day.”

Madison's smile matched hers. "He knows there's a specific window of opportunity, right?"

"He considers the rest of the time practice. Like training for a marathon, he claimed. Pray for me that I survive."

They laughed, even though both their hearts smarted. Madison looked forward to being an aunt, almost as much as Genny looked forward to being a mother.

"And the other thing?" she asked her friend.

"It's Mr. Pruett."

"Oh, dear. Did he go off on another one of his tangents?"

"That's just it. I don't know. I haven't seen him since Saturday."

"This is only Tuesday. I'm sure there's nothing to be concerned about."

"You don't understand. That man comes in here every Monday without fail. We're closed on Sunday, so he says he can hardly wait to get a decent meal by the time we open back up on Monday. Something is wrong. I can feel it."

"Have you tried calling him?"

"No answer."

She could see her friend was genuinely concerned. "What can I do to help?"

"I want you to go with me to his house and check on him."

"We could call Brash," Madison suggested. "He could do a welfare check. That way, if he needed to go inside, he would have a legitimate reason."

"We have a legitimate reason."

"Do you have a key?"

"No," Genny admitted.

"Then let me call Brash. It's not breaking and entering if you have a badge."

"What if you have an ax?" Genny asked in a sweet voice.

It was an effective argument. With a heavy sigh, Madison said, "Point taken. When do you want to go?"

"There's no time like the present."

"Do you even know where the man lives?"

"I have a general idea. You can google it on the way. I'll drive."

"Our leader is back," Madison mumbled, but she wore a smile as she followed her friend out.

Tom Pruett lived in a modest house on one of Naomi's back streets. Like everything else about the man, the house was nondescript. Beige shutters against beige siding. A brown composition roof and a carport with beige railings. No window boxes or colorful flowerbeds. The lawn was neatly trimmed but without ornamentation. The few trees in the yard didn't bear fruit and were trimmed to have a slim silhouette.

"His car is in the carport," Genny said. Her voice reflected the sudden bout of nerves assuaging her.

"It's not too late, Gen," Madison reminded her softly. "We can still call Brash."

"He's my friend," she said stubbornly. "I should be the one to find him. Look for him," she corrected hastily.

"Okay. Let's do this."

They went to the front door and rang the bell, not expecting an answer. They weren't disappointed when no one answered. The same could be said for the side door off the carport.

"I wonder if he keeps a key hidden somewhere," Madison said, looking around for an obvious hiding spot.

"The man is obsessed with conspiracy theories. If

he does have one, it won't be anywhere we would expect. Think unexpected," Genny advised.

"Maybe his car is unlocked. Maybe there's an extra set of keys inside."

It wasn't unlocked. They searched for several minutes, running their hands along uneven grooves, looking under railings and eaves, shaking and rattling to see if anything was loose and hid a spare key. Each time, they came up empty handed.

"Let's go around back. Maybe he left a window open."

"Tom Pruett? The man who sees a 'scandal of grave magnitude and an investigation that will rock this town' at every turn?" She imitated his voice. "Not likely."

"And yet, just look at that," Madison said with a smug smile.

Genny followed her gaze, a deep scowl tugging at her mouth. "That looks like a bathroom window. I seem to recall us having trouble with one of those in the past."

"In all fairness, the house was on fire, and our lungs were filling with smoke. We weren't at our best."

"In all fairness," Genny said, "my hips are just as wide now as they were then. They're not going to fit in such a narrow space."

"They fit that night, didn't they?"

"We were desperate."

"Okay, then call Brash."

Genny wrinkled her nose in distaste. "I'll see if I can find something to crawl on."

Their search turned up two five-gallon buckets with lids.

Even with her long legs, Madison couldn't scale the two stacked together. "I'll stand on this one, and you can balance the other one to the side, just enough for me to get a foothold," she suggested. "I should be able to boost up and over. I'll go in and open the door for you to come in."

"No." Genny shook her head adamantly, sending her blonde hair into a dance. "He's my friend. If he should be... dead... I should be the one to find him," she insisted again. "I won't have you in there alone with a dead body."

Madison gulped, having not thought through that aspect of her plan. "What if—what if he's in the bathtub and the window is above the tub?" she worried. The thought of landing on a dead body made her stomach roil.

"Can you see inside?"

If she put her face against the window and squinted just right, she could make out the shadowy interior of the bathroom. The lights were off, and the room was vacant.

"No tub at all," she reported. "It's a half bath. And this is a fairly large window." She removed the screen and pushed the pane open to its full extension. "I'll need the other bucket."

After considerable effort, they had the buckets in place and Madison atop the taller one.

"Here goes nothing."

It took a lot of grunting and groaning, pushing and pulling, but she finally managed to crawl through the window. Once on the inside, she caught her breath and peered out at her friend. "Are you sure you don't want me to open the door?" she offered again.

"I'm doing this, one way or another," Genny said with determination. "I may not be able to walk tomorrow, but I'm doing this."

After a few false starts, Genny hoisted herself up and over the window ledge. She wasn't as agile as her friend and her legs weren't long enough to offer a final boost from the bucket. When she floundered on the windowsill, half in, and half out, Madison tugged her through. She came in headfirst, like a big fish hauled into a boat. Momentum carried her forward. Despite Madison's efforts to catch her, they both crashed to the floor, narrowly missing the sink and commode.

They lay on the floor for a long moment, laughing, panting, and catching their breath.

"This—This has to rate pretty high up on our list of cr—crazy stunts!" Genny hooted, holding her stomach while she laughed.

"I—I just hope there wasn't a surveillance system that caught us in action!" The thought brought another gale of laughter, until they eventually remembered why they were there in the first place. They instantly sobered.

"Help me up, girlfriend," Genny said with determination. "Let's get this over with."

She opened the bathroom door, stepping gingerly into the hall. "Mr. Pruett?" she called. "Mr. Pruett, are you in here?"

"It smells okay," Madison murmured, drawing a sharp look from her friend. "Hey, I watch TV," she defended herself. "After two days..." She didn't point out she had been the one to find Ronnie Gleason. Of course, he had been inside a chicken house, where it reeked with or without a dead body. "With any luck, he's just fallen and knocked himself unconscious," she offered.

With that cheery thought, they moved forward. After a thorough search of the house, they saw no signs of Tom Pruett.

"I don't get it," Madison said, standing in the middle of the living room. "There are no signs of a struggle. No signs of someone breaking and entering." She looked around with thoughtful eyes. "In fact, there's not much signs of anything."

"It is rather sparse, isn't it?" Genny murmured, her gaze taking in the hollow room. It held only skeletal furniture and a sad lack of personal decoration.

"Are you sure he still lived here?"

"I'll look in the bedroom, you look in the kitchen."

They met back to report their findings.

"An adequately stocked kitchen, consistent with someone who eats most of his meals out. There is, however, a distinct lack of pots and pans." Madison arched her brows in speculation, recalling Mr. Pruett's wild claim of midnight raiders.

"His closet and medicine cabinet are full. There's a suitcase under the bed, so I don't think he went on a trip. Not a planned one, at any rate."

"Then where is he?" Madison wondered aloud.

"I don't know, but his car is here. He either left on foot or with someone else."

"We should talk to his neighbors."

"Okay, but first, let's look around. Maybe we'll find a clue as to where he may have gone."

Moving to the side tables flanking either end of the sofa, Madison muttered, "A note would be nice."

"While you're wishing, wish for a map with a big X circled on it," Genny suggested.

They made a second sweep through the house. With only two bedrooms and one and a half baths, it didn't take long.

Genny stood in the hallway, hands on her hips, waiting for Madison's exit from the second bedroom.

"Did you see these?" she asked, tipping her head toward the framed photos marching along the wall.

Madison nodded. "It looks like we owe Mr. Pruett an apology. Unless those are excellent forgeries, he really did serve in the Secret Service. Possibly the FBI, too, or one of those other alphabet agencies.

Apparently, not all his stories are fantasy."

"It's crazy, right? We just blew him off, assuming he was delusional. I feel terrible."

"Don't beat yourself up. Some of his stories may have been true, but there are plenty that weren't. The Nazi warplanes flying overhead, for instance. If he was even born then, he had to have been very young. He's not remembering that, Gen. He's flat-out making it up."

"Maybe," Genny said, sounding unconvinced. "But if you're going to tell tales, shouldn't you at least tell them in the right century? He can't seriously think there are Nazi warplanes in current times. That suggests a definite nod toward senility, wouldn't you say?"

"Maybe he's a history buff. Maybe it had to do with some case he worked back in the day, and he's getting it confused in his mind."

"I've heard that, for the sake of national security and for their own personal safety, top-level agents are brainwashed to forget sensitive information."

"I've heard that, too." Madison studied a few of the photos as they wandered down the hall. Most were in black and white, dating them mid-twentieth century. Tom Pruett had dark hair in the photos, but his wardrobe was as bland and dependable then as it was now. Back then, he wore dark, nondescript suits with a white shirt and a dark tie. "It's like he simply faded through the years," she murmured. "Bleached out, to gray and tan."

"In that line of work, I guess it makes sense not to call attention to yourself," Genny agreed. "But you'd think *inside* the house, where no one else can see, he would have some sort of personal effects. I don't even see signs of a hobby in here."

"That is rather strange." Madison pursed her lips. "I

wonder if there's a basement. And if so, where? My guess is it would be off the kitchen."

Genny trailed behind her friend, muttering, "Great. Crawling through a bathroom window wasn't enough. Now we're going down into another basement. It's our past adventures, come back to haunt us."

After a futile search, they came up empty handed.

"Well, that idea fizzled out," Madison admitted.

"Knowing Mr. Pruett's fascination for conspiracy theories and hidden agendas—and now finding out he really does have a secret past—I half-expected a hidden dungeon somewhere." A giggle escaped Genny's lips, but it had a nervous warble to it.

A light went on in Madison's eyes. "Hidden. That's it! He has a hidden room somewhere!"

"But where? This is a small house."

"Yes, but..." Her voice trailed off as she hurried from the room and down the hall. Genny followed in time to watch her stop just outside the half bath and study the wall.

Madison poked her head into the spare bedroom beyond and turned back with a brilliant smile. "Just as I thought!"

"What? What is it? Hidden stairs to the basement?"

"I don't know, but there's a false wall in the bathroom." Madison led the way inside the bathroom, pointing to her rationale. "See those tiles? On these three walls, there's a pretty little border. On this blank wall over here, no border. I noticed them when my face was squashed against them at an up close and very uncomfortable angle." She aimed a pointed look at her friend.

Genny offered an apologetic wince. "Sorry. You're the one who pulled."

"True. Anyway, I thought the placement of the window was a little odd. It's jammed up against this wall, instead of centered in the room. Obviously, the wall was added later. I imagine a bathtub once sat along this wall.

"But there's no door."

"No, but there's a full-length mirror."

"I did notice it had an elaborate frame," Genny murmured, watching as Madison's fingers worked along the mirror's edge and gently tugged. "The rest of the house is Plain Jane, but this one mirror is Fancy Nancy."

One solid yank, and the mirror swung out to reveal an opening sawed into the wall. "Hel-lo, Nancy!" Madison whistled.

The hidden room was tiny and compact, but it housed a network of fancy computers, monitors, and electronic gizmos. Worried her elderly friend might be inside, Genny shoved Madison aside and stuck her head through the space.

"He's not here," she said, her voice a curious mix of relief and disappointment. She had hoped to find him inside, safe and sound, but had feared the opposite.

Madison stretched on her tiptoes to peer over her friend's head. "This is... incredible."

With an abundance of caution, Genny stepped over the threshold. The doorframe rose several inches from the ground, hidden behind the mirror's facade. There was hardly room for one person inside the narrow space, but without a word, Madison crammed her way in beside her.

There was a long counter running the length of the room, serving as a desk for his collection of electronics and scattered paperwork. Short filing cabinets sat beneath either end of the desk, while a rolling chair made easy work of sliding the distance. The walls were plastered with whiteboards and monitors. In lieu of a corkboard, pegs punched directly into the sheetrock.

Photographs, reports, and bulletins hung from their colorful stubs.

"This looks like some sort of command center," Genny breathed. "Is that... is that one of those old ham radios?"

"Actually, it doesn't look too old," Madison murmured in wonder. "None of this stuff does."

"You're right. This looks like state-of-the-art equipment. But... what in the world is he doing with all this?"

"I'd say he's working a case."

"Real, or imagined?" Genny wondered.

"Good question." Madison bent forward to get a closer look at some of the papers pinned to the wall. "That report is dated 1933. And that... oh my gosh! That's a copy of Executive Order 6102!"

"So? What's Executive Order 6102?"

Madison put a hand to her forehead, her thoughts spinning.

"Maddy? What's wrong? Why has your face turned so white?" Blue eyes darted back to the writ pinned to the wall. "What's Executive Order 6102?"

"It's, uh... It's... I'll—I'll explain later." Using the tail of her blouse to cover a telltale fingerprint—*better late than never*—Madison pressed the Enter button on the keyboard nearest her.

The monitors sprang to life, washing the tiny space with their many bright pixels.

Over Madison's gasp, Genny's voice was incredulous. "Why does he have pictures up there of that horrible necklace? Are those diamonds? Rubies? That's... that's almost a criminal waste of precious jewels!" Genny stepped to her left to peer at a second monitor. "Who's this guy, I wonder?"

She pointed to the man on the screen. It was obviously an old photograph, grainy and captured on black and white film. If nothing else, his slicked-back hair and sharp attire dated the look to the ‘30s era. Genny moved down to the next screen and briefly scanned the document.

“It says his name was Abel Cartwright. He was a jeweler in downtown Bryan.”

22

"Maddy? You look a little green now. What is going on?" Genny demanded.

"We, uh, need to... go. We have to get out of here."

"But we still don't know where Mr. Pruett is!"

"But he's not here, and we shouldn't be, either."

Genny crossed her arms over her chest and took a stubborn stance. "I'm not budging. Not until you tell me what's going on."

"Not here." *What if the room was bugged?* Madison's mind screamed.

"Madison Josephine!"

"Please, Genny." Madison took her friend by the arm and pleaded, "Trust me on this. Not here."

Genny huffed out a silent protest, but she turned to make her way through the crude opening. Once both women were on the other side, they swung the mirror back in place and made their way to the side door.

"The alarm wasn't set," Madison pointed out. "Either Mr. Pruett forgot to set it when he left, or whoever he left with didn't give him time to do so."

"As much as I want to question the neighbors, I want to question you more." Genny's tone was blunt. "Are you going to tell me what's going on, or not?"

"I will tell you," Madison promised, "but not until

we get to Granny Bert's."

"What is so dad-burn important that you had to pull me away from my Tuesday afternoon Bunco group?" Granny Bert wanted to know, stomping into her kitchen with noisy protest.

"We may have a problem."

"May? *May*?" the older woman demanded. "I was on a hot streak! I was coming back after your great Aunt Lerlene rolled snake eyes and cost us all our points! I rolled three buncos in a row and had us back up to within two points of the other team when you called. I got so flustered that when I rolled another bunco, that Bettye Hooper stole the dice out from under me and won the game." She all but glared at her granddaughter. "I hope you're happy. I was playing for the top prize. It was a DVD of that movie about the male strippers, and it came with two tickets to a show in Houston with the same name. I was going to take Sybil there for her birthday next month."

Madison put her hands over her ears, even though it came too late. "Why do you tell me these things, Granny? That's definitely more information than I need to know."

"What I need to know is why I had to come home in such a rush. We hadn't even had our margaritas yet," Granny Bert complained. "And Sister Caroline makes them nice and strong, just the way I like them."

"Sister Caroline, the preacher's wife?" Genny clarified.

"That's right. She's the one who won the top prize, thanks to Madison's call."

Madison shook her head, hands still to her ears. "Didn't hear that," she claimed.

Speaking louder, Granny Bert repeated, "I said,

Sister Caroline won tickets to the male str—"

"Please! Don't say it again. I heard you the first time!"

"Then stop all this nonsense and tell me what's going on. What's this all-important problem you have?"

Madison took out her phone and showed a picture to her grandmother. "Do you know this man?"

After studying it for a moment, Granny Bert shook her head. "Who is he? He looks sort of like a movie star from the silver screen."

"Wrong profession. Right era." Before following her friend from the secret room, Madison had snapped pictures of the computer screens. "His name was Abel Cartwright, and he was a jeweler in Bryan from 1914 until the mid '40s."

"And?"

"And he was under suspicion for aiding and abetting citizens in their attempts to hoard gold. He had a marked increase in business immediately after the Executive Order was issued. They could never prove he did anything illegal, but according to the report, he kept a lot of late-night hours in his basement workroom, doing 'questionable' work. He was even held in jail overnight while they raided his business."

Granny Bert darted a nervous glance at Genny, wondering why her granddaughter broached the subject in front of her friend. She trusted the baker implicitly, but a deal was a deal. They had agreed not to tell another soul of their find.

"Genny and I found this," Madison explained, "on Tom Pruett's computer. In a secret room inside his house."

"Why were you at Tom Pruett's? And why does that man have a secret room? You know he's not rowing with both oars in the water."

"Mr. Pruett is missing, and Genny was concerned, so we went to check on him."

"With an ax?" her grandmother guessed, not too far off the mark.

"No. By aid of two overturned buckets and an open window. But that's beside the point. The point is this picture and this newspaper article were on two of the monitors. *This* was on the third one." She turned her phone so that her grandmother could see the necklace.

"Ouch. It's even uglier than I remembered," Granny Bert mumbled.

"You've seen that necklace before?" Genny's voice revealed her surprise. She crossed her arms again, glaring back and forth between the two women. "Are you two going to tell me what's going on? What couldn't you tell me back at the house?"

Madison shot a questioning glance at her grandmother. When Granny Bert nodded in agreement, she continued, "Sit down, and I'll tell you all about it."

"I'll get my part of the show and tell," Granny Bert offered, disappearing from the room.

"You remember that chair I told you about? The one I found at *New Again Upholstery*? Well, I went back and bought it, and Derron helped me bring it here to Granny Bert's to recover."

"Yes." Genny nodded. "You told me that the day you brought it home."

"I did? I guess it slipped my mind. A lot has happened since then." Madison massaged her aching head with splayed fingers. "Once I got it here, the seat wasn't nearly as comfortable as I remembered. I decided something must have shifted during transport. Then Granny Bert recognized the chair as one that used to belong at the Big House, so we turned it over to see if it had the mark of the craftsman who made it."

"Wait. The chair originally came from the Big House?"

"Yes, but that's not even the big news."

"That's pretty huge!" Genny protested. "What are the chances of you buying a chair in another town, only to discover it once sat in the house you now own? How did it even get to Navasota?"

"I'll explain that later. Right now, you need to know what we found when we turned the chair over."

"The craftsman's mark?"

"No. Well, yes, but we found something more. Something inside the chair."

Granny Bert returned and held both hands out, her palms curled upward. "This," she said, unfurling her fingers.

Genny stared at the oddly shaped rocks she held in her hands. Her brows puckered in confusion. "What are those? Why did someone spray paint them gold?"

"They aren't spray painted, girl. They're solid."

"You—You're kidding. Right?"

"I never kid where a fortune is concerned. And given the weight of these two rocks and the two others we found, whoever sat in that chair was sitting on a fortune."

"There's *more*?" Genny gasped, whipping her gaze around to Madison. "But—But—" Words failed her.

"There was something else, too," Madison told her, as Genny reached out a tentative finger to touch the golden nuggets. "We found a necklace. *This* necklace." She flashed her phone's screen again. "The one from the computer screen."

Genny's frown deepened. "I don't understand. Why would Tom Pruett have a picture of a necklace that was hidden in your chair? How would he even know about the necklace? And why, by the way, was there even a necklace *in* the chair? None of this is making sense!"

she accused.

"We don't have a lot of answers. It's as big a mystery to us as it is to you."

The three women sat at Granny Bert's table, going over the few facts they knew, questioning the ones they didn't. Their thoughts and suggestions were fragmented.

"Maybe the necklace was stolen."

"Maybe the owner of the gold took the smaller of the nuggets to the jeweler and had him disguise it as a piece of jewelry."

"An ugly piece, at that!"

"Maybe this was one of the pieces he worked on, late into the night in his basement."

"If I made something that ugly, I'd hide my face, too." This, from Granny Bert.

"Maybe it was some of the jeweler's early pieces. *Before* he perfected his craft."

"If that's a sample of his work, there's no way he stayed in business for all those years."

"Maybe this was some of the 'questionable' work the article was referring to."

"But who would have commissioned him to do the work?"

"Someone who could afford all those diamonds and rubies. In the middle of the Great Depression, there couldn't have been many people with that kind of money."

"Miss Juliet. Her sister Naomi. Possibly one or two others, but it's doubtful."

"And it was Juliet's chair."

"There is that," Madison agreed.

"But, why?" Genny demanded. "Why would she hide a fortune in gold and jewels in the cushions of a chair and never go back to retrieve them?"

"We've asked ourselves that, a hundred times."

"Then there's the matter of Mr. Pruett, and how he plays into this."

"Maybe it was a case he was working on." Belatedly, she thought to tell her grandmother of their other discovery. "It turns out we owe Mr. Pruett an apology. Some of his tales may be true. If the photographs on his walls are to be believed, he once worked for the Secret Service and in several other highly confidential positions."

"Well, butter my buns and call me a biscuit!" her grandmother gasped. "I'd have never believed it."

"I know. But the photos look authentic. We even saw a medal of honor," Genny added.

Granny Bert detected the fault in Madison's logic. "But it couldn't have been his case. He was born a decade or so too late for that."

"It could have been a cold case," Genny suggested.

"They overturned the Executive Order," Granny Bert pointed out. "That would be like going back and trying to catch bootleggers after prohibition ended."

Madison stood and moved about the kitchen. "But would Mr. Pruett have realized that? If he does have dementia—"

"No ifs about it," Granny Bert harrumphed. "He thought he saw Nazi and Japanese warplanes flying the friendly skies."

Genny understood where her friend was going with the thought. "So, he's clearly been confused about what year it is."

"Exactly. If he can believe it's the 1940s and we're at war with Germany and Japan, he could easily believe it's 1933 and the Executive Order is still in place."

"He may believe it's his sworn duty to track down hoarded gold."

"But... how would he know it was here? In this chair?"

"He found it, same as us," Granny Bert reasoned. "You heard Hank and Virgie. They sold him the chair in a yard sale. At some point, that crazy old coot found the gold. He probably remembered the basic history of the Executive Order and dug into it."

"And at some point," Genny reasoned with an air of sympathy, "got confused and believed it was a current event."

"That would explain some of his crazy ramblings. That bit he gave Latricia the other day at the café, urging her to hide her gold."

"Wouldn't that be taking the other side?" Granny Bert pointed out. "If he believed he was acting on behalf of the government, he would be trying to confiscate the gold, not encourage people to hide it."

"Who knows what he might think? Clearly, he's delusional."

"And yet, at times," Genny argued, "his mind is as clear as a bell. He's like a walking calculator. He can add his tab faster than I can put the numbers into the register."

"The mind is a complicated piece of machinery," her surrogate grandmother reasoned. "Even with our modern-day medicines and all those doctors with their fancy degrees, they still can't tell us exactly how the mind computes the data we put into it."

"That's true," Madison agreed. "Maybe Mr. Pruett has trouble deciphering what's from the past, what's in the present. He certainly wouldn't be the first person to get it confused."

"Maybe what he doesn't remember, he just makes up. Maybe his wild stories are his way of filling in the gaps," Genny suggested.

"You mean like creating his own version of the truth?"

"Something like that."

"And we all know the government goes in and erases an agent's brain," Granny Bert threw in.

"I don't know about erasing their brain..." Madison protested.

"Okay, their memory. Same difference. I've heard tales all my life, about how they brainwash their agents so they can't reveal items of national importance."

Madison contemplated the thought with a twist of her lips. "Genny and I were talking about that earlier. I wonder what happens when someone like that becomes senile? I wonder if their brain ever short-wires and resets, bringing back things they were supposed to forget?"

The thought startled Genny. "That could be a hot mess!"

"Yes, but it's like Granny Bert said. What if Mr. Pruett can't remember how to compute all that data rolling around in his brain? Think about it. He had a career handling highly sensitive material. He has to have a trove of information locked away in his head."

"He just can't remember it," Genny empathized.

"Right. But whether he's forgotten it by design or by nature, what if he remembers just enough to truly muddy the waters? He could have access to things the rest of us would never know, but, because of his dementia, he wouldn't know what to do with that information."

"What are you getting at, girl?" her grandmother asked.

"Maybe he found the gold, like you said. Maybe he recognized the necklace from old files. Or maybe he just knew that people hoarded their gold by disguising it as jewelry. Maybe his brain knew there was something secretive about it, but he couldn't remember what. Maybe for that reason, he chose to keep it hidden. He could have discovered the gold and decided to leave it there in the cushions."

"That's a lot of maybes, girl," Granny Bert scoffed.

"Maybe you have a better explanation?" she asked, pinning her grandmother with a sharp gaze.

Genny broke into their staring contest. "Even if that's what happened, how did the chair get to Navasota?"

"Mr. Musa said someone brought it in. They traded it for some sort of locker."

"Did he remember who?"

"A gray-haired man, maybe with a beard."

"Could it have been a mustache? Did he get the man's name?"

"Yes. Paul Revere."

"Great!" Granny Bert snorted. "Now he's reverted back to Revolutionary days!"

"*If* it was Mr. Pruett who traded in the chair."

"Unless there's another chair thief on the loose in The Sisters, I highly doubt it."

Her grandmother was right. It was unlikely someone had stolen the chair. Then again, she never would have suspected anyone would take Mrs. McSwain's orange and white monstrosity of a chair. It had been handcrafted for the proud parents of a Texas Longhorn football star and taken from her living room.

"You have a point," Madison conceded. "But why would he trade a chair holding a half-million-dollar fortune for a locking cabinet?"

"Dementia, girl." Granny Bert clucked her tongue in empathy for the other senior. "The mind is a terrible thing to lose."

23

After leaving Granny Bert's, Genny reminded her friend, "All these theories still don't explain what happened to Mr. Pruett. I'm still worried about him."

"You'll be even more worried when I tell you about the black car."

"What about the black car?"

"One followed me home from Granny Bert's on Friday. She saw it circling her house a few times. That was *after* a strange woman was peeking through her windows. And before the same car made almost ten laps around the Big House. Brash was counting."

"Brash knows about all this?" Genny asked sharply. "I thought you said you and Granny Bert agreed to keep it a secret."

"He doesn't know about the gold. But I couldn't keep him from seeing the car."

"I guess not. Do you know who it was?"

"I assumed it was Lamont, but now I'm not so sure."

"You think the car and the necklace have something to do with Mr. Pruett's disappearance?"

"Honestly, I don't know what to think. All of this is giving me a major headache."

"Why don't you take me back to the café? You go on home. I'll take my car and go back to question Mr.

Pruett's neighbors."

"Not by yourself, you won't."

"I'm a big girl, Madison. I can make a few house calls on my own."

"I could have rescued a dog on my own, too, but I didn't. You helped. Just like I'm going to help you."

They returned to Meadow Street to visit the few houses on the block. Genny fished a Styrofoam box from her backseat and gave it to Madison to carry. "Whatever you do, under no circumstances do you allow anyone to eat one of those cookies," she instructed her friend.

"Why? What's wrong with them?"

"They're at least three days old. Maybe four."

"So?"

"I am not about to risk my reputation on a four-day old cookie!"

"Oookay. Then why did you hand these to me?"

"You'll see."

Genny knocked on the first door, smiling brightly when the homeowner answered the door. "Hello, Mrs. Morse. How are you today?"

"Why, I'm fine, Genny. Just fine. And Madison." She acknowledged her with a nod. "Won't you come in? I'll make tea."

"We'd love to, but we're just making a delivery. Tom Pruett ordered a dozen cookies, but when I rang the bell, he didn't answer. Do you happen to know if he's home?"

"Is his car in the carport?"

"Yes, ma'am."

"Then he's home. He never goes anywhere afoot," the neighbor said with confidence.

"Does he ever get a ride from some of your neighbors? Maybe someone runs him into town from time to time?" Madison inquired.

"No, not that I'm aware of. He doesn't have much interaction with the neighborhood, I'm afraid. Keeps to himself mostly."

"If you should happen to see him, would you please tell him I dropped by?"

"Sure. Say, if you'd like to leave those cookies here, I'd be happy to deliver them for you." The woman eyed the box greedily.

"Thanks, but I'd better not."

There weren't many houses on this back street of town and of those, half or more of the homeowners weren't home in the middle of the day. When a rare door opened, the occupants had no helpful information.

Two houses down, they heard a similar story to Mrs. Morse's.

"Beats me. The lights are on at night. Maybe he's just not answering. Tom's a loner."

"Does he ever have company?"

"Not that I ever see. Other than his 'business associate,' I never see anyone come by the house."

"What business associate?" Madison asked, her interest piqued. She noticed the way the man said the words, as if mimicking Mr. Pruett's stern tone.

"That Andrews fellow, the one that owns the pawn shop in town."

"Lamont Andrews? Do you mean the *Gold and Silver Exchange*?"

"He may call it that, but it's just a fancy name for what it really is. A pawn shop."

"And he and Mr. Pruett are business associates?" Madison questioned.

The man laughed, but the sound was condescending. "According to Tom, they had some 'serious business matter to attend. A matter of great importance' that he wasn't at liberty to talk about." He snorted out another chuckle. "You know Tom. Always some grave and important matter."

"Do you happen to know what he did before he moved here?" Genny wondered.

"I know he *didn't* lead no all-female orchestra," the neighbor sneered. "The man can't carry a tune in a tow sack."

"Thank you for your time."

"I'd be happy to take those cookies off your hand, being as you wasted a trip and all."

"Thanks, but Mr. Pruett already paid for them. I wouldn't feel right about giving them to someone else."

"Oh, I'd pay for them."

"I could bring you out some of your own," Genny offered, "but this dozen is spoken for."

They turned to leave, before Madison swung back to ask, "One more thing. When was the last time you saw Mr. Andrews visiting down the street?"

"I believe it was... Saturday? No, Sunday. I was watching a fishing tournament on television. Heard him peel out from the driveway and go racing down the street."

"Could you tell if anyone was with him?"

"No," he admitted. "But I knew it was him; he always runs the same stop sign. Never bothers to stop, just guns the motor as he makes the corner."

"Sorry to have bothered you," Madison mumbled.

After making the rounds, their last stop was to the house across the street from Mr. Pruett's.

"Excuse us, Reverend Green. We don't mean to disturb you, but—"

"Not at all, not at all. Come on in here, young ladies!" the older man said in his deep, booming voice. Jamal's grandfather's voice always reminded Genny of James Earl Jones' pleasant bass. "I just made fresh coffee."

"Oh, thank you, but we were actually trying to deliver these cookies to Mr. Pruett. He doesn't seem to be home. You don't happen to know where he is, do you?"

"Cookies, you say?"

"Yes, sir." When the reverend's eyes lingered on the box, his look almost sinful, Genny prodded gently. "Your neighbor? Do you happen to know where he's been the last couple of days?"

"Who, Tom?" Eyes still on the box, he licked his lips.

"Yes, sir. It seems he hasn't been home for the last few days."

The reverend's eyes shot to Genny's. "Then how did he order the cookies?"

"It—It was a pre-order," Genny stammered, uneasy with telling a fib to a man of the cloth.

"No, I have no idea where Tom went." After one last glance toward the cookies, the older man transferred his gaze across the street. He stared at the house as if reading a hidden message upon the beige siding.

"Do you recall the last time you saw him?"

The reverend thought about it for a moment before scratching his chin and determining, "I remember waving to him on Sunday when we came home from church. Now that you mention it, I don't recall seeing him since."

"What was he doing? Was he getting in the car with someone, maybe?" Madison suggested.

"No. That woman had come to the door again, but he didn't open it until she was well down the street. He gazed after her, then turned around and went back inside."

The two friends looked at one another in confusion. No one else had mentioned a woman. "What woman was this?"

"I didn't know her. The first time she came, I

thought maybe she was his daughter. You know. The one that raises that expensive beef. Raises the cattle in a sterile barn, wearing one of those hazmat suits when she feeds them. Gives them a fancy diet that includes champagne. Never heard of such foolishness myself, but Tom's quite proud of her. Says the meat sells for a hundred dollars a pound."

Not knowing how to respond—this was one story she had never heard before—Genny said, instead, "The first time? The woman's been here before? And I'm assuming you decided this wasn't the daughter?"

"I hope not, at any rate. The first time she came, Tom slammed the door in her face. After that, he refused to answer. As proud as he is of that little girl, I can't see him leaving her to stand out there on the sidewalk."

"Does Mr. Pruett have many other visitors?" Madison asked.

"Not many. I've seen Lamont Andrews drop by a time or two, and his cleaning lady. But that's about it. Sad, that no one ever comes to visit the old guy." He opened the door wider in invitation. "Are you sure you two ladies don't want to come in for coffee?"

"Thank you, but we should go."

"About those cookies..."

Hurrying back to the car, Madison couldn't help but giggle. "Good grief, Genny! You could singlehandedly put the Girl Scouts out of the cookie business. Maybe you should consider adding door-to-door cookie delivery to your business plan."

"I'd be so busy baking and delivering cookies, I'd never have time to cook for the café. And speaking of the café, I must get back. They probably think I've skipped town."

"You, at least, have a job to get back to. I've just realized that while I thought I was so smart finishing up early at *Marvin Gardens*, it wasn't a very wise move on my part. Now I'm out of a job."

"No problem. I'll hire you."

Madison gave her friend the *Mom Look*. "Genny. We've talked about this. I'd make a terrible waitress."

"Not at the café, silly."

"Then, what?"

"I have a crazy-busy week ahead of me, but I'm worried about Mr. Pruett. The obvious solution is to hire you to do it for me!"

She knew she would never accept money for helping Genny look for the elderly gentleman, but Madison finally agreed to 'take the job.' It was the only away to appease her best friend. She knew from experience that once Genny got something in her head, it didn't do much good to argue with her. Genny had her hands full running the restaurant and preparing for Virgie Adams' birthday party this weekend, and Madison happened to have some free time.

Both women knew the logical thing to do was call Brash and report Mr. Pruett missing.

Neither woman claimed to be the voice of logic. Not always.

The elderly gentleman might not be missing, they reasoned. He may have gone somewhere with a friend or the elusive daughter/niece he often spoke of. In all truth, Genny didn't know much about the man's personal life. She wasn't privy to his schedule or his social calendar; he didn't owe her an explanation for missing his usual Monday lunch at *New Beginnings*.

Besides, nothing in the house suggested a struggle. His neighbors hadn't seen anything suspicious. Except for the fact he hadn't visited his favorite restaurant in two days, nothing was amiss. Brash would immediately call attention to that fact. He or his deputies would conduct the customary welfare check, but unless they had reason to suspect foul play, there wasn't much they could or would do.

Did the women want to burden the police department with the matter? Wouldn't it be best if Madison did a preliminary investigation herself? Save the taxpayers' money on something that could have a perfectly good explanation?

Most importantly, Madison reasoned as Genny dropped her off at her car, if she accepted her friend as a client, she would feel less guilty about keeping even more secrets from Brash. She could cite client confidentiality, if only to her own conscience.

Madison wasn't thrilled with the idea, but she knew her only lead in Mr. Pruett's whereabouts was Lamont Andrews. Despite her vow to never again darken his door, here she stood. About to step inside the patchouli-tainted air.

Madison gathered a deep breath and opened the door. She saw Lamont at the back counter, talking to a customer. It was a young man, probably not yet out of his teens, and he was shopping for a necklace for his girlfriend. Madison stood back and waited her turn.

When Lamont noticed her standing there several minutes later, a distinct chill moved into the air. He shot her an unwelcoming glare, and his nostrils flared with silent hostility, but he said nothing while servicing the customer.

The moment the young man left, that changed. Lamont crossed muscular arms over his chest and spat, "What brings you back? I told you to stop harassing me."

Biting back a retort, Madison reminded herself to relax. She would never get any information by being confrontational. She even attempted a half-smile. "I'm not sure where we got off track, but I never intended to harass you, Mr. Andrews."

Could he make the same claim?

With a smirk, the proprietor replied, "It may have been when you came in here, accusing me of doing something to the mutt. Or maybe it was when you came to my house. Or when you plowed me over outside in the parking lot. What were you doing that day? Spying on me again?"

"Not at all. I was working for Marvin Combs."

"You work next door now?" He clearly hadn't expected that answer.

"Not exactly. He hired me for a temporary position, but I'm done now. You may remember, I own *In a Pinch Professional Services*." Madison made a motion with her hands. "Honestly, when I saw you in the parking lot, I wasn't following you."

She couldn't tell if he believed her or not. "What do you want this time?" he asked, but his voice was slightly less demanding. His arms relaxed a bit.

"I have a new client who's trying to find a friend. I understand you may be able to help with that."

"Oh, so you want my help," he smirked. His arms tightened again in a defensive stance. "That's what this is all about."

"The life and safety of an elderly gentleman may be at stake. Any help you can offer would be greatly appreciated."

His chin came forward. "Who's the old man?"

"Tom Pruett."

Something flashed in Lamont's eyes, but his facial expression could have been carved from stone. "What makes you think I even know him, much less know whether or not something happened to him?"

"Mr. Pruett often referred to you as his business associate."

At this, Lamont hooted. "I buy one or two pieces from him, and suddenly we're business associates? The old man ain't right in the head. Everybody knows that." Dropping his arms, Lamont moved away from the counter with exaggerated ease. His lax posture suggested the conversation was too laughable to take seriously.

"But you have had some business dealings with him, is that right?" Madison pushed.

"Very few."

"That was last week, correct?" Madison knew he wouldn't offer any direct details, but that didn't mean she couldn't still fish.

"I haven't seen the old coot in a week or two."

And yet, you were at his house two days ago. What else are you hiding? She wondered.

"I know Mr. Pruett dabbled in jewels and precious stones." Madison amazed herself by sounding so convincing. She knew no such thing. "Were those part of your business transactions? Is that where you got the fancy dog collar?"

The businessman snorted. "Believe me, the old cat didn't have anything that classy," Lamont drawled. "The necklace he tried selling me was costume jewelry. A child's dress-up toy, next to that collar."

She had a nibble! Heart thumping crazily in her chest, Madison attempted a casual grin and reeled him in. "That tacky gold piece with the supposed diamonds and rubies, huh?"

"The gems looked real enough, but it was the setting that gave it away. It looked like someone melted a glob of gold and stuck a few gems on it, hoping to turn a sow ear into a silk purse." He shook his head in stupefaction.

Keep cool, Madison reminded herself. *Tilt your head and look perplexed. Sound surprised when you ask*, "When was this? I thought he sold that necklace months ago."

"It was awhile back," Lamont agreed. "I don't know who was fool enough to buy it, but it wasn't a reputable dealer, I can tell you that."

"Why do you say that?"

"It only took one look to know it was either a complete fake or a stolen piece that had been modified—badly, at that—to avoid detection. Most likely a case of insurance fraud. No reputable dealer wants to get tangled up with that."

Madison truly was perplexed now. She hadn't taken Lamont Andrews for a particularly reputable businessman; she assumed he valued profits over ethics. Had she pegged him wrong? Or was this all a cover? An act he had perfected for law enforcement? *And their wives.*

"Do you have any idea where he got the necklace from?" she asked.

Lamont Andrews didn't realize he was helping the woman he had sworn to forswear. He was busy mocking his troubled 'business associate.'

"Depends on which day it was. The first time, he told me it had 'ties with a top-secret government controversy.' Another time, it was a family heirloom passed down to the next generation from a jeweler's personal collection. One day, he mumbled something about discovering it in a chair cushion. I could never get a straight answer out of the cat, but there's nothing unusual about that. He tells one wild story after the next."

On that, Madison had to agree. "He does have a good imagination, doesn't he?"

"The old cat's crazy."

"What about his other collections? Were they any better?"

"I wouldn't know. He was all talk, no show."

Madison decided to press her luck. "Is that why you

were at his house Sunday? To see his other collections?"

His obsidian eyes filled with suspicion. "Why do you think I was at his house? What are you accusing me of now?"

"Nothing!" she was quick to assure him. "Neighbors remembered seeing you stop by his house. Other than a woman no one could identify, they didn't recall him having any other visitors that day. Or any day, for that matter."

"So? I went by his house a time or two. Doesn't make us buddies. I don't keep up with his comings and goings. And before you ask, he wasn't home Sunday. I knocked on his door, but he didn't answer."

Sensing she would get nothing further from him, Madison sighed and handed him a card. "Here's my number. Please, if you see him, would you please call me? Mr. Pruett hasn't been seen or heard from in several days. My client is worried."

"I'd say good riddance," Lamont muttered, all but snatching the card from her hand.

As Madison thanked him for his time and left, she realized he had made no promises.

24

"I hope this works." Madison's voice sounded doubtful.

"Trust me. It will."

It was the next day, and Genny still hadn't heard from her most faithful customer. Pulling up in front of his house, she put the car in park and killed the engine. She turned to her friend and flashed her dimples. "Show time."

With two takeout boxes in hand, Genny made her way to Tom Pruett's front door. When there was no answer, she turned to retrace her steps, only to 'accidentally' drop her load. Cookies and assorted pastries scattered on the ground.

No one watching could possibly know the delicacies were stale and not suitable for consumption. While Genny stood in dismayed frustration, staring down at the mess and the 'ruined' food, Madison jumped from the car and came to her friend's rescue. She carried the large black trash bag casually, as if it didn't hold a short, lightweight aluminum stepladder. Together, the women stooped to pick up the mess and sweep it into the bag.

Madison disappeared around the side of the house, presumably to find a trash can. Genny returned to the car and made a show of taking more boxes from its interior. She turned to count the houses along the street, her arm extended and her finger dancing. She then made a show of counting boxes. Pretending a discrepancy, she repeated her actions.

For good measure, Genny started down the sidewalk with a wobbling tower of boxes in her arms, appeared to think better of it, and returned to her car. She loaded up with a more reasonable amount and started back on her way.

By that time, any nosy neighbors watching her escapades were all but salivating, wondering what the renowned baker was doing with so many cookie boxes. Who was the lucky recipient? No one gave another thought to her friend.

As Genny knocked at every house along the street and made a surprise delivery to anyone answering, Madison took her ladder to the back of the house, climbed through the window, and paid Tom Pruett's empty house another visit.

They decided that if the elderly gentleman hadn't surfaced by tomorrow, they would alert Brash. Before the police made their official welfare check, however, Madison wanted one more peek inside. The police's presence would only muddy the waters, stirring up her deeper suspicions that what she did technically fell under the 'breaking and entering' clause.

If only in her own mind, she rationalized that today's excursion was a friendly visit to a friend. Okay, so she knew he wasn't home, and she crawled in by way of an open window. Wearing plastic gloves, but, so what? She hadn't broken a thing while entering. And she wasn't tampering with evidence, because the police weren't involved, and it wasn't a case.

No case, no evidence.

The rationale worked for her.

Madison started in the master bedroom, doing a more thorough search for hints about the man who lived there. She snapped pictures of the prescription drugs she found, few of their names familiar to her. She looked for an address book or phone directory. Carefully sorted through drawers and neatly organized shelves, hoping for photo albums or scrapbooks. Anything that hinted at a family or close friends. The best she found was an emergency call list with the names of his physicians, a few photos of whom she assumed was his late wife, and a single album containing pictures from his career.

Genny texted several times, updating her progress with the cookie delivery. The coast was still clear. No one mentioned seeing her accomplice and no one paid attention to the house at the far end of the street. She'd warn her if an issue arose.

In route to take a second look through Mr. Pruett's kitchen, Madison paused in the living room. The room held a formal seldom-used sofa, one well-worn recliner, a large flat-screen television, and little else. If the red velvet chair had sat in this room, it had been the only splash of color. Perhaps the color had been too lively for the older man and a contributing factor to its removal, Madison mused. On a whim, she turned on his television to see the last channel viewed.

She wasn't surprised to see he was a fan of *Mysterious Past*, a cable program that highlighted unsolved mysteries, curious happenings, and past conspiracies. She hit the 'recall' button, bringing up a thumbnail review of the six previous channel changes. Again, no surprise to see his favorites were a cable news channel, the History Channel, and two channels known for their documentaries and focus on historical myths and mysteries.

Madison didn't find a phone book, but she did find

a date book from the previous year. She snapped pictures of several pages, but she held little hope of gaining insight from the calendar; most of the scribbled handwriting was written in code. A magnetic dry-erase calendar clung to the refrigerator but offered little information. Some of the dates were circled, some starred, some marked with a diamond icon, but few had words written within their squares. Other than 'buy groceries,' 'pay bills,' 'trash day,' and 'dentist,' she had few clues about his plans for the month.

One drawer revealed three takeout menus from *New Beginnings*, one from *Montelongo's*, an old calendar with handy tips on car service from *Rudy's Tires*, and a local shopping guide put out by the Chamber of Commerce each January. Madison snapped a picture of the guide, thinking she might check with the businesses he had circled. He may have mentioned plans to go out of town to one of them.

She saved the hidden room for last. She took photos of almost everything but didn't go so far as to search his computer. When Genny texted to say she was almost done, Madison went out the way she had come, donated the ladder to the homeowner, and waited until Genny was back to the car before joining her.

"You walked slow enough," Genny grumbled. "What if someone saw you?"

"Are you kidding? I'm sure everyone is happily munching on their cookies about now. In fact, I may be insulted. What does that say for me, if I can be overlooked so easily in favor of a box of cookies?"

"It worked, though, now didn't it?" Genny's previous frown turned into a smug smile as she pulled away from the curb.

"Like a charm."

"So? Did you find anything?"

"Nothing of significance. I didn't even find a cell

phone."

"Which could be a good sign," Genny pointed out. "If he has his cell phone, he must have left willingly."

"And police could possibly track it, assuming it is charged and has a signal."

"Did you search his computer? If you sent the files to your email, I can help you go through them."

"I didn't. And don't look at me like that. I didn't want to leave an electronic trail. Nothing that pointed to us being in that house. But I took a ton of pictures with my phone. I tried to capture all his notes, screenshots of the open windows on both monitors, the file names in his filing cabinets, anything I could see. I also took photos of his doctors' names and the medications he's on. Maybe something will give us an insight into his whereabouts."

"Hmm. I never thought of the medical aspect. I know he didn't call an ambulance, or it would have come across Cutter's radio, but I suppose he could have gone to the hospital on his own."

"His car is home, remember?"

"I know there aren't any local share riding services, but someone could have come from Bryan-College Station."

"I've already called the hospitals there and asked to be connected to his room. None of them had a Tom Pruett registered."

"What about the VA Hospital in Waco? He claimed to have been in the Army or the Navy. Possibly both."

"It's worth a shot. I'll also look his doctors up and see what hospital they're affiliated with."

"Hey, you're getting pretty good at this PI stuff!" Genny beamed. "You should seriously consider getting your license."

"Then why am I having such a hard time putting this all together? Tom Pruett obviously had possession of the necklace at one time. He either found it in the chair or put it there himself. I'm unclear if he knew about the nuggets, as well. I know that at some point, he tried selling the necklace to Lamont. Lamont thought the necklace was too hideous to be real and declined the offer. It's after that point that everything gets fuzzy."

"Maybe Lamont convinced Mr. Pruett it was fake, so he put it back in the chair and either forgot about it or thought it would be a fun joke to play on the next person who found it," Genny suggested.

"Maybe." Madison chewed on her lip. "That's assuming he didn't know about the nuggets or thought they were fake, too. But for whatever reason, he still had a picture of the necklace pulled up on his computer."

"But if he's senile and having trouble with the concept of time..."

"There's still the black car, the woman, and the blackout at the library."

"I thought you suspected it was Lamont in the car, an overzealous believer, and what about the blackout?"

"I didn't tell you this before. But that day the lights went out, I could have sworn someone else was in the library with me. I heard several sounds. Not creaky, old building sounds, but brush against something sounds. The tiniest of grunts. Something. Or someone."

"Three blind mice?" Genny offered with a sheepish grimace.

"I wish that were all, but I can't shake the feeling that someone was there. It was while I was searching the web for a match to the necklace. What—What if someone saw my search and wanted to stop me from investigating further? I had been looking up gold nuggets the day before. Maybe someone hacked into the library system and thought I was getting too close to... I don't know what," she admitted, "but to *something*. Something they wanted to remain hidden."

"I hate to break it to you, but I doubt the Juliet Municipal Library is a hotbed for routine hacking activity. If someone hacked into your search, they would have had to know you were there and researching the gold. I don't think that was it."

"But maybe that's what the message was talking about. Maybe someone knew I was looking up information about gold and searching for the necklace online."

"What message?"

"Did I not mention that, either?" she winced. Shaking her head, Madison groaned. "I'm telling you, Genny, keeping a secret from Brash has made me a nervous wreck! And that was when I only had the gold to worry about! Before all this business of old men going missing, cars circling the house, hiding a fortune in my house, lights going out, threatening phone calls, and this new nasty habit I've picked up of breaking and entering. I have a perpetual headache from the stress. It's getting harder and harder to remember a thing."

"Again. *What* message?" Genny demanded. "What threatening phone call?"

"Someone called my phone on Friday. Repeatedly. Never said a word, except the final time. They told me to take some *golden* advice. Back off."

"Golden?" Genny gasped. "How could anyone know?"

"I have no idea. Granny Bert thought it still could have been Lamont, playing on the *Gold and Silver* aspect. But I'm not so sure. Especially now. I don't think it's a coincidence that Mr. Pruett is missing and the last thing he looked up on his computers was the necklace."

"To be such an obnoxious piece, it certainly has

created a commotion," Genny murmured. "Just imagine the drama if it had been well designed."

"I do have to wonder what the jeweler was thinking, creating that piece."

"He probably wasn't thinking. He was probably working as quickly as possible so he wouldn't get caught. If the feds were on to him, and he was operating in his basement like the article suggests, he was probably trying to get in, slap on a few gems to make it look like an authentic pendant, and get out."

"You're probably right. If no one is home, I'll take you up to the library and show you the thing in person. I think the photograph may be more flattering than it deserves."

"Is that even possible?" her friend murmured. "The picture was pretty bad."

"I'm afraid so," Madison chuckled. "I'll spend the rest of the afternoon following up what little I found at the house."

"And tomorrow, after I try calling Mr. Pruett one more time, I'll call Brash. I think it's time to file an official missing person's report."

The medications she discovered at his house gave Madison more insight into Tom Pruett's health status. Most of the medicines were used for treating symptoms of dementia such as delusions, paranoid behaviors, and irrational beliefs, all of which the man possessed. Madison wasn't certain if he had sleep disturbances, aggressive behavior, or restless wandering, but she thought some of the behavior she had witnessed fell under "disinhibited behavior." All were classic symptoms for patients suffering from Alzheimer's or other dementias.

Reading the side effects of each medication was

scary enough, imagining them together as a whole was a potential nightmare in the making. What was beneficial for one symptom was prone to make another worse. All cautioned the increased risk of confusion. All warned that treatments should never end abruptly, but gradually tapered off under a physician's watchful eye. Unless Tom Pruett had a second set of meds with him or was under a doctor's care, Madison worried about the consequences of him going cold turkey.

Judging from the emergency contact list, the man saw a variety of doctors. Research revealed the list included a cardiologist, psychiatrist, and a neurologist. His primary care physician was a geriatrician in Bryan, but most of the other specialists practiced in Houston.

Madison ruled out the probability of a ride share service making the three-plus-hour round trip, but he could have taken a bus. She doubted the transportation line would give information to a civilian, so she left that lead for her husband and his deputies to chase.

In the meantime, she *could* contact the Houston-area hospitals used by his doctors and ask the operators to connect her to his room. Houston had 2.3 million residents, not to mention the thousands of people from around the world visiting the Bayou City's renowned doctors and hospitals. Knowing there could be multiple patients with that name, she specified that he 'was admitted on Sunday or possibly Monday.' Even within that parameter, she was connected to three others with that same name plus a female Tommie Pruett, but none was the right person.

Madison breathed a sigh of relief when Thursday morning arrived. Today, Genny would call Brash and report Mr. Pruett missing.

Brash would know exactly what to do.

25

"And when did you first notice he was missing, Genny?" Brash's tone held the appropriate concern, but Madison couldn't detect an undercurrent of suspicion. *So far, so good.*

She came with Genny to file the report, sensing her friend could use the moral support. Plus, if Brash should discover their duplicity, Madison felt she should be the one to deal with the fallout, not Genny. Who better to reason with the chief than his newly wed wife?

"I was surprised when he didn't come in Monday for his normal chicken-fried steak. I tried calling him that afternoon, just to make sure he was feeling well. No answer. By Tuesday, I was concerned. I even asked Madison to run over to his house with me that afternoon. We knocked on both doors, but he never answered. By Wednesday, I was worried. Still no word from him. He's *never* gone this long without coming in for at least one meal. Even the time he suspected Shilo Dawne of trying to poison him with tainted jalapeno juice—long story, don't ask—he only stayed away two days. But he hasn't been in since Saturday, and this is Thursday."

The friends had agreed to tell as much of the truth as they could, without implicating themselves in their unorthodox 'visits' inside the house. As she recited the edited chain of events, her hands twisted in her lap and her blue eyes clouded.

"I'm worried, Brash," she concluded.

"Why didn't you mention this earlier, Genny? Or Maddy? Why did you wait so long to bring this to my attention?" His voice was still gentle, but the concern now edged toward judgmental.

"And say what? That a customer didn't eat at my restaurant? Even though it's a Monday tradition, it's not a mandate. He's under no obligation to eat at *New Beginnings*. I appreciate his loyalty, but he hardly owes it to me."

"That being the case, why are you here today? Like you say, he can take his meals anywhere he chooses."

Genny glanced at Madison, trying to judge whether the chief was attempting to trick her. "That's absolutely true," she agreed with an animated nod. "And that could very well be the case. But he's not answering his phone or his door, and none of his neighbors remember seeing him since Sunday."

"And you know this *how*?"

Madison slowly crossed her legs before offering a simple explanation. It took a moment for her husband's eyes to release the image of her long, slender legs and focus on her words. His gaze was like a caress, momentarily distracting them both. "While we were in the neighborhood, we knocked on a few doors and asked. Reverend Green remembered waving to him on Sunday after church. No one else had much interaction with him. Ever, apparently."

"Did I mention that his car was still parked in his carport? Since we have no local taxis or Uber here, we think he must have left with someone else." Genny stated the obvious, but she was nervous. Brash's sharp, watchful gaze danced between the two women as if he suspected they were hiding something.

"What makes you think he's not visiting relatives?" Brash asked.

"He could be." She was quick to answer. Slower to add, "He's mentioned a daughter, but to be honest, I'm not sure she exists."

Brash nodded in understanding. He was familiar with Mr. Pruett's many versions of his life.

"We know he uses doctors in the Houston area," Madison pitched in. "For all we know, he took a bus down there and has checked into a hospital for routine tests."

"Or, with any luck, to a mental facility where he can get help and supervision," the police chief muttered.

A frown marred Genny's forehead. "I hadn't considered that."

Brash released a sigh. "I'll check into it. He lives on Meadow in Naomi, right?"

"Yes. Last house on the right. Directly across from the Reverend."

"I'll send one my officers out to do a welfare check. We'll see if we can find his whereabouts for you, Genny."

"It's not just for me. I'm getting truly concerned for his safety. What if he doesn't have his medicine with him? What if he just wandered off?"

Brash was kind enough not to point out that reporting him missing earlier may have prevented all of that. He still wasn't completely convinced his wife and her best friend were telling him the whole truth.

Madison presented him with a beaming smile. "Thank you, sweetheart. We knew you could help."

"I'm not sure how much I can do or if I can locate him, but I will try," he promised.

Genny stood to leave. "That's all I can ask of you."

"Maddy? A word?" Brash said when she would have

followed her friend out the door.

Genny turned to see Madison, her back to her husband, mouth the word, “Uh-oh.” She pasted on a smile, said, “I’ll be right out, Gen,” and whirled to face the firing squad.

“Want to tell me what’s really going on?” Brash asked with a shrewd look on his face.

“We told you. No one has seen or heard from Mr. Pruett since Sunday, and Genny is concerned enough to file a missing person’s report. It could be nothing, but she’s worried.”

“Why do I think there’s something you two aren’t telling me?”

“I don’t know. Why?”

“Don’t play dumb with me, Mrs. deCordova.”

“I wouldn’t dream of it,” she murmured demurely.

“Okay, so now I *know* something is up!” His bark of laughter lacked amusement.

Having anticipated his suspicion, Madison had her response planned. She looked momentarily torn before she admitted, “Okay, you’re right. I told Genny you would see through us. The truth is, she’s hired *In a Pinch* to look into his disappearance, as well.”

He arched that imperial brow of his. “She doesn’t trust the department to do our job?”

“It’s not a matter of trust. It’s a matter of knowing how busy you are and how few resources you have to dedicate to the investigation. Since my schedule is currently free, I’m able to give it my undivided attention.”

“And what has your undivided attention turned up?”

“He hasn’t been admitted to any of the local hospitals, the VA Hospital in Waco, or to these facilities in the Houston area.” She presented him with a typed list. “There are plenty of others, but these are all I’ve had time to check." This was true. She just hadn't bothered checking with the hospitals not affiliated with his doctors. She couldn't volunteer that information to her husband, however, so she left it at that. "I didn't bother with the bus station angle, because I knew they wouldn't release such information to a civilian. You'll have to chase that one down."

"Very good, my love," he commented.

"Thanks. Genny says I should go for my PI license," she said, a proud twinkle in her eyes. One look at her husband's solemn expression doused the light. "We'll discuss this later." Quickly changing the subject, she stretched upward to give him a kiss. "Don't forget, Blake has a game this afternoon. Love you."

"Love you, too, sweetheart."

Madison scurried from the room, thankful to have narrowly escaped her husband's razor-sharp intuition.

She missed the way his eyes narrowed as he watched her retreat.

Nor did she hear his muttered words.

"I wonder what my beautiful but curious wife and her faithful sidekick are up to *this* time."

They were in bleachers cheering on the home team when Brash took a call from his deputy. He couldn't hear well for the noisy crowd, namely his wife. Blake was having a particularly good game, which hadn't escaped the attention of his most devoted fan. While there were plenty of high school girls cheering for the talented athlete, Madison was doing her part and more.

"Hold on. I'll have to call you back, Abraham." Brash was already up from the bench.

"Trouble?" Madison asked, dividing her attention between his answer and Blake's pitch.

"I don't know yet. I can't hear."

"Sorry about that. *Way to go, Blake*!" Her attention shifted at the speed of a fast pitch. "One more!"

Brash sat back down to watch their son strike out another batter and end the inning. He then stood again and wove his way among pumped arms and excited fans.

When he returned a few minutes later, Madison immediately noticed the dark look on his face. "What's wrong?" she asked.

"That was Officer Abraham. She made the welfare check as requested."

Madison knew Mr. Pruett wasn't in the house—or hadn't been yesterday, at any rate—but Brash's brow had puckered into a frown. "What—What's wrong?" she asked. Her attention transferred from the game to her husband's pending answer.

"She didn't find Mr. Pruett, if that's what you're thinking," he was quick to correct. "But she did find something else."

Madison was impressed. *Had she found the hidden room that quickly?* Maybe the woman was more than a pretty face, after all.

When Misty Abraham joined the force a few weeks ago, Madison was the first to admit she wasn't exactly thrilled at the prospect. After all, the woman and Brash had once dated, no matter how casually and how sporadically. Maddy knew the woman was still attracted to the handsome chief of police—*and who could blame her?* —but she had been nothing but respectful toward Madison and the sanctity of their marriage. For his part, Brash paid the curvy blonde no more attention than he paid the other two officers on the force. His wife held his undivided attention and affection.

"Oh? What was that?" she asked now, trying to sound casual.

"The house had been ransacked. The entire place tossed."

"What!" Her shocked cry was utterly real.

When did that happen? Her mind raced with possibility, probability, and cause. *'Cause someone has been following you,* Madison reminded herself bitterly. *They watched you go in the house and wondered why. You led them right to his house, and they trashed the place.*

Unless...

Unless she had been right, and Mr. Pruett was somehow mixed up in this whole messy gold business in the first place.

"But... why? How?"

She was talking to herself, but Brash didn't know that. His release of breath sounded weary. "Because my life isn't complicated enough right now. Because we need one more thing on our plate to juggle." He rubbed his hand over his suddenly haggard face and shook his head. "I know I should be ashamed, making this about me. A man is missing, and considering this discovery, there may very well be foul play involved. I'm sorry."

Madison slipped her hand onto his leg. "You don't have to apologize, sweetheart. I know you have enough to deal with, without this."

"I need to go. I need to make sure the scene is processed properly."

A line appeared between Madison's brows. "Does that mean... fingerprints?" She had worn gloves the second time, but not on that first visit.

"Maybe. I guess that depends on how big of a mess they left. If it was a professional, they would have known to wear gloves."

Another reason you have no business playing private eye, Madison scolded herself silently. *You're obviously not a professional, or you would have known that.*

Aloud, she tsk-tsked her disdain. "Why do you think someone would do something like that? Why would they kidnap an old man and toss his house?"

"Like we've said before. With all the crazy claims he makes, someone may have been just foolish enough, or greedy enough, to see if they were true." He leaned over to brush a kiss across her lips. "Tell Blake I'm sorry. I hate to walk out in the middle of a game, but duty calls."

"He'll understand. Be careful."

"Will do."

His feet barely touched dirt before Madison texted her best friend.

Have to talk.

Bubbles appeared on the screen a few seconds later.

What's up?

Madison glanced around, making certain no one watched the exchange.

Someone broke it to TP's house.

More bubbles.

Well, duh.

Madison shook her head, even though her friend couldn't see.

For real. Tossed the place.

Her phone rang immediately. Madison answered with, "Give me a second." She picked her way off the bleachers and found a semi-private place to talk.

"Brash just got the call. They were waiting on the locksmith to come from Riverton and open the house. Misty took the welfare check and found the house ransacked. Brash is headed over there now. Gen, what if they take fingerprints? Mine will be all over the place from that first day!"

"So will mine!"

"Yours could be explained. For all anybody knows,

you made a home delivery in the past. I, however, have absolutely no reason to have been inside that house. Ever."

"Let's not worry about that until it happens. The place may be too trashed to give a complete print."

"What about the windowsill? My prints will still be all over it!"

"Maybe not," Genny said with a hopeful whine. "With my graceful belly flop over the edge, I may have wiped out all traces of those suckers."

Madison's lips twisted in memory. A tiny giggle escaped, easing some of the worry gathered at the base of her spine.

"That offers a little hope," she agreed.

On a gasp, Genny asked, "Did they find the secret room, I wonder?"

"I have no idea. And I can't come out and ask. I'm not supposed to know about it."

"Aside from possibly exposing our own little adventure, there's a bigger concern," Genny pointed out. "Who did this? And why?"

"I'd say whoever kidnapped Mr. Pruett."

Another gasp from the other end of the line. "You know for certain he was kidnapped? Brash said so?"

"No," Madison admitted. "But it makes sense. The man is a creature of habit, but he misses his standing Monday ritual. The lights are still on, the car is in the driveway, and the alarm wasn't set. No one has seen or heard from him in days. Now his house is ransacked. I think—" Madison paused as someone passed within earshot of her hushed conversation.

She stepped further away from the ballfield. "I think," she continued, "someone kidnapped him to find either the necklace, or those fabulous collections he's always bragging about. Or maybe even both. When he couldn't take them to it, they came back to search the house."

"They didn't leave a note," Genny pointed out.

"I don't think this is a kidnap for ransom situation."

"Then, what?"

Madison lowered her voice, trying to break the news as gently as possible to her friend. "I hate to say this, Gen, but I'm afraid it's worse than that. I think it's a 'you give me your valuables or I'll kill you' situation."

26

Brash came home late that evening, but Madison was there to greet him at the door.

"Dinner's waiting in the microwave," she said as she accepted his kiss.

"Is Blake still up? How did the game wind up?"

"I think he just laid down. We won, 11-4."

"Did he pitch the entire game?" he wanted to know, pulling his starched uniform free of his belt.

"They brought in a relief pitcher halfway into the sixth inning, once it was obvious we had the game under control."

"I'm proud of my boy!" Brash beamed. "Are you sure he's in bed? I can just poke my head inside his room..."

When he would have turned to take the back staircase up to the second floor, Madison grabbed his arm. "Not so fast, Mister. You can talk ball over breakfast, same as every morning. I want to know what happened at Mr. Pruett's."

"That." Just one word, but full of weariness. Shaking his head, Brash tucked his arm around her waist and asked, "Do you think I could have my supper before I go into the details? And a big, tall glass of sweet tea?"

"We'll compromise. You can talk *while* you're having supper." She slipped out of his reach and hurried to the refrigerator. "One glass of tea, coming up."

Settling his large frame into a seat in the breakfast nook, Brash waited for the promised glass. He stretched his neck and rubbed at his eyes. "It was a huge mess," he volunteered, even before she placed the bribe before him. "I don't think they left a single thing untouched. Tables turned over, shelves knocked off the wall, pillows ripped, drawers upended."

"Mirrors, too?" She tried to sound casual as she punched buttons on the microwave.

"Most of them busted," he agreed. "One or two knocked off the wall."

"Really?" she squeaked. "Why?"

"Probably looking for a wall safe. Some of them were the perfect size and location."

"Lo—Location? Like where?"

Brash shrugged. "Usually it's the bedroom or a hallway. Sometimes it's in the bathroom where a medicine cabinet should be."

Her heart stalled at the mention of the bathroom, where her prints surely paraded all over the windowsill and the floor tile. Not to mention the long, full-length mirror. "Oh, so the smaller ones," she managed to say, gathering his eating utensils. The microwave beeped before she had her voice schooled enough to sound natural. "Did they find anything?"

"No idea what the thieves found, but *we* didn't find a thing. Thanks, sweetie." He smiled as he accepted the plate she offered.

"None of those grand collections he bragged about?"

"No, but we did find some interesting photographs in the hallway. It turns out, Tom Pruett really did have a long and distinguished career in the Armed Forces, the Secret Service, and in national intelligence."

"You're kidding."

"Nope. While the officers finished up, I went back to the station and made a few calls. Despite the late hour, I confirmed everything with DC. Including the fact that Pruett was an alias."

Madison's gasp was sincere. "Honestly?"

"Honestly."

"So, all those crazy stories..."

"May not have been so crazy," he completed her thought. "I have no idea if he collected half the things he claimed, but the truth is, he did travel to a lot of different countries and saw a lot of amazing sites. When he squawked about conspiracy theories and the government watching, he may not have been as delusional as we all thought. According to my buddy in Washington, he worked on some high-profile and sensitive missions."

"I feel terrible," Madison admitted. "All this time, we thought he was crazy."

"About that." Brash pushed back his plate and looked at his wife with a serious expression. "It appears that Tom Pruett, as we know him, does have some severe issues with not only his memory, but with his mental wellbeing. He's in the early stages of Alzheimer's, but he's been battling dementia for a while now."

"Your contact told you all this?"

"I asked. I found Pruett's medicine and looked up what the pills were prescribed for."

"That was fast," Madison murmured, impressed with her husband's detective skills. It only took him a couple of hours to accomplish what had taken her half a day.

"Without his medication, Pruett becomes a wild

card. He could as easily turn comatose as he could volatile. We need to find the man as soon as possible." Brash took her hand in his and stared into her eyes. "So, I'm going to ask. What is it you're hiding from me?"

Madison resisted the urge to jerk her hand away. "Hiding?" She knew her voice came out unnaturally high.

"Yes, Maddy. Hiding. I know there's something you and Genesis aren't telling me."

"I, uh, told you. She hired me to find Mr. Pruett."

"And I believe you. I also believe that's not the entire truth. There's something you haven't told me yet."

Suddenly suspicious, she pulled back. "You already know what it is?"

"No, that's why I'm asking you. But I know there's something you aren't telling me. Talk to me, sweetheart. Tell me what it is."

"Did you... take fingerprints?" She studied the large hand engulfing hers, pretending to look for the telltale black dust.

"The team did. But quit changing the subject. Tell me what you're hiding from me."

After a long moment, punctuated by a sigh of defeat, Madison caved. "I may as well tell you. You're going to know soon enough. When Genny and I went to check on Mr. Pruett, we sort of... let ourselves in."

"Genny has a key? Why didn't you say so? I had to track down a locksmith in Riverton, wait for—"

Madison shook her head, interrupting his exasperated comments. "No key."

The slow, precise annunciation of his words revealed his growing suspicions. "Then *how* did you get inside?"

"We didn't break and enter. We just... entered. The

bathroom window was open."

"Madison, that's—"

She broke in before he could explode. "I know. I know what we did was wrong. I know what we did could be construed as unethical as well as slightly illegal, but—"

"No *slightly* about it!" he bellowed. He jerked his hand away and fell back against the chair. Hard.

"But there were extenuating circumstances," she went on calmly, as if he hadn't interrupted her with his outburst. "We were worried about Mr. Pruett. Genny truly thought we would find his body inside. She thought that, as his friend, she should be the one to find him."

"That's hardly the point, Madison."

"It's the whole point. We were going the extra mile for a friend. Being loyal and dedicated to the end. The very thing we teach our children to do."

"Not to break the law, we don't!"

Before Madison could come clean—before she could tell him the house wasn't ransacked until last night, or that there was a secret room, or that the mystery went deeper than Mr. Pruett's disappearance—Madison's cell phone rang. She glanced down, seeing Bethani's name pop up on the screen.

"What's she still doing up?" Madison muttered. "I thought she went to bed an hour ago." One glance at Brash's thunderous expression, and she hit *Ignore*.

The phone immediately rang again.

"Yes?" she answered tersely.

"Mom? I feel sick," the teen mumbled, her voice sounding terrible. "Can you come up here?"

Her mom instincts on full alert, Madison felt guilty about her sharp greeting. "What's wrong, sweetie?"

"Don't know." Her voice was low and groggy. "So

cold. And my stomach..."

"Okay, Bethie. I'll be right there." She was already sliding out of her seat.

Overhearing the exchange, Brash frowned. "Is she okay?"

"She sounds terrible. I know you think I'm running out on the conversation—"

"Go," he interrupted her. "This conversation isn't over, but it can wait. Go check on our girl."

Madison brushed a kiss across his lips before she left. "If I'm too long, don't wait up."

Despite a fever of 101, Bethani still complained of freezing. Madison layered another blanket on her bed and tucked it in close, just as she had done when the girl was a small child.

"Thanks, Mom." The teen's smile was weak.

"You're welcome, baby. Does your throat hurt?"

"Not really."

"Your head?"

"Feels like a ton of bricks."

"What about your stomach?"

Blue eyes fluttered closed. Madison thought she had fallen asleep until she finally answered, "Not happy. Cramping."

"Do you know if there's a stomach bug going around? Or the flu?"

Her answer was an indistinguishable moan.

Mopping her daughter's feverish brow, Madison offered, "Would you like some Sprite or soda water to settle your stomach?"

"Not sure it would stay down." She mumbled something more, but Madison couldn't understand the words. After a long pause, Bethani moistened her lips and asked weakly, "Did Daddy D get home?"

Touched by the girl's concern, Madison smiled. Not so long ago, the relationship between Bethani and Brash had been strained. Understandably, her father's death shattered the teen. It wasn't easy for her to accept a new man in her mother's life, but Brash had slowly won the girl over with his patience, understanding, and with his good and loving heart. There was still something about a pony, some private joke between the two of them, but Madison allowed them their secret. It helped strengthen the newly formed bond between the two.

"Yes, he was having his dinner and heading up for a shower. He's worried about you, too, honey."

A pleased smile lifted one corner of the girl's mouth as she drifted in and out of sleep. She awoke with a start, several minutes later. "Mom?" Her voice sounded worried.

"Yes, sweetie?"

"Stay?"

"Of course. I'll be right here if you need me. You get some sleep. I'm not going anywhere, sweetheart."

It was a long night. Bethani slept in bits and pieces, alternately freezing and burning. The Sprite, intended to help, didn't stay down.

By morning, the fever had broken and her stomach settled, but Madison kept her home from school. The best thing for them now was rest.

It was late in the morning before Madison was up and moving. After her second cup of coffee, she called Genny.

"Sorry, but we're already slammed with customers," her friend said when she answered. "I can't talk long."

"Do you want me to call back after lunch?"

"I don't know if that will be any better. My entire day is crazy. That party is tomorrow night, and I still have to prep."

"I'll make it quick, then. I had to tell Brash about our visit—the first one, anyway. I didn't have time to fill him in on the room or what we found on the computer because Beth got sick. It's been a rough night."

"Ah. Bless her heart." There was a loud crash, followed by Genny's rare oath. "I'm sorry, Maddy, but I really have to go."

"I'm still going to tell him, Genny. I have to."

"I'll back you any way I can, girlfriend. Just say the word."

"I appreciate that. Bye."

The call to her grandmother didn't go as smoothly.

"You promised me three weeks," the older woman said stubbornly. "You said until Brash's birthday."

"Which is Monday," Madison reminded her. "His party is Sunday."

"But not today."

"A man's life could be at stake, Granny. Mr. Pruett is missing, and now someone has ransacked his house. I'm sure they're looking for the necklace."

"So, the damage is already done. No reason to rush now."

"Except that he's been kidnapped!" Her cry was filled with exasperation.

"Do you know that for a fact?"

"I think it's rather obvious, don't you?"

"Not necessarily," Granny Bert challenged. "Someone may have seen he was gone and decided to rob his house. Doesn't mean something bad happened to him. He may have taken one of those bus tours to Louisiana to do a little riverboat gambling."

In truth, Madison had never considered that option. She knew plenty of local seniors who did just that. Granny Bert, in fact, had joined them year before last, but decided to drive herself after that. She claimed hanging out with a bunch of old people cramped her style.

"Does he gamble?" Madison questioned.

"Beats me, but Genny says he's a whiz with numbers. Makes sense. Say, you don't suppose that's where he got the necklace, do you? He could have won it in a poker game, and now someone wants it back. Maybe he's mixed up with the mob." There was an undertone of excitement in her grandmother's voice, as if she hoped that were the case.

"Granny! What a thing to say!" She heard a noise behind her and turned. "Oh, look. Here's Beth, wobbling her way into the kitchen. She was sick all night but looks much better now."

Hearing the claim, the girl gave a lackluster thumb's up.

"I've got to go, Granny. Remember what I said."

"Monday, girl. You promised me Monday."

"That's three days out, and all bets are off. I'm telling Brash. Today."

27

Except, she didn't.

She never had the opportunity.

It was Friday, and even though it wasn't the thirteenth, it felt that way.

Blake was the next to succumb to the stomach flu. He came home in the middle of the day, swore off food, and didn't emerge from his room until the next morning. If there was a bright side to the malady, this strand was short lived.

A wreck on the highway kept Brash out late again that night. Between the wreck and a sick son, Madison only spoke to her husband in passing. He was on duty Saturday and made it home just in time to dress and leave for Virgie Adams' birthday party.

"Wow. This place looks great!" Madison said in breathless appreciation. "Genny continues to amaze me with her talents. And those retractable panels Cutter made are awesome."

Putting his welding and steel-working skills to use, Cutter had fashioned a wall, of sorts, to separate the back section of the restaurant. Ornately attached against the exterior brick walls, the lattice-type panels could pull and retract to stretch the distance. By the time Genny added yards of gauzy material, twinkling lights, and whatever decorations the occasion called for, the panels gave the illusion of privacy.

"It does look great in here," Brash agreed. He gave an appreciative sniff as his stomach growled in response. "It smells even better. I haven't eaten since breakfast, and I'm starved."

"Why didn't you eat? You're not getting sick, too, are you?" she fretted.

"I have an iron stomach," he claimed. "We were too busy to stop for lunch."

"Really? What was going on?"

"Don't even get me started. I don't want to talk shop tonight. I want to have a nice, relaxing evening with my gorgeous wife and a roomful of friends." He let his warm gaze run over her. "You, by the way, look particularly ravishing tonight."

"Thank you." She glowed under his attention. "When Derron insisted on buying this for my trousseau, I was afraid I wouldn't have anywhere to wear it."

"We'll have to do something about that, now won't we?" When he would have nuzzled her cheek and promised to take her out soon, their hosts for the evening spotted them and made their way over.

"Miss Virgie, Happy Birthday!" They took turns hugging the eighty-year-old and shaking hands with her husband.

"A little birdie tells me this wasn't exactly a surprise," Madison said, eyes twinkling.

"This one," Virgie scoffed, putting her arm through her husband's. "He never could keep a secret. Sixty years of marriage, and he's never once surprised me with a gift. Can't keep his lips zipped long enough not to spoil the surprise."

"At least it gave you time to find a lovely dress," Brash said with a smile. Winking at the older man, he said, "Hank, I do believe we have the two most gorgeous dates at this party. Not bad for a couple of old country boys, huh?"

Brash was in such a good mood that evening, Madison couldn't bring herself to spoil it. He needed at least one night without stress and worries. Although he carried it well on his broad shoulders, the weight of his responsibilities was heavy. The community depended on him not simply for their safety, but also for his guidance. He was like their lighthouse on a foggy shore. He loved his job, and he loved his community, but everyone needed time off now and then.

They mingled among the crowd, visiting with what seemed like half the community. Madison wasn't sure if anyone was left to dine on the other side of the wall, but it sounded like the entire place was packed. Genny had extra staff on hand but still ran back and forth between the two rooms, lending a helping hand where needed.

"Poor Genny," Madison commented as she and Brash finally seated themselves at a table. "She's going to run herself ragged before the evening's half done."

"She loves every minute of it, and you know it. I was surprised to see her newest busboy, though."

"Who's that?"

His brown eyes twinkled with humor. "Cutter. It appears he traded in his bunker gear and welding helmet for an apron."

"You're kidding! I've got to see that!" Madison clapped her hands together with glee, laughing as she imagined the handsome heartthrob clearing tables. "I bet the women love that!"

Brash shook his head with a chuckle. "The man is officially whupped," he claimed. "The things we husbands do to please our wives."

"And vice versa," she reminded him, patting his

arm. "Speaking of pleasing the women in your life. Your mother is really excited about throwing you a birthday party tomorrow."

"Don't remind me."

"Come on. The girls are so excited about baking you a cake. Just in case any tainted air is still lingering in the Big House, I don't feel right inviting a bunch of people over. Your mom was delighted to move the party out to the ranch."

"I'm sure she was. She can invite both my brothers and my sister that way," he grumbled, "plus half the ranch employees. Blow this thing up to a big production."

"Think of it this way. More gifts," Madison grinned.

"I have you and the kids. That's everything I need."

"Don't deny your mom this pleasure. Or your girls. Megan and Bethani are excited about this."

Beside her, Brash grunted, but she knew it was all an act. He enjoyed a birthday celebration as much as anyone did.

As they enjoyed their meal, Brash watched a middle-aged woman deposit a gaily wrapped present onto the table after greeting the birthday girl. Even though the invitation insisted no gifts were necessary, most of the guests brought some token, and the pile of presents continued to grow.

"That was nice of her to come," Brash murmured.

"Who is that?" Madison asked. Something about the woman was vaguely familiar, but Madison was certain she had never met her. She had the look of someone who was harried and exhausted and running on fumes. Streaks of gray hair blended with brown to pull into a messy bun. Madison wondered if it had started that way or if she had had a difficult day. Judging from her stiff movements and the visible scratches on her hands, she suspected the latter. The woman looked like a hard worker.

"Their ex-daughter-in-law," Brash answered. "She and Gerald have been divorced for years. Even though they have Paul as a connection, it's nice to see she keeps in touch with her ex-family."

"I don't remember seeing her at the trial. Then again, I concentrated on the attorneys and nothing else. I wanted nothing to do with the circus outside that courtroom."

"Because of its ties to the TV show, it naturally got more attention than most cases," Brash agreed.

"At least the judge didn't allow cameras in the courthouse. But I still don't remember seeing her there."

"Neither do I, come to think of it. Maybe she had to work. Or maybe she couldn't stand seeing her son and the father of her children on trial and facing prison time."

"Maybe she knew they were guilty and didn't want to jinx their fate. Jurors watch the families' faces, you know."

Brash grunted in disagreement. "I doubt that. Maybe she didn't condone their methods, but she supports the underlying message. She's always maintained the Adams family was swindled out of their inheritance. I wouldn't be surprised if that wasn't why she married Gerald to begin with, thinking he would come into Miss Juliet's fortune. They never seemed particularly happy together. She left him when Paul was still in school. She didn't come back here until a few years ago."

Madison studied the woman again. "Maybe that's why I don't recognize her."

"She's one of those who likes to keep the old feud oiled up and running," he added. "She can't just get over it and let bygones be bygones."

"Water under the bridge," Madison agreed, recalling a similar conversation with Marvin Combs.

"I'm going back for more barbecue. Would you like something?"

"No, thank you. I'm stuffed, and they haven't even cut the cake yet."

That night, Madison had a dream about Mr. Pruett. He was somewhere in a dark room, surrounded by upturned tables and scattered papers. A blindfold wrapped around his eyes, secured by a gaudy gold necklace.

As morning sun streamed into the room, she vowed to tell Brash the full truth. Between sick children, his work schedule, the party last night, and the temporary reprieve she granted for his own benefit, the urgency of the situation had slipped past her. The truth was, however, that Mr. Pruett could still be in danger. They still had no idea if he was on vacation or if he had been kidnapped. The more information she gave Brash, the better equipped he would be to find the missing gentleman.

She knew there was the possibility that her input would make little or no difference. So far, she hadn't made much progress in connecting the dots, but Brash was a trained professional. He could catch things her amateur eye didn't see.

Promises to her grandmother and birthday surprises aside, it was well past time she did the right thing.

When Madison rolled over in bed, however, the pillow beside her was empty. Instead of his dark head, she found a note, anchored by a chocolate candy kiss and written in her husband's masculine hand.

"Sorry to leave, but I didn't want to wake you. Fire

broke out at Gold and Silver Exchange. Huge mess. If I don't make it to church, I'll try to meet you at the ranch. This kiss doesn't love you as much as I do, but at least it's sweeter. Your adoring husband."

Madison smiled, touched by his thoughtfulness. Propping herself up on pillows, she called her best friend.

"Did you survive last night?" she asked with a smile.

"Barely!"

"It was wonderful as always, Genny. The room looked fantastic, and the food was delicious. I don't know how you do it."

"I had a lot of help. Cutter was a godsend. I may make a restaurateur out of that man yet!"

"I saw him cleaning tables," Madison giggled. "Speaking of your groom, I hear there's a fire at *Gold and Silver*."

"He got the call about three this morning. He's still not back."

"I know what you went through when your house burned. I'm not a fan of Lamont Andrews, but I'd never wish that on anyone, not even him. Was it a total loss?"

"No, I don't think so. They were able to get some of the stuff out, and I know there are at least three walls still standing. I'll forward you the pictures Cutter sent me."

"I hope it didn't spread to *Marvin Gardens*."

"No, it was contained to the one building."

"Do they know what started it?"

"This can't go any further than us. But between you and me, they think the cleaning service may have left something flammable behind. It's too soon to say, and the fire marshal hasn't gotten here yet, but that's the theory they're leaning toward. And of course, Lamont is breathing fire."

"I guess that explains Brash's mention of a huge

mess."

"How did he take the news of the gold? Has he already made you turn it in? Does it offer any clues to Mr. Pruett's disappearance?"

"I haven't told him yet. These last couple of days have been so crazy, I just never had an opportunity. I know it sounds like a copout, but it's true. Between the fire and the party, today isn't looking too favorable, either."

"I just hope the guys finish in time to come. We can't very well have a birthday party without a birthday boy."

Madison crawled from bed and padded into the library turned personal office where she had a coffee maker. She loved this room, with its rich paneled walls and built-in nooks and crannies. Unlike its larger and more formal counterpart downstairs, this one was scaled for a woman, making the space feel cozy and inviting.

The gold nuggets beckoned to her. Knowing she would soon reveal them to her husband anyway, Madison decided to take them from their hiding spot. This time, she used the library ladder to access the sliding panel.

"This is much easier than a stool," Madison realized aloud, reaching around the journals to find the box. "I should have been doing this all along." Making her a few inches higher than when on the stool, the additional height offered a different vantage point.

As Madison fished the box out, she saw a piece of paper in the far back of the cubby. "Hmm. Wonder where that came from? I wonder if it's been here all along, and I'm just now seeing it." She stood on her tiptoes, stretching to touch the paper with her fingertips. "Almost. Just a little... there! Got it!"

She glanced at the paper as she backed her way

down the ladder. It appeared to be the same quality of paper as the journal entries. Hadn't she noticed a couple of torn-out pages? A stickler for appearances, Juliet recorded her thoughts in a flowing, even hand. Madison had marveled at the lack of errors and cross-outs in the many documents. If Miss Juliet made a mistake, Madison had no doubt she ripped the pages out as not to mar the perfection of the others. Perhaps this had been one of those error-tainted pages, she mused.

Madison sat at her desk and carefully emptied the contents of the box. With the same sense of wonder and awe as the first time, she tested the weight of the golden nuggets in her hand. What was even one of these worth? A college education? Three cars, for three teenagers? A debt-free future? She allowed her mind to wander at will, imagining the possibilities if the gold were hers.

There was that huge two-letter word. *If.*

She pulled the necklace from its tissue, questioning its origin. Such an odd piece. Valuable, without a doubt. But still so awkward and gawky.

"How do you tie into Mr. Pruett?" she wondered aloud. "What did he know? Did it get the poor man killed?"

The diamonds had no answer. They winked at her in the light, brilliant and sparkling despite the abuse they had suffered. The rubies glistened with a low red glimmer, bringing to mind blood and, for some reason, the racing stripe on Lamont Andrews' white sports car.

Startled at the path of her own thoughts, Madison traded the necklace for the discarded piece of paper. She unfolded it and read the familiar script of Juliet Randolph Blakely.

Word came today that President Roosevelt has rescinded that dreadful Executive Order. It was indeed a sad and dark day in our country's illustrious history when our government seized property from its devoted and most lawful citizens. It pleases me to know the order has been rescinded, but the damage has been done. Those more loyal to their country than I have already relinquished their property. I knew I took a great risk, refusing to heed the call, but I could never surrender my beloved's inheritance. It was Darwin's dream to use his uncle's generosity to promote and provide good health to those less fortunate.

I couldn't allow the government to take his gold. To lose it, to lose hope of giving Darwin his dream even in death, would be like losing my beloved all over again. I had to protect the gold at all costs. It was my duty as a wife. Mr. Cartwright tried to help, but the results were less than satisfactory. The only option was subterfuge. I had no option left but to hide the gold. It shall remain hidden until I can use it to make Darwin's dream a reality.

One day, Darwin Blakely's destiny shall be fulfilled.

Madison stared at the entry in disbelief. For whatever reason, Juliet had chosen to rip this page from her journal. Perhaps she feared someone finding the note, and what consequences it would bring. If the knowledge fell into the wrong hands, the reader might tear the mansion apart, looking for the hidden treasure.

Who would think to look in a chair? A desperate sort might rip out the exquisite burled wood panels. Splinter intricate woodwork. Shatter inlaid marble. Rip out polished brass sconces. Pluck crystal chandeliers from their sockets. Tear out parquet patterns and polished hickory floorboards. They might destroy the integrity of the grand old dame without once thinking to pluck the cushions from a favored chair.

It had been Darwin's chair, of that Madison was certain. The sentimental widow had hidden her husband's inheritance in his favorite wing chair, and then... then, what? Madison wondered. Had she, indeed, forgotten of its existence? Given up on the dream? Become too old and too feeble to see it through? Had the cost of construction outweighed the market value of gold? Or had she, in her bitter later years, no longer wished to honor the man who had fathered her sister's child?

Madison would probably never know. Unless there was another page, another entry ripped from the journal for secrecy sake and inadvertently left behind, she would probably never understand Juliet's ultimate decision to leave the gold hidden in the chair. But one thing was now clear. The gold, and the necklace, had belonged to Juliet.

The knowledge was slow to sink in.

The gold, and the necklace, had belonged to Juliet.

Juliet left her home and its contents to Granny Bert. Her grandmother sold them to Madison. Even though the chair changed hands a couple of times, carrying the hidden treasure along with it, Madison had purchased it back. There was only one deduction to make.

The gold was hers! All four nuggets and this tacky, tasteless necklace belonged to her.

The knowledge was stunning. Madison grabbed for the desk to steady herself, even though she remained seated. This couldn't be happening. This couldn't be real!

And, yet, it was.

Suddenly, Madison couldn't wait to share the full story with Brash.

28

Lydia deCordova was in her prime, having all four of her children and most of her grandchildren together again. It was like Christmas all over, she beamed. She prepared a huge feast, followed by the cakes Megan, Bethani, and Brash's niece Ava had baked with such enjoyment. A handful of friends joined the family celebration, including Cutter, Genny, Matt and Shannon, and their son. Granny Bert even brought Sticker along, their differences patched for the time being.

Madison had a token gift for her husband to open at the party, but she told him his real present was too large to wrap and was waiting for him at home. The wicked gleam in his eye brought a blush to her face, but most of the guests knew about the chair. His father, both brothers, and a nephew had carried it from Granny Bert's garage and deposited it, for now, in the downstairs library. Madison thought it poetic justice that the chair had come full circle, returning to the very room it once sat in.

She didn't mention its secret, of course. The fewer people who knew about the gold, the better.

She enjoyed the day with his family, but she thought it would never end. When the men went down to the fishing hole, she smiled and shooed her husband away, pretending she didn't mind. When Andy deCordova insisted they stay for leftovers, Blake answered for them. After skipping a full day of eating, the teen had meals to make up for and food to eat. As an afterthought, he asked his mom if it was okay. She nodded and lied through her teeth, her smile never giving away her impatience and her jumbled thoughts.

If she thought keeping a secret from her husband was torture, it was nothing like wanting to share the truth with him now! The day dragged by, minute by minute, while her mind and her emotions bounced all over the place.

They could buy those cars.

They could pay for college.

They could be debt free.

They could spend their fortune any way they chose. They could start with that long-awaited honeymoon.

By the time they finally made it home, Madison was antsy. She dragged her husband to the formal library and presented the charcoal-tweed chair with a flourishing hand movement. Brash was thrilled with the chair and duly impressed by her newly acquired upholstery skills. The chair's history, sans gold, amazed her audience, much as it still amazed Madison. The full story, the one including the gold, was for Brash only, and not the three teens. After another round of birthday wishes and hugs all around, the girls disappeared to the third floor, and Blake helped Brash lug the heavy chair up to the master bedroom to begin its reign there.

With the kids settled and the house quiet for the night, Madison smiled at her husband. "I have one more present for you, Mr. deCordova."

That wicked gleam returned to his dark eyes, and he reached for his wife. "I was hoping you'd say that, Mrs.

deCordova."

She accepted his lingering kiss before amending, "Okay, maybe two more. But let me give you this one first. I promise. You will like it."

"I'm sure I will," he murmured, nuzzling her neck as he deftly edged her back toward the bed.

Madison twisted from his arms. "Not yet. First, I have something to tell you."

A strange look crossed Brash's face. His eyes darted to her flat stomach. "I, uh, know now might not be the right time to mention this... We never really talked about starting over, but... but..."

Realizing where his thoughts led, Madison burst out laughing. "No, silly! I'm not pregnant."

The relief on his face was laughable. "Whew. I love you, sweetheart, and I'd love making a baby with you. But I'm not as young as I used to be."

"You're right, we haven't talked about it. I'm not saying I'm totally opposed to the thought..."

"Nor am I. But the three kids we have are more than enough to fill my heart and make me the proudest dad around."

"I feel the same way. So, at least for now, you can wipe that petrified look off your face."

"No offense, but I'm not sure I'm up to those midnight feedings again. Megan had her days and nights mixed up for the first two months of her life. And if we start over with a baby, I might never be able to retire."

"Not necessarily," she contradicted mystically. "Here, have a seat in your new chair and let me tell you the *rest* of the story."

When she was done, Brash's mouth hung agape. If not for visual proof, he would have thought she had taken a play from Tom Pruett's book and made the entire thing up. He questioned everything, but Madison had answers for his inquisitive mind. Knowing how her husband's mind worked, she had anticipated most of them.

"Now do you see why I've been so distracted and testy lately? I hated keeping a secret from you, sweetheart. The guilt was crippling. But I promised Granny Bert."

"She still has two of the nuggets?"

"Yes. I worry about her, having something so valuable at the house, but we thought it was best to split it up. Genny is the only other person I've told, and I didn't do that until a few days ago. The fewer people who know, the better."

"Agreed. This must be kept under strict wraps."

"What do we do now?"

"I suppose we'll need to report it to the proper authorities."

Madison gave him a sharp look. "That's exactly what Granny Bert said you'd say, and the whole reason I didn't tell you in the beginning!"

"But, the gold..."

"Belonged to Miss Juliet." Madison crossed her arms over her chest in a show of stubbornness. "Brash, I'm not turning that gold in."

"We don't know for a fact that it belonged to Miss Juliet."

"I found the note, Brash! Weren't you listening? Darwin's uncle was a gold miner in Alaska who hit it rich. Darwin dreamed of using it to provide better health care for the less fortunate. Miss Juliet admitted to hiding it until she could make that dream come true. She never did, hence the gold still in the chair, almost a hundred years later."

Brash gave his auburn head a couple of slow,

deliberate shakes. "I guess I'm having trouble absorbing it all."

"I know." Her voice softened, and she sank to her knees in front of him. She cradled his hands in hers. "I know, sweetheart. I feel the same way. I know this is all new to you, and it's overwhelming. I've had a little more time to adjust."

"So, is the gold yours? Granny Bert's? Both of yours, since you found it together?" He still looked dazed.

"She insisted it's mine. Said she sold me the house and all its contents. Skeletons, spiders, first-edition books, hidden treasure, and all. I told her to keep the two nuggets she has, but she refuses. So, I suppose they're ours."

"Yours."

"What's mine is yours, what's yours is mine. Ours. That's how a good marriage works, sweetheart."

He shook his head again, this time in wonder. "This is still just too unbelievable."

"There, uh...is more..."

He heard the tentative tone in her voice. "Of course there is." His sigh was weary. "And if I read you correctly, it means trouble. Is that why you were so eager to share? Split the gold, split the trouble?" he teased.

"That, too, is how a good marriage works," she answered smoothly.

"Just tell me and get it over with. Does the gold come with some sort of a curse?"

"Possibly. It's already stirred up quite a bit of trouble."

She told him about the first time she had seen the black car and the sinister message on her phone. She knew he would be angry. She knew he would fuss at her for putting herself in danger and ignoring the safety measures he had tried teaching her. She knew he would be angrier still, perhaps with good reason, about Mr. Pruett and the things she hadn't told him.

"How could you, Maddy? You may have put that man's life in danger!"

"I know. I've been so torn. Once I decided to tell you, regardless of the consequences and regardless of the promises I made Granny Bert, there just wasn't a chance. With the kids being sick... and you working so much... and both birthday parties... Look. I know it was wrong to withhold the information. But the truth is, we still don't know if he's actually missing."

"But he knew about the necklace. He may not have known about the nuggets, but he knows about this necklace, awful as it is." He held up the offending piece, allowing it to sway back and forth from its long chain.

"It is pretty terrible, isn't it?" She couldn't help the giggle that bubbled out. "Can you imagine Miss Juliet's face when the jeweler presented that abomination to her?"

"The thing is this has to be worth a small fortune all its own. Besides the weight of the nugget and the thirty-or-so-inch chain, those are real diamonds and rubies."

"Please tell me that is not my punishment for keeping the truth from you. Please tell me you aren't going to make me wear that!"

"It would serve you right." He grinned, slipping the necklace over her neck. "There. It looks... awful."

He gathered her up and pulled her onto his lap, wrapping his arms around her. "You know I have to go back to the house now. I need to see if the intruders found the secret room. While the computers are still on and running, I need to back up all the information, in case they're password protected. I'll probably end up taking it all down to the station so we can comb through them there. Maybe we'll find a clue as to his whereabouts."

"Do you have to go tonight? But it's already so late. And it's your birthday!" Madison protested.

"If you had told me this on Thursday, or, better yet, on Tuesday when Genny first noticed he was gone, I wouldn't have to. The information would have been much more useful then." Despite his gentle tone, his eyes held a light of accusation.

"I know. I'm sorry. Can I go with you?"

"It's a police investigation, Maddy."

"I know. But I've worked with and for the department several times. Consider me a consultant on the case."

He was slow to agree. "That might work."

"Of course it will. And you really don't want to make your deputies get out at this time of night."

"Abraham is on duty tonight."

Madison never missed a beat. Wrapping her arms around his neck, she said, "And I really don't want you cooped up in the tiny little room with that woman."

"Maddy, I've told you a hundred times—" he started in exasperation.

"—what you really want for your birthday," she finished for him, already loosening the top button of his shirt. "We have a few minutes, don't we?"

It would take a stronger man than he to resist her offer. "We've wasted this much time," he murmured. "What's another hour? And Maddy?"

"Uhm?" she asked in distraction, working more buttons loose.

"I can think of one way to make that necklace look better."

The impossibility of the notion captured her attention. "How's that?" she wanted to know.

"Make it the only thing you're wearing."

Brash called in his intentions to revisit the house on Meadow. Officer Abraham offered to assist, but he assured her it wasn't necessary. When he stopped by the station to get the newly made key, she offered a second time. He asked her, instead, to keep an eye on the *Gold and Silver Exchange*, making certain there were no looters.

He and Madison picked their way to Pruett's guest bath, where she showed him the hinged mirror.

"Good eye, sweetheart. How did you know this was here? We all missed it."

"It made sense. Tom Pruett loves conspiracy theories and all that secret spy business. He's just the type to have a super-secret room. When we didn't find a basement, I remembered the tile didn't match up in here." She pointed to her proof. "Watch your step. And your head. Come to think of it, your shoulders may not fit, either."

It was a tight fit, but Brash made his way through the crudely carved opening.

"Wow. This is impressive," he said, once they were inside the tiny space. "I can't turn around in here, but those are some serious machines he has."

"And look." She touched a button, bringing the screens to life. "There can't be two necklaces on earth that are *that* ugly." She pointed an accusing finger.

"I don't know," Brash said. A twinkle came to his eyes. "The way you wear it gives me an entirely new appreciation for the piece."

"Get that look out of your eye," she warned. "No room. And what if there's a hidden camera?"

"Hey, I wonder if Pruett had any cameras in other parts of the house. Maybe it caught the intruder on tape."

"I can't imagine how. This entire house is trashed. If there was a camera, it's buried in a heap somewhere by now." Her voice was sad. "The house was plain, but neat as a pin. That is such a shame out there."

"When the investigation is done, I'll see about getting someone to come in and put it to rights. Maybe the same cleaning service that half the town uses. *Coming Clean*, I think it is."

"Do you have those thumb drives? I can save all the data from this computer, if you want to do that one."

Together, they backed up as much information as they could. "By the way, I already have photos of everything," Madison offered. "I'll send them to you when we get back home."

"Let's just hope it's not a reminder to me of how angry I still am at you for keeping this secret for so long."

"Remember what we said last night? Water under the bridge," his wife reminded him.

"Yes, but this water is still running. Let's just hope it doesn't drown us both."

29

It was very late—or early, depending on one's perspective—when the weary couple returned home. Madison peeked in on the sleeping teenagers before falling into bed beside her husband.

They awoke just a few hours later, forced to face the new workweek.

"Since you are apparently a consultant on this case now," Brash informed his wife in a dry tone, "you'll need to earn your keep. Can you come down to the station today and go through Pruett's computers?"

At the thought of being officially involved in the case, Madison perked up. "Absolutely!"

"I'll see you at the station, then. Kiddos, have a great day." He mussed Blake's head before collecting kisses to the cheek from both girls.

"Happy birthday, Daddy!" Megan called after him.

"It looks like I have just enough time to get dressed before dropping you off at school. Clean up after yourselves but don't worry about loading the dishwasher. Dishes are clean."

"You know, Mom," Blake started in. He never missed an opportunity to say, "If you'd buy me a truck, you wouldn't have to bother with taking us to and from school."

As always, his mother had a ready reply. "It's no bother, honey. It's my pleasure to haul your smiling faces around."

Still, as Madison jogged up the stairs to the second floor, she considered the luxury of not being her children's personal taxi service. What if the kids had their own car to drive? Not three of them, mind you, although Megan probably needed her own, as she split her time between her parents' houses. And if Megan had one, why shouldn't each of the twins?

Would one of the gold nuggets cover the cost of three used vehicles? It could be worth mentioning to Brash.

Just a thought, she assured herself, hurrying to her closet.

It turned out to be a busy day. Tom Pruett's computer was password protected, but the code was easy enough to decipher. The man was certainly obsessed with Executive Order 6102, so it seemed logical he would use it as his current password. Madison typed in the numbers, and the blank screen churned to life.

She worked most of the day without pause, pulling information from the many and varied files. Like his mind, Tom Pruett's digital research was all over the place, covering a multitude of topics that spanned several decades. As she looked through them, a pattern emerged.

There was a story of a man in Dallas who led an all-female orchestra.

There was a file on how to build your own helicopter.

One on Executive Order 6102.

A file for unmanned military drones.

A file on Kobe beef.

Files for making jewelry and files for mining gold.

Details on Nazi and Japanese warplanes, and all things World War II.

A file on Paul Revere and his metal workmanship.

The files were like a road map. They led from one of Tom Pruett's fantastical stories to another. It seemed that when the man researched a topic, he then imagined himself playing that role in real life. Sorting through file after file, Madison could hear his voice in her mind, reciting much of the very same information she found within. He claimed to have lived out the events, but they were nothing but files on his computer.

Oddly enough, the most interesting and impressive careers of all, those in the Secret Service and the Armed Forces, were the only ones that were real. Brash's contact confirmed he traveled the world, so his claim of exotic collections could very well be true. Why he felt the need to embellish with other stories could only be answered in his twisted mind.

Madison's phone rang early in the afternoon. She was surprised to see the home number for Monte Applegate.

"Miz deCordova?" a timid voice asked.

"Yes. Is this Monte?"

"Yes, ma'am."

"How are you today, Monte?"

"Not good. I have the stomach bug, and I'm home from school. But that's not the problem. The problem is Pup is missing again!"

"Oh, dear. That's not good," Madison murmured as she saved another file, this one on Smithsonian exhibits. Hadn't she heard Mr. Pruett talk about that, just a few weeks ago?

"I don't know how he got loose this time. I know I had him tied and tied good. But I came home from school last Monday, and he was gone."

"He's been gone a full week?"

"I kept thinking he would come back," the boy said in a glum voice. "Plus, it took me awhile to get enough money together to hire you. I only have twelve dollars. Is that enough?"

Madison pretended to consider the offer. "Let me see. With the repeat customer discount, and with the fourteen-day window policy..." She punched a few keys on the keyboard, acting as if it were a calculator. "Your follow-up case would be nine dollars," she told the hopeful-sounding boy. "Eight, if you're paying cash."

"Really? That's awesome!"

"I can't make any promises, Monte, but I'll see what I can do."

"Thanks, Miz deCordova. You're the best!"

"Again, I can't promise the same results as last time."

"But you can try. With his business burning down and all, I'm afraid what kind of mood Ol' Man Andrews will be in."

His parting comment haunted Madison. The more she thought of his sorrowful voice, the more she worried. How *would* Lamont Andrews react to finding Pup on his property again? He might very well make good on his threat to ensure it was the last time.

She left early and drove out to the old barn, just to make certain Pup wasn't trapped inside again. She called Genny on the way.

"Do I need to come with you?"

"Thanks, but I'm good. I'm coming prepared this time. I stopped by the house and raided Brash's tools. I have a claw hammer, crowbar, and a pair of wire cutters, just in case. Oh, and a flashlight and water boots to wade the grass. If Pup is trapped inside the barn again, it should be an easy rescue."

Genny's voice sounded doubtful. "If you say so."

"I'm almost to the *Exchange*. If Lamont's car is

there, I'm good to go."

"Okay, but be careful. If at any point you need backup, give me a call."

"Will do. Thanks, Gen. I'll call you when I'm done."

Turning the corner, Madison saw the destruction. The front of the *Gold and Silver Exchange* was boarded up with shiny new plywood, a stark contrast to the smut-covered cinder block walls beneath it. Some of the blocks crumbled near the top. Overhead, the roof was charred and, in some places, caved inward. Curls of pale smoke wafted up from the heavily damaged building. On the air drifted the stink of burnt electrical wires, charred wood, and patchouli.

"What a mess," Madison muttered. "And what a shame. I must say, I feel sorry for Lamont." She drove around back, to confirm his car sat in the parking lot. Even the white sports car had traces of smut and ash on its hood.

Confident Lamont was occupied at his store, Madison turned down Sawyer Road. As her tires gobbled up the distance, her mind was on Tom Pruett and his complicated mind. She imagined the man had been brilliant at one time, before age and disease ravaged his memory and ate away at his cognitive skills.

Like Granny Bert said, a mind was a terrible thing to lose.

As before, Madison parked at the edge of the public road. Gathering her supplies, she sprinted through the tall grass to the back of the old barn. Lamont Andrews still had not mowed this side of the driveway.

"Pup?" she called quietly. "Are you in there, boy?"

There was no sound from within. Madison thumped the wall and called again. This time, she was rewarded with Pup's sharp bark.

"It's okay, boy. I've come to get you."

Madison found the knothole from before and peered inside. Too dark. She shared the space with the beam of the flashlight, allowing her to see shadows and lumpy forms.

From the sounds of his excited whimpers and barks, the dog ran around in circles before racing to the back where she was. She heard the click of claws on wood and the thump of his paws as he reared up on the wall. Pup whined and barked, begging for attention.

"Give me a minute, boy. I'll have you out and back home in no time." Madison lifted the hammer and attempted to pry the boards apart with the metal claw. When it didn't work as easily as she had imagined, she added, "I hope."

A few more futile attempts and Madison stood back, surveying the side of the old structure. "Maybe this isn't the right section of boards. Maybe I was... there." She moved over two feet, spotting a board whose nails were missing or wallowed out. "Ah. I think this is the place."

Pup ran back into the interior of the barn, still whining and apparently running in circles again.

"He must have his rabbit in there with him," she murmured. She wedged a flat end of the crowbar between the boards and pushed. Nothing happened.

Madison got a better grip on the iron handle, squared her shoulder, widened her stance, and pushed again. Pulled. Pushed and pulled, wiggling the bar back and forth. She heard a groan. Felt the wood shudder. Watched as a small opening appeared.

"Come on, Pup. Here, boy. This way." When the dog didn't come to the call, she whistled. "Here, Pup. Monte is anxious to see you. Come on, boy."

The more she coaxed and pleaded, the more the dog barked and whined, but from a distance. He didn't hurry to her the way he had to Genny.

"Come on," she groaned, more to herself than to

him. "Don't make me call in reinforcement. I could bring Genny or even Monte out here, but it would be much easier if you would just... Come on! Come on, boy! Let's go." She whistled again.

The excited dog finally ran to her. Just as Madison wiggled one hand between the boards and touched her fingers to his fur, he pulled away. He raced back to the interior of the barn, clearly wanting her to follow.

"I do not want to see your rabbit," she informed the dog. "Or, worse, your rat. Come on, boy, please. Let's go, boy!"

When the dog clearly had other plans, Madison huffed out a tired breath. Wedging the pry bar just *so* to keep the boards splayed, Madison flattened her body against the grass so she could peer into the dark barn. She shone her flashlight into the interior but still couldn't see much. She wiggled further, pushing her head inside. From this vantage point, she finally had an illuminated view.

The first things she noticed were the rows of metal shelving lined neatly along the perimeters of the walls. One was a narrow cabinet, reminiscent of old school lockers. Locks and all.

A sense of unease moved up Madison's spine. She attributed it to the damp grass tickling her tummy and the small stone pressed into her thigh as she slithered closer. If the boards snapped together now, they would close on her neck. She shoved the tip of one shoulder forward.

She moved her light along the shelves, seeing all manner of assortments. Some held boxes with unknown contents. Some held vases and urns. When the beam of light glinted off something metallic, her discomfort grew tenfold. One set of shelves held pots and pans of the household variety. The kind with copper-clad bottoms. The brand, she thought, that had

Revere in its name.

Paul Revere.

"Someone broke in and took my best pots and pans!" Mr. Pruett's fantastical claim rang in her ears. *"This is a disgrace. A matter of national crisis. It has the earmarks of a conspiracy. Mark my words, there will be an investigation into this, and when the truth is revealed, it will rock this entire community!"*

She had thought it was all in his head. He was delusional, at worst. Sleepwalking, at best. However, there had been a sad lack of cookware at his house. That looked like a full set, there on the shelves. And the man who had traded the red chair—her chair, the one Tom Pruett bought at a yard sale—for a cabinet with a lock had called himself Paul Revere.

It made sense, and yet, it didn't. Why would his cookware be here, in Lamont Andrews' old barn? Why would the locker be here? Had he staged his own theft and brought it here, thinking to make an insurance claim?

Something light colored caught her eye. Pup danced around the lumpy object resting on the ground, barking and yipping, becoming more animated in his excitement. He darted back toward Madison, keeping just out of her reach, never slowing as he made a wide arc and raced back to his find.

"I really don't have time for this, Pup," she groaned. "Come on, boy! Now! Let's go!"

The dog barked again. His teeth latched onto the light-colored blob and tugged. Madison couldn't see it well enough to make out any details, other than it lay in the shadows between two sets of shelves. The dog growled and shook his head, teeth still latched on, growing more agitated by the moment.

So did Madison. "I'm not staying here forever, Pup," she warned. "Here, boy. Let's go home." Her shrill whistle echoed in the empty cavern of the barn.

She thought she had finally made progress. The brown and white dog started running her way, carrying something in his mouth. She kept up an encouraging call, coaxing him forward, but he suddenly stopped. He had dropped it. He nosed around on the floor, pushing something with his snout. Madison watched as the dog twisted and turned his head, managing to pick the something up with his teeth. That was when she realized he was bringing her a gift.

"Please don't be a mouse. Please don't be a mouse." By now, her head and both shoulders were inside the barn. There would be no hasty retreat if her gift were alive and wiggling.

Instead of a mouse, Pup deposited a piece of material in her outstretched hand.

Even in this light, she knew it was khaki.

"Mr. Pruett?" she called. "Mr. Pruett, are you in here?"

Pup barked and sprinted to the darkened cavity of the barn.

Heart in her throat, Madison followed. She belly-crawled forward, pushing the hammer ahead with one hand, the flashlight with the other. She had stuffed the wire-cutters into one back pocket and her cell phone into the other. She felt the cutters snag now on a board and fall free.

"Hope I don't need those," she grunted, twisting and wiggling her hips through the narrow opening. She doubted the crowbar would hold much longer. One more push and slide, and she would be inside.

She fought down a sense of panic as she heard the crowbar tumble away and the boards snap back together. She looked back in time to see the slice of daylight shrink to a mere sliver. She started to turn back and retrieve the tool that laid on the other side, but a noise from inside the barn drew her attention. It sounded like a moan.

"Mr. Pruett?" she called. Madison scrambled to her feet and dusted off her clothes. She scooped down to grab her flashlight and hammer, shining the light into the darkness. It bounced wildly off shelves and walls before zeroing in on the light-colored heap.

Madison ran forward, calling his name. "Mr. Pruett, are you okay? Can you talk to me?" Pup danced at her feet, leading the way to his bounty.

Tom Pruett sat slumped over on the floor, his body looking like a discarded rag doll. If not for the low moan rattling his chest, Madison might think him dead. His clothes were filthy and disheveled, his hair matted in all directions. For once, the man had some color. His skin was as ashen as ever, making the blood appear all the darker. There was a dried patch on his shoulder, some smeared down one pant legs and on his hands, but the worst was from a gash in his head.

"Mr. Pruett! What happened to you?" Madison sank to her knees, trying to assess the worst of his injuries. She unfolded his body with gentle hands and patted at his cheeks. Was he even conscious?

"Mr. Pruett! Can you hear me?" She spoke in a loud voice, hoping to penetrate the fog of his injury. "It's Madison deCordova. I'm Genny's friend. You know, Genny from *New Beginnings*? She's been very worried about you."

The old man's head moved. He tried to speak, but his mouth was dry and his voice hoarse. A few tries later, he managed a mumbled, "I'll have my usual."

Grateful to know he was halfway coherent, Madison reached for her cell phone. She would call for help and have him out of here in no time. Reaching into her pocket, she pulled the pair of wire cutters from her pocket.

"Oh no! That was my phone that fell out," she realized. "Wait here," she told the man, already on her feet. "I'll be right back."

She ran to the back of the barn and pushed on the loose board, but nothing happened. After several attempts she managed to move it a fraction of an inch, but the phone was still out of her reach. She needed the hammer.

Madison dashed back to Mr. Pruett's side and would have retrieved the hammer, but he was mumbling again. His moan was filled with pain.

"Where do you hurt?" she asked, kneeling beside him again. "Is anything broken?"

"Head."

Whether or not his head was broken was debatable, but that was beside the point. Madison ran her hands over his body, applying just enough pressure to detect trouble spots. He cried out when she touched his shoulder and his leg. Both places were near the dried pools of blood. His hands and fingers were bloody, but she saw no obvious injuries, other than raw knuckles. She suspected most of the blood was transfer from other places. The place on his head was the worst and needed medical attention.

"I'm going to see if the door is unlocked. You stay right here."

"Locked," he mumbled, but she stood and tried anyway. She rattled the massive old doors, watching as the entire wall swayed and gave just a bit beneath the onslaught. The locks held steady.

Madison walked along the wall, looking for a weak board. She banged and rattled, pounding her fist against rotted areas and kicking here and there. The walls shuddered, but nothing gave way. They were locked inside.

Had Mr. Pruett locked himself inside (either accidentally or on purpose) or had someone secreted him away and locked the door?

The answer didn't take much thought. His car wasn't outside. It was at his house. The same house someone ransacked.

Someone had brought him here, and they had left him here, knowing he was injured and in need of medical treatment.

"Who did this to you, Mr. Pruett?" she asked as she turned away and retraced her steps to his side. "Who hurt you and left you in this place? Was it Lamont Andrews?"

His only answer was a moan.

A quick survey of the barn revealed a jug of water, a stack of disposable paper goods, and a few food items. Madison grabbed the half-full jug and carried it to him. She poured some into a cup and insisted he drink, helping hold the cup to his parched lips. Trails of liquid dribbled across his dirt-streaked face to leave muddy tracks. If she managed to get as much *in* him as on him, it would save him from dehydration. After he drank his fill, she dampened a paper towel she found and worked on cleaning his head wound.

He could offer little information to her steady barrage of questions. How had he gotten here? How long had he been here? What was the last thing he remembered? Who had been here with him? Did it hurt when she did this? What about when she pressed here?

And *what* was that terrible racket?

"Door," he mumbled feebly. "Opening door."

30

The chains around the door rattled and fell, banging against the wooden barn door with a noisy clatter. Years of moisture and neglect made the door swell and warp; it no longer aligned with the slightly listing doorframe. Opening the door required a yank and a tug. It, too, was a noisy process. Massive hinges, rusted and worn over time, creaked and groaned in protest. The door scraped against the ground and rubbed aggressively against wood.

There was no sneaking into the barn via the front door.

As the door opened and a large rectangle of light filled the space, Madison felt the older man cower in fear. All she saw was a looming body, silhouetted against the harsh glare of sunlight.

Belatedly, Madison dove for her flashlight, but it was too late. She had exposed her presence and there no time to look for cover. Two thousand lumens of brilliance lit up the dark barn, radiating from a hand-held lantern.

Madison pulled herself to her feet. If she had to face Lamont Andrews' wrath, she would do it standing up to the man.

"Well, well, well. What have we here?"

The voice wasn't right for the black man. In fact, this voice sounded distinctly feminine.

Rough, but feminine.

Was it the woman from Granny Bert's sprinkler? The unseen driver behind darkened windows? Could this woman be Lamont's girlfriend? His accomplice in crime?

On the off chance she was none of the above, Madison motioned to the man cowering on the ground beside her, his body once again curled into itself. "We need your help. This man is hurt. He has a nasty gash on his head."

The woman stepped forward, allowing the door to bang shut behind her. The chains rattled again, and the wall shook. It was a heavy door.

"He'll be okay," the woman said with confidence. "I have everything under control."

Hearing her calm reassurance, Madison felt a rush of relief. She had no idea who the woman was or why she was here, but she would help! "Oh, thank you," Madison said with gratitude. "I'm so glad you're here."

"Really." It hardly sounded like a question. It sounded... unbelieving. More than skeptical. Not quite surprised. It sounded sarcastic, but for the life of her, Madison couldn't imagine why.

"Of—Of course. You'll help us, won't you? Mr. Pruett needs medical care."

"He definitely needs help," the woman agreed.

As the woman stepped closer, Madison caught the familiar stench of smoke. Funky ash. Smoldering wires. Melted tar. Charred remnants of patchouli. Madison turned her head to sneeze, her gaze falling upon the forgotten hammer. She wasn't sure why, but instinct urged her to hide the potential weapon. As her senses went on high alert, her foot edged the tool beneath the nearby shelf.

Madison's earlier relief melted into wariness. Beside her, Pup growled and backed up, the hair on his back as stiff and ridged at Madison's nerves.

The unknown woman reached into her pocket and pulled out some dog treats, tossing them into the darkness. The dog hesitated before hunger and curiosity lured him beyond the circle of light.

"Who are you?" Madison asked, trying to hide her growing apprehension. "You'll help us, won't you? You'll get this man the help he needs."

"*No one* can get him the help he needs!" the woman spat. "That fool is beyond help."

"Could you at least help me get him to my car? I can take him from there."

"Princess, you ain't goin' nowhere. And neither is the old man."

It was the word *princess*. Warning signs went off in her head. Big, yellow, cautionary signs, written all in caps. They flashed in Madison's head, alerting her to danger.

Gerald and Paul Adams called her a princess. Both men vowed war against "Her Highness."

"I—I don't understand."

"You never do. None of you Hamiltons and Cessnas *ever* understand! You go about your pampered lives, lording your greatness over the rest of us lowly peasants, looking down your noses at us. You think you're better than us!" she accused.

The angry tirade came out of nowhere. Madison had no time for comment.

"When I needed a loan, just enough to get my business up and running, who do you think turned me down? Joe Glenn Cessna, that's who! It wasn't enough to get turned down by a loan officer; the bank president had to swing the ax." The woman's voice was bitter as she recounted the many sins of Madison's family.

"Who refused to give me store credit? Jubal and Lerlene Hamilton, that's who. When I wanted to look at houses, who showed me the sorriest, saddest houses on the block? Larry Cessna, the local real estate mogul. Who refused to date me back in high school, even though I was good enough for a few cheap thrills under the bleachers? Bobby Joe Hamilton. It's been that way my whole life. It's always been that way. Just because Rose Hamilton wormed her way into the Big House and stole it from the Ford family, it don't make her better than them!"

Madison groaned aloud. Would this ridiculous vendetta never end? "Seriously?" she muttered. "This again?"

"It may seem petty to you," the woman allowed. "You sit in your princess tower and look down over the town. You and your hotshot husband. You've had everything given to you your entire life! You don't know what it's been like for me. I worked for the old woman for a while, cleaning floors at the Big House. She treated me like the dirt she tracked in. But I showed her. I married into the Ford family. An Adams, heir to the throne. Until your grandmother stole it from us!"

As the woman lowered the lantern, Madison finally saw her face. "You're Hank and Virgie's daughter-in-law," she realized aloud. "You were married to Gerald. I saw you at the party Saturday night."

"That's right. And you're Bertha Hamilton Cessna's little princess. You're the woman who put my boy behind bars. You ruined his eyes!" she accused.

Madison saw it differently. "I'm the woman your son and your ex-husband tried to kill," she pointed out.

"Too bad they didn't succeed," the woman spat.

Her cold response drew a gasp from Madison. No one had ever said such a blatantly hateful thing to her. Blinking away the sting from the words, she tried reasoning with Paul Adams' mother. "Look, Mrs. ... I don't even know your name. Do you still go by Adams?"

"I don't want no reminders of my time with that good-for-nothing man. The one good thing to come of it, my boy Paul, even turned sour. I go by my second husband's name. Henry."

Madison had heard the name recently, but she couldn't remember where. "Mrs. Henry," she began again, "all of this is ancient history. It happened *a hundred years ago*. I can't be held responsible for something my ancestors may or may not have done in the past. I wasn't even born yet."

"Maybe not," the woman snapped. "But you sure reap the rewards, when the rest of us are left to do without! My life could have been so different, if not for your family."

She was as small-minded as her ex-husband. She blamed the Hamilton and Cessna families for her plight in life, allowing bitterness to replace ambition. It was easier to blame others for what could have been than to work for what could be. She accused them of supremacy and intolerance, but she was the one prejudiced against anyone bearing those names. She was blinded by hatred.

To try to reason with her was a waste of breath and good time. The best Madison could do was appeal to her sense of compassion. "Please, Mrs. Henry. This man is suffering and needs a doctor. You don't even have to help me. If you could just move aside, I'll take care of him myself."

"I told you, Princess. You ain't going nowhere." A gun appeared in her hand, punctuating her claim with deadly aplomb.

Several thoughts swarmed through Madison's mind.

She has a gun! This crazy woman just pulled a gun

on me!

...Wait. I've seen that gun before. I recognize the pearl handle.

And her face... I've seen her before, too. Before the party. Wasn't she...

"The library!" Madison gasped. "You were the woman cleaning the library."

"That's right. That's me, the invisible woman in the background. The cleaning lady. The one no one ever really sees."

Madison was totally confused. More confused, at the moment, than she was afraid, even though the woman was armed and clearly unstable. "*Who* did you say you were?"

"Sandy Henry. Owner of *Coming Clean*."

The pieces of the puzzle floated around in Madison's mind, but she still had trouble making them all fit.

"You clean several of the businesses around town. You left *Marvin Gardens* to open your own business. You're the one who called in a couple of alarms at the *Gold and Silver Exchange*." Inadvertently, Madison's eyes went to the fancy pearl handle in her hand. Was that where she had seen the gun before? "You were at the library that day. You overheard me and Miss Sadie discussing local gold mines."

"Who knew?" Sandy Henry mimicked Madison's own words from that day in an overly sweet, little-girl voice. Then her voice hardened, and her face twisted into a sneer.

"You'd be surprised at the things you overhear when no one thinks you're listening," she said. "People assume the cleaning woman is deaf. That she's too stupid to understand what they're talking about. People say all sorts of things in front of the invisible cleaning lady."

"But... what does this have to do with Mr. Pruett? Why are you holding him here? Why do you need the gun?"

"Because I'm tired of waiting! I want the necklace!"

"The... necklace?"

"Don't play dumb." It took great restraint for Madison to stand her ground when Sandy Henry moved forward. Close enough to kick Mr. Pruett's foot. "Do you know how much time I've wasted on this fool? I saw the pieces he brought to Lamont Andrews. Some of those were worth twice as much as Lamont paid him. He said there were more where those came from. And I saw the necklace. I made a point to befriend him after that. I've spent hours listening to this fool drone on about his fortunes. Hearing him talk about his grand collections, his many treasures. Waiting to get my hands on that necklace."

"You and Lamont Andrews are partners?" Madison guessed, her voice squeaky.

"He was manager for my ex. I guess I'm *his* manager now," Sandy decided, "even if Mr. Andrews doesn't know it." A cunning smile touched her face. "Yeah. I like the sound of that. You could say I've become his manager. I've learned a lot of things by being invisible there. In return, I may have *managed* to take a few slow-moving pieces off his hands. When you think about it, I did him a favor, setting that fire. He'll make more on the insurance claim than he ever made in that two-bit store!"

Madison's eyes widened. "*You* set the fire?"

"I couldn't get the stupid case open," she complained. "He changed the codes again, and this was one I couldn't crack. So, I cracked the glass to get to this little jewel." She waved the pearl-handled gun in the air. "I had to cover my tracks. A fire seemed the easiest solution."

Done with his treats, Pup came back to circle and sniff around their legs. Sandy kicked him away in aggravation.

"Why did you keep stealing the dog?" Madison asked. So many things didn't make sense. So many of the puzzle pieces just didn't fit.

It was Sandy's turn to look confused. "I didn't steal the dog. That's his dog."

"No. This dog belongs to a little boy down the road."

Sandy shrugged. "Whatever. I assumed the mutt was his, here to protect his treasures. Treasures that turned out to be nothing but trash! *These* are his grand, priceless collections!" She waved her arm in the air, indicating the shelves filled with their random offerings. She set the lantern on a shelf so that it still illuminated the space, freeing her hand to pick something up. "This isn't a valuable copper vessel, handcrafted by Paul Revere's own hand. This is an ordinary stockpot!"

Angered, she flung the pot down atop the prone man. He grunted as he absorbed the unexpected blow. As the pot hit and rolled away, Pup growled in protest. A single glare from the madwoman sent the dog cowering to Mr. Pruett's side.

"He told me he had Ming vases and exquisite urns brought back from his travels in the Middle East. He told me he dabbled in gold and precious gems. He said they were priceless. Turns out he told me lies, but I saw the necklace." Her eyes sparkled with greed. "Not up close, mind you. I was in the back cleaning, being invisible. But I saw the way it glittered. Lamont laughed and said it was a fake. And I would have believed him, if it hadn't been for you."

"M—Me? What did I do?"

"There you go, playing dumb again. You *know* about the necklace. You have a picture of it. You were looking up information about local gold. I never believed that story the Adams family told. They said it was their insurance that the old broad would leave the house to them, but you know how *that* turned out. Until you started snooping around, asking questions, I thought they were just blowing smoke. But thanks to you, I realized that old story was true."

The more she talked, the less sense she made. Madison struggled to keep up. "What story?"

"Gerald remembered his grandfather talking about it. Truman Ford was Juliet's most trusted employee. He was the one she trusted to handle her sensitive business, even things that weren't strictly legal. He told about a secret package he once took for her to a jeweler in Bryan. The old woman vowed him to secrecy. He said it was dangerous mission, because there was some sort of new law making it illegal for her to own any gold.

"The jeweler made him wait in the basement until closing time. Without a word, the jeweler came downstairs, went into a different room, and left Truman to wait there in the dark. The man came back out, handed Truman a box, and said just four words. 'You were never here.' His grandpa said he knew he shouldn't have looked, but he peeked into the box before giving it back to the old woman. He said it was a necklace. Diamonds and rubies around a gold nugget. He said Juliet was really worried later on, because the jeweler went to jail. Something about conspiring against the government for helping people hoard gold. That was why he knew she would leave him the mansion, because he kept her secret about the necklace."

The words were weak, but from the floor, Tom Pruett took up his old fight. "It's the only way to preserve our constitutional rights. We have a duty to our forefathers to resist the call..."

Sandy kicked at his foot, ending his weak mantra. "Listen to that old fool," she scoffed. "Crazy as a bed bug. But when I saw you upload that picture to the computer—"

"That was you that day!" Madison gasped. "You killed the lights!"

"I didn't want that photograph getting out on the web, not once I realized where the necklace came from and how valuable it really was. If there was gold found locally, then Grandpa Truman's story was true. I tried to play nice. I tried convincing this old coot to show me his collections. I finally tricked him into coming out here. That's when I realized how crazy he really was, and that the necklace was either hidden somewhere else, or he had already sold it."

"So, you ransacked his house."

"Didn't find a thing," she snorted in contempt. "Which could only mean one thing. He had sold it. And since *you* had the photo, and *you* were the one researching gold, I realized that *you* are the one with the necklace."

Swallowing nervously, Madison took a step backward, attempting to put more distance between them. Distance that hardly mattered when one of them had a gun.

Particularly when that gun now aimed directly at her abdomen.

"I guess you're real proud of yourself," Sandy sneered. "Your grandmother cheated the Adams family out of the house, even though they proved their loyalty by keeping quiet all those years. That house should have gone to my Paul one day. But you got your greedy hands on not just it, but now the necklace, too. I can't let you take it all. I can't let you keep stealing from my family. This invisible woman is going to stop you."

Sandy waved the gun, but its aim stayed true.

"I. Want. That. Necklace." The words came out in a slow, guttural growl.

"I—I don't have it." Unfortunately for Madison, she wasn't a very convincing liar.

"I don't believe you."

"It's true."

"I told you. I'm tired of wasting time. I'm tired of being invisible. Tell me where the necklace is." Her eyes bore into Madison's.

"I don't have it!"

"Fine. I'll just shoot the old man." Her tone was so nonchalant, so casual, it had to be a bluff.

She never broke eye contact. Sandy simply aimed her gun at the ground and fired.

Madison shrieked in surprise and no small amount of terror.

Mr. Pruett roused to see what the commotion was about; the bullet had missed him by several inches.

Pup barked and ran around in circles, adding to the chaos.

The air still quivered with the gun's echo.

Time stuttered.

Seconds later, the door jerked open, and someone rushed through.

31

Madison saw an opportunity and took it. When Sandy Henry whirled around, Madison swooped down, grabbed the hammer, and slung it with all her might. It struck the woman in the back and sent her toppling to the ground.

"Quick!" Madison cried to her unknown savior. "She has a gun."

"Not no more."

Lamont Andrews leaned down and scooped the gun up from the ground. The gun had flown from Sandy's hand when she fell, skittering along the floor to land at the man's feet. "Hey. This is my gun," he said darkly, recognizing the pearl handle with its one-of-a-kind marking.

Madison had never been so happy to see the sour-faced businessman as she was now. Taking big gulps of air, she nodded and managed to say, "She stole it. Right before she set your building on fire."

Lamont narrowed his eyes and looked at the woman on the ground. She writhed in pain, cursing and moaning and complaining about a broken back. "I suspected the broad was stealing from me," he admitted, "but I never could catch her in the act."

"She knew your codes," Madison offered. She knelt

beside Mr. Pruett, tending to his injuries again. "This man needs a doctor!"

Sandy attempted to sit up, but a large foot came down on her injured back and held her in place. "You stay where you are," Lamont told her. He used the gun as extra incentive. The large man appeared unfazed, his manner as casual and nonchalant as if he did this sort of thing every day.

He pulled out his phone and hit redial.

"This is Lamont Andrews again. We need an ambulance."

At Madison's questioning look, he explained, "I called 9-1-1 as soon as I heard the shot."

"I'm so glad you came home when you did!"

Pup circled Lamont's feet, barking his dislike for the newcomer. He raced over to Madison and Mr. Pruett, yipped, and started back toward Lamont. Madison managed to grab the dog and keep him beside her. After all, the glowering man had a gun, and there was no love lost between the two.

She worked to quieten the dog as Lamont asked, "Is that the dog you accused me of stealing?"

"Yes. I don't know how he kept getting locked in your barn, but this is the second time I've found him here."

"This ain't my barn."

"Then whose is it?"

"His." He pointed to Mr. Pruett. "My property ends at the drive. I keep asking him to mow his side, but he never does. He usually only comes out here at night, so when I saw all the cars, I was curious what was going on. But when I heard the gunshot, I knew something was up."

"Again, I'm so glad you came home!" Relief gathered in her eyes and threatened to leak out. She concentrated on roughing the dog's fur. "I came out to rescue this little guy, but thanks to him, we rescued Mr. Pruett. And then you rescued me." She lifted her eyes to the man, no longer ashamed of her tears. "Thank you, Mr. Andrews. I owe you a debt of gratitude that I can never repay."

He eyed her for a long moment. "I don't know about that," he finally drawled. "We caught this one." His foot tightened on Sandy, causing her to cry out. "I think my insurance company will be very interested in what you're able to tell them."

Madison and Brash soon thought of another way to show their appreciation to her unexpected savior. They asked Lamont Andrews to act as broker for the sale of four gold nuggets. The sale gave him a generous commission and a newly found air of legitimacy and respectability.

On Lamont's suggestion, they opted against an outright sale of the necklace. With the mystique of legend behind it (no one would confirm or deny exact facts and dates, due to legal concerns,) the horrendous necklace took on a new quality of intrigue. Lamont suggested the item be auctioned by a reputable auction house, after suitable hype and legend was put in place. So far, the plan was working beautifully, and there had been great interest in the piece. Madison was astounded when the insurance company suggested a policy of no less than one million dollars. In exchange for publicity that would carry with the sale, they offered the policy at no cost.

Mr. Pruett had no serious injuries from the ordeal, but it was evident that the man could no longer care for himself. He required a doctor's care and close monitoring, particularly if he were to be a candidate for a promising new drug on the market. A niece was in the

Houston area who agreed to act as his guardian. She promised Genny regular reports on her uncle's progress and his move into an assisted-living facility.

As a show of appreciation to the community for finding and rescuing her uncle, the niece donated his state-of-the-art computer systems to The Sisters Police Department. She also gave a small cash reward and a year's supply of kibble to Pup and Monte Applegate.

Pup, it was determined, was regularly lured to the old barn with treats and his new favorite kibble. When he was quick enough, the dog could escape capture by the older gentleman. Occasionally, however, Tom Pruett got the upper hand, and the carefree canine had to serve as a guard dog to his 'treasures.'

The treasures were a mixture of fact and fantasy. Some of the items he collected—the vases and canvased artwork, the artifacts and some of the jeweled baubles—were, indeed, valuable. Most came from his travels abroad. Some of the items—the copper pots, the stamp collection, and much of the modern art—were practically worthless. Their grand worth existed only in his mind. As his disease progressed, he became obsessed with the need to hoard things his mind deemed as treasures.

Sandy, in her greed and in her own obsession with the unfairness of life, believed the poor man's illusions. She saw him as the means to an end, the one big break she had needed to get ahead. When she realized the fortunes weren't real and the man didn't offer the golden opportunity she anticipated, something in her broke.

Even though she was correct about Madison having the necklace, she erroneously came to that conclusion based on hatred and her age-old vendetta against the Hamilton-Cessna family. She believed that, once again, they had denied her of what could have/ should have been. She had no way of knowing about the chair or the secrets it held.

When Brash came to arrest her, she denied her rights to an attorney. She gave her statement there in the old, ramshackle barn, beneath the beam of the LED lantern. She admitted to kidnapping Mr. Pruett and tossing his house. She admitted to setting fire to the *Gold and Silver Exchange* and stealing various items, including the gun. She admitted to tampering with the internet at the library and leaving Madison a threatening message. She admitted intent to do bodily harm to both Mr. Pruett and to Madison. If Madison hadn't turned over the necklace, she was prepared to kill them both.

She denied any knowledge or involvement in peering into Granny Bert's house or driving the phantom black vehicle. Records supported Lamont's claims of innocence, as well. He had traded his black car in for the sportier white model, one day before the mysterious sedan appeared.

For now, who drove the car and why remained a mystery.

After much debate, and with her husband and grandmother's full support, Madison decided how best to spend the money from the gold. Cars, debts, and college tuition aside, she could think of only one way that felt right.

It was a big day for the community. Their first-ever *Gold Rush Bonanza!*

The massive old cotton gin connecting the two towns hosted an arts and crafts fair. Special events included a Golden Baby Contest, costume judging, and period games. Mr. Jenkins' high school science class presented an impressive exhibit on gold, and the One-

Act Play cast and crew performed a skit about striking it rich in the gold mine.

The Big House opened for limited tours and refreshments served on the lawn, something Juliet was known to do upon occasion. Across the street, the Juliet Municipal Library had readings from Darwin Blakely's medical journals and a prominent feature of his library section.

With the renewed interest in gold mining—again, no one would confirm whether the gold came from local mines or the Yukon—*Muehler Creek Mining* opened for the day, offering tours and relay races centered around panning for gold. There was even talk of re-opening the business on a limited basis.

The final event of the day was the parade, announcements of the winners in all contests, and the moment Madison had been waiting for. A moment one hundred years in the making.

With Brash at her side—Granny Bert refused to join her, insisting it was her time to shine—Madison made a brief but eloquent speech in front of the Tuesday/Thursday Clinic. Together with a smile, she and her husband tugged away the heavy tarp.

Against the rays of a golden afternoon sunset, the letters sparkled on the building, sure as gold.

Today was the dedication of the newly renamed and expanded *Darwin Blakely Memorial Clinic.* At long last, Juliet Randolph's promise to her true love was kept, and his dream became reality.

Destiny had been fulfilled.

With fantastic readers like you, who needs hidden fortune? Your support means more to me than a thousand gold necklaces. The real 'jewel in my crown' is when you take the time to leave a review, or to drop me a line. I value each of you more than you know.

Thank you for spending yet another adventure with us here in The Sisters. There's more fun and hijinks in *Rose by Any Other Name*.

YOU MAY NOT KNOW...

They say that truth is stranger than fiction, and that just may be true.

* Executive Order 6102 is a true piece of our nation's history. I found it so interesting/appalling, I also incorporated it into my award-winning *Tangible Spirits*. (Don't let the cover scare you; Mac is more like a guardian angel than he is a ghost.) The book is full of historical facts and local lore, making it so much fun to research.

* I can't take credit for Mr. Pruett's entertaining imagination. His character is based on a real-life customer I had at my restaurant. The fantastical tales are compliments of Mr. D, who I fear suffered the same sad disease but who kept things interesting, nonetheless.

* Gold can, indeed, be found in almost every state in the US, but I sincerely hope there is no such thing as a Lost and Found Registry.

If you've forgotten how the diaries, and Gerald and Paul Adams fit in with the skeleton found at the Big House, check out Book 3, *Stipulations and Complications*. With Books 1-4 now available on audio, catching up on the backstory is easier than ever!

And, lastly, but still so very important, if you

enjoyed this book, please say so in a brief review on Amazon. (And/or Goodreads and BookBub.) It means the world to me, helping with sales, rankings, and visibility. More importantly, it lets me know if I'm writing the stories *you* want to read.

Thanks again, and drop in for an e-visit anytime at beckiwillis.ccp@gmail.com/ or www.beckiwillis.com. Sign up for my newsletter, too!

ABOUT THE AUTHOR

Becki Willis, best known for her popular The Sisters, Texas Mystery Series and Forgotten Boxes, always dreamed of being an author. In November of '13, that dream became a reality. Since that time, she has published numerous books, won first place honors for Best Mystery Series, Best Suspense Fiction and Best Audio Book, and has introduced her imaginary friends to readers around the world.

An avid history buff, Becki likes to poke around in old places and learn about the past. Other addictions include reading, writing, junking, unraveling a good mystery, and coffee. She loves to travel, but believes coming home to her family and her Texas ranch is the best part of any trip. Becki is a member of the Association of Texas Authors, the National Association of Professional Women, and the Brazos Writers organization. She attended Texas A&M University and majored in Journalism.

You can connect with her at http://www.beckiwillis.com/ and http://www.facebook.com/beckiwillis.ccp?ref=hl. Better yet, email her at beckiwillis.ccp@gmail.com. She loves to hear from readers and encourages feedback!

Made in the USA
Las Vegas, NV
24 July 2023

75192398R00154